# ZOMBIE INC

# Chris Dougherty

A special thank you to the early readers, Anne Francemore, Bob Dattolo, and Rich McGee. Thank you for your patience and the use of your brains.

# Prologue

"Look at it! Look! At! IT!"

Carl looked to where the angry homeowner–clad only in an open bathrobe and loose boxers–pointed. Not that Carl needed the direction. The problem was plenty obvious.

Two legs waved sluggishly from a sewer grate in the curb.

"Yessir, I see it," Carl said, and propped his hands on his hips. He hadn't brought the trainee with him from the car. Not yet. He wanted to get a good rapport with the homeowner and an audience or any show of bureaucracy about to swing into action would only infuriate the man further. "Did the collar not pop him at all or don't you know?" Carl smiled a puzzled half-smile. An 'I'm just doing my job here, buddy' smile.

"I don't know," the homeowner said on an outrushing sigh as his shoulders relaxed. "I came out this morning to get the paper and saw him kicking around in there."

Carl and the homeowner turned their gazes back to the legs. A low moan issued from the grate, echoing and lost. It still had its head. That much was obvious. They couldn't groan like that without their heads.

"Well, you were lucky. I can tell you that," Carl said. He scratched his ribs and nodded thoughtfully. He made some notes on the clipboard. This was a nice neighborhood, at least one in every five or six houses still standing. This guy was either government or he worked at one of the power companies.

"Don't I know it! Sucker coulda come right after me if it hadn't tumbled into the sewer there. I was hardly awake!" This time, the homeowner's squawk was excited, a 'can you believe it? I can't believe it!' exclamation.

"Huh. You were lucky for sure. No question about it," Carl said. Big house, landscaped nice. Plenty of money here. Good grid system, expensive. The houses on either side and across the street were burned to the ground. Anything unoccupied after the plague had been demolished to control infestation and looting.

Three more zombies stood in the front yard, spaced out like checker pieces. They moaned and swayed, their attention fixed on the two men. One quarter of the yard was conspicuously empty.

"Well, let me get this written up and taken care of for you," Carl said. "How's the rest of the system been? You've had it– what? Six months or so? Any problems?" He liked to ask this to remind customers that there were, in fact, very few occurrences of this nature.

The homeowner shrugged. "Nope, no problems. Wife hates it, but..." He shrugged again. His belly, a pugnacious basketball, rose and fell. "The ladies are a little soft sometimes. You know. They don't understand security as well. That's why I made sure we got all menzies." A small, unconscious moue of disgust crossed the guy's face, and Carl understood it. He and the homeowner were probably about the same age, early fifties. Same generation, at least. Some of the terms nowadays: menzies, womzies, kidzies...there was something decidedly wrong with a term almost of endearment associated with those shuffling monstrosities. "She didn't even want us to have guns in the house much less these here yard zombies."

Carl nodded in sympathy, but of course, his thoughts went to Annie, his wife. He'd lost her twenty-six years ago now, in the first wave. She'd been so young. They'd all been so young.

Carl shook off the thought and put his hand out. "I'll be in touch, but take my card. My scan code is right there. Call if they haven't set you back up in a few hours."

"Well, thank you. Thanks. I'll do that." The homeowner pulled his bathrobe together and bent to retrieve the paper. He went up the driveway, whistling. The remaining zombies–one on one side and two on the other–tracked his progress with their hungry, empty eyes.

*Newspaper*, Carl thought. Guy must have the big bucks. Probably a government worker, then. Four yard zombies just in the front? Most likely eight out back. Totally unnecessary, but that's overzealous sales for you. Maybe Candy. She'd be just this guy's type. He probably hadn't been able to get his nose from the woman's cleavage long enough to say no. Course, he wasn't one of the millionaires, the really high-ups. Those people all had Ze Sheds. Much more attractive than having corpses standing around your yard twenty-four seven. At least with Ze Shed, you could put the damn things away once in a while.

Not that anyone was having garden parties.

Not anymore.

Carl grinned and went to retrieve the trainee and the clipboard. Hopefully, the kid had brains enough to do some of the prelim paperwork. Most likely not, though.

Trainees weren't known for their overabundance of brains.

# ONE

### Ze Popper!®

Zombie, Inc., introduces the newest in home security with **Ze Popper!**® line of defensive containment. Keep your home safe with your own personal army of the dead! Robbers will move along when they see you're protected by ZI mobile corpses.

A discreet system of lasers is installed around your property to create fixed and/or flexible boundaries. They are custom-matched to your yard size, lifestyle, and budget. You can set the system up in zones, or simply surround the perimeter (if you are using in conjunction with Ze Shed® system).

Your zombie(s) come completely trained. A tone accompanied by a charge alert your zombie(s) to the presence of the laser boundary–factory conditioning keeps them in!* Zones can be cleared for homeowner access with the in-home control pad or Ze Panic!® mobile remote.

***You'll sleep in comfort when you have the Zombie, Inc., Ze Popper!® system securing your worldly goods!***

*A permanent collar of small charges instantly decapitates any collared zombie that wanders over the laser line, rendering the zombie harmless** to you and your family. Simply contact your Zombie, Inc., representative via their customer care scan code and the team of Zombie, Inc., Recovery Specialists will take over.*

****A beheaded zombie could potentially pose a threat if you come in close contact with its mouth.*** Keep children and pets away from a decapitated zombie, and DO NOT attempt* *containment yourself. The ZI team of Recovery Specialists is here for YOU!*

*All warranties implied or written become void if system is not installed by Zombie, Inc., licensed and certified contractors. For a list of ZI Ze Popper!® and Ze Shed® installation specialists, please use the scan code in this brochure under "CONTRACTORS". For general questions or to set up a free, in-home, no obligation consultation, simply use the scan code under "TELL ME MORE!"*

— — —

The SUV was a Mazda Zecon with black-tinted windows and a complete black wrap with the Zombie, Inc., logo on each side in white, an Assessment Team scan code on each door panel, and a photo-realistic, life-sized horde of zombies plastered across the entire back. *Classy*, Carl thought and popped the passenger door open. The trainee sat in the driver's seat, wide eyed and shaking. She had a small Ze Cross!® gas canister crossbow and bolt trained unsteadily on Carl's head.

Carl raised his eyebrows. "Don't get out much, Dillalia?"

She lowered the bow and breathed out a long, shaky whistle of air. She smiled, but even the smile was tentative. Carl had come to believe that people of Dillalia's generation were hardened, insensitive. Not this one, though. She was smallish, not more than five four. Thin but strong looking and neatly turned out in the ZI Assessment Team uniform of white button-down Oxford, and tan khakis. It was an old-fashioned outfit, a throwback to the '20s and before, when service-people in many fields wore such things. Of course, Carl remembered when men (mostly) had worn them in earnest. It hadn't been a uniform back then, it had just been business casual.

"It's ze-cedure, though," Dillalia said. Her tone was questioning. She was looking for confirmation, instruction. "It's right in the handbook to be on the defensive when you're in the wild."

Carl snorted and slid heavily into the passenger seat. "The wild, huh? That what you kids are calling it these days, Dill?" He shook his head. "That meant something entirely different when I was your age."

"Right, I know. Jungles and stuff."

Carl snorted again. "Well, kind of. Not really, though." He shot her a look. "And please don't call it 'ze-cedure' again. Just call it '*pro*cedure'–call it what it is. Believe me, all the 'ze' this and 'ze' that is not going to catch on if it hasn't yet."

"But the handbook–"

"The handbook is ninety-nine percent crap once you're in the field," Carl said. "File it away for the information regarding health care and whatever, but I'll tell you one thing right now that will help us get along–don't contradict me with handbook bullshit. Okay?"

Dill nodded, her face untroubled but intent, and Carl wondered what his reputation at ZI had become. Of course, everyone in Field Assessment was considered a little bit of a loose cannon. Assessment was the front line, the ones who left the safety of the ZI compound to do the dirty work. Assessment decided next steps, further measures and compensation. It took a lot of training, a lot of practice. There had been two trainees before Dill that hadn't made it. One dead, one quit, and they both went against Carl's record. It wasn't bad over the course of a career to lose one or two, even four or five depending on how long you were training and the adversity of your territory, but to lose two in a row had been bad luck.

There was every possibility that Dill, herself, was Assessment, too–*Employee* Assessment–the most hated and feared group in ZI.

"Scan for the Wranglers," Carl said. Time to get down to business. "We've got a menzie stuck head first in a sewer grate."

"Collared or…?"

"Yep, pretty sure. Not popped from what I can tell. One Wrangler truck is enough."

Dill flipped down the visor and touched the corner of her eye. A laser bloomed from the small scanner tucked next to her eyelid, and she trained it on the code under WRAN. A blip came from the vicinity of her ear, and she touched her earlobe lightly with two fingertips. "This is FA 12382, and we are requesting one Wrangler truck. Location broadcast."

"Okay, Field Assessment, Wrangler truck on the way." The automated voice was good, very close to human, but there was always a hitch when it switched. "Is this containment?"

Dill glanced at Carl and without looking up from his clipboard, shook his head. "It's already contained itself," he said, muttering distractedly. "There's nothing to panic over."

"No," Dill answered the voice and removed her finger from her earlobe, ending the call. "What's next? Do we go wait out near the one in the gutter?"

"Christ, no," Carl said. "We wait until the Wranglers–" Carl shuddered, "–get here."

"Are they really that bad?"

Carl raised his eyebrows at her. "You haven't seen the Wranglers yet? No? Well, they're just, you know, *different*. Not as bad as the Cleaners, but you wouldn't want to hang out with Wranglers on a regular basis."

"I've heard that about them."

"Okay, so, procedure, see here? This form? This is the first one filled out. Always. On site and in front of a homeowner if it's regarding a defect or perceived defect in a system."

"Assess first, though, right?"

"Yeah, well, shit, of course. You have to assess to be able to fill the damn thing out."

Dill nodded again, unperturbed, her eyes on the clipboard. Carl swallowed his impatience. It was his own fault. He wasn't explaining things right, and also, she hadn't been with him. How would she know?

Okay, so he was a little rattled. There seemed to be more riding on her success because it impacted his.

"Listen, Dill, I could tell from the guy's tone when he called that it would be a bad idea to give him an audience. You'll learn that. Next time, you'll come with me, okay?"

Dill nodded again. Carl couldn't get a good read on her. She was self-contained enough to be Employee Assessment but seemed too young. She'd been scared to be in the SUV by herself, but that could be an indicator of anything. The only ones who weren't skittish outside company walls were Wranglers, Cleaners, and of course, zombies.

Gave you an idea where the Wrangler and Cleaners' heads were at.

"Once you have everything down on the clipboard," Carl continued, "then you input it into the tablet."

"Why not just put it into the tablet in the first place?"

Carl sighed, but it was a reasonable question for a young person. Most of them had probably never used pens, pencils, or paper. "It's part of the service, part of the...what the hell is it called the, uh, the–? The mystique! Just like the khakis and the Oxfords. We're going for old-fashioned. We're going for reassurance."

"I wouldn't be reassured by a clipboard," Dill said.

"No, I guess you wouldn't," Carl said, "but you're not in your fifties. You don't own a house or–" He cocked an eyebrow at her. "Do you own a house?"

She looked at him as if he was crazy. Her first real expression if you disregarded the fear earlier.

"No, see?" Carl continued. "That's what I mean. Our territory is almost entirely houses, homeowners, richies who can afford the big systems. See what I mean? They want to see a goddamned clipboard and some chop-chop. It makes them feel good. More secure."

Dill nodded and turned her eyes back to the clipboard. She was ready to learn. That was good, because she had a long way to–

A gas engine roar made her jump. Carl couldn't see the Wrangler truck from here, but he recognized it nonetheless. Wranglers had actually fought for and won the right to the old gas vehicles. That's how crazy they were. It was as if they *wanted* to attract zombies. Crazy.

"Okay, they're here," Carl said. "Sneak on up there."

Dill pressed the steering wheel at the top. The car hummed and rolled forward, slowly gathering momentum. She rounded the corner, and the Wrangler van came into view. Her eyes widened.

"What the fu–?"

Carl laughed. He'd been watching her face, waiting to see what happened once the Wranglers were in sight. "Something else, huh?"

She glanced at him and then turned her stunned gaze back to the vehicle twenty-five feet down the road, turned sideways curb to curb. It was a big pickup truck, flat black, with the Zombie, Inc., logo on each door panel in red. The tires were easily four feet high with heavy, studded tread, and the body of the truck sat an additional eighteen inches over the tires. A cowcatcher grill, also flat black, covered the front, and a rack of bullhorns with zombie heads on each of the two points sat above it like something from a wild-west nightmare. A red cap on the back had the word 'Wrangler' in loopy writing made to look like rope.

The engine roared, shaking the truck, and then the sound died. In the sudden silence, Dill took a breath to speak, but then the doors of the Wrangler truck opened. Two Wranglers tumbled out.

The men were dressed as old-time bikers in heavy blue jeans and leather chaps and leather vests over bare skin. Their forearms were laced up in black leather, they wore studded collars around their necks, and the sun glared and sparked off the metal spikes. Steel-toed cycle boots with chains and do-rags of flat black emblazoned with red skulls completed the look.

They ran, whooping, toward Carl and Dill.

"They…they, uh…" Dill stuttered. The Wranglers looked like bandits, like pirates, hooligans, ruffians. "Are they coming to kill us?"

Carl's shoulders rose and dropped. "Man, you just never know," he said, and then his door clunked open, and he pointed to the legs in the sewer grate, redirecting the Wranglers' furious attention.

They turned like flocking birds and their whoops increased in both volume and frequency when they saw the legs. One or two 'yee-haws' popped out of them like uncontrollable burps.

"I'll be back," Carl said and began to close the door.

"Wait!" Dill said, her voice edged with panic. "What about me?"

"You'll be okay. You have your crossbow, right? Keep it handy."

"Yeah, but what about, you know, learning the job?"

"Do you *see* those two?" Carl asked and hooked a thumb back over his shoulder. The Wranglers had the errant zombie by the ankles and were pulling as they laughed, dragging it from the sewer. "Shit, Dill, you're going to have plenty of on-the-job, okay? For now, just observe, okay?"

Dill nodded and sat back in the seat. She scanned the rearview and big side mirrors. Always be aware of your surroundings. Alertness was the number one rule when you were outside the compound wall. It wasn't written specifically anywhere in the training materials, but the stories of lives lost through sheer inattention were many and frightening. Even if at least half of the stories were more office lore cautionary tale than factual account.

The Wranglers nodded to Carl and resumed their tugging. The zombie finally pulled free and one of the Wranglers stumbled back and landed hard on his ass. The standing Wrangler bugled a laugh as the grounded Wrangler cursed.

"Haw! You idiot! Watch where yer own big damn feet is, idiot!"

"Fuck you, Floyd! It wan't my feet the problem! It was this 'un!"

"Floyd, this old feller never got nowhere near them bloated boats you calls feet. Now get on 'em boats, and let's get this feller took care of." The standing Wrangler turned and spit a thick stream of tobacco onto the road. He turned back and grinned broadly. "You idiot."

The grounded Wrangler cursed again and turned the zombie's foot with a sharp, businesslike twist, snapping the ankle. The standing Wrangler crouched and twisted the zombie's other leg in a similar fashion, snapping the other ankle, splintering the fibula with a crunch. Then the Wranglers stepped back.

The zombie pushed, grunted, and gained his knees. His head dangled almost to the ground. The Wranglers crossed their arms over their burly chests and tilted their heads in observation. They were quiet, watchful. All pretense of idiocy and rambunctiousness seemed to have drained away clean.

"The collar only half popped would be my guess."

"Yeah, mine too. Charges mighta wore out?"

"Not supposed to, not on the new models. See that blue tag there? That collar ain't but a month old."

"Shitfire, you're right about that, Floyd. We'll have to pluck that sucker offa that guy. Get the collar back to ZI so they can figure out why the poppers didn't pop 'im."

"Well, that's what we're about, Floyd, so let's get about it. Let's wrangle this sucker!"

The Wranglers turned to Carl. "Keep an eye on this one while we get the gear, would you, Abby? There's a good girl."

Carl gave them the finger, and they broke up laughing and bashing each other on the shoulder as they trotted back to their truck.

Wranglers were mystifying. They all called each other 'Floyd' and called everyone else–for reasons unknown–'Abby'. They were a tight, secretive bunch, and Carl pitied the HR rep in charge of them. For years, the company had tried to move a Wrangler into management specifically for the HR job, but there were no takers amongst the Wranglers. The job was currently being handled by a young man who was rumored to be near suicidal because of it.

The Wranglers came back, one carrying a long pole with a rope on the end. A dogcatcher, it was called in the old days. Carl remembered them well. Now there were no more dogs, or at least, not many. After the plague, dogs had been drawn to the rotting zombies, drawn by the smell. It had not been uncommon to see a dog chewing the leg of a shuffling zombie or trying to roll on the less ambulatory ones. But zombie meat was poison to animals.

A lot of the ASPCA equipment had been bought up by Zombie, Inc., at pennies on the dollar. It translated well to zombie containment.

The other Wrangler carried a thin baton and a long Taser. They approached the struggling zombie like animal trainers in a zoo for the insane.

"We don't need your help, Abby," the Wrangler addressed Carl without looking at him. "Get back in your pussy-mobile, and wait for the report. This one's gonna be easy!"

"You said it, Floyd," the other Wrangler said. "Half the head gone already? I like those odds!" He swung the pole in a circle over his head, and the loop hissed and snapped. "Half the head gone; half the job done! Haw!"

"Catch hold on 'im and stop runnin' yer mouth, Floyd. He's gained his feet somehow."

The zombie stood swaying on the stubs of his ankles, feet pointing off in different directions, the twisted bones of his shin poking through the skin. His head dangled against his chest, the back of his neck having been blown off by the collar. Shards of bone entangled with ribbons of rotting skin hung around his shoulders like a macabre scarf. He moaned, and it was muffled in the old corduroy jacket he wore. A substance that looked like a mix of coffee grounds and drying blood clots trailed down his back. He swayed and shuffle-hopped toward the Wranglers, leaving one foot behind. A coffee-clot about the size of an eyeball fell to the pavement with a slucking sound.

"Shit, sucker's got a little life in 'im yet, I reckon."

"Just get 'im looped up, Floyd, for fuck's sake, quit yer dickin'!"

"I got 'im, I got 'im, quit yer cry babyin', ya' loose stool." He swung the loop of rope and twirled it down over the zombie's dangling head, but the zombie lurched to the left, and the rope skidded down his side.

"Aw, fucker! Hold still, ya' oily cunt rag!" He raised the loop again–the pole was long and unwieldy–and this time, the zombie feinted backward, and the loop tripped uselessly down his front. Then the zombie lurched forward, swinging his arms and groaning as his head rocked side to side on his chest.

"Jesus! Quit fucking around, and LOOP that thing!" Carl said as he fumbled at his belt for his pistol.

"Shut up, Abby, Floyd's got 'im! Go sit in your pussy-wagon if you can't–"

The zombie tumbled, one of its reaching hands tangling in the Wrangler's vest. The Wrangler roared like a surprised lion and jumped back as the other Wrangler stepped in with the Taser. "Floyd! Be careful! Sucker almost got you!" He jabbed the Taser into the zombie's arm.

The zombie's arm jerked up and back, flinging wildly. The Wrangler pushed closer and jammed the Taser into the open cavity at the zombie's neck. Blue fire zizzed and flashed, and a stink of hot, rotted flesh combined with ozone made Carl gag.

"Loop 'im, Floyd! Loop the fucker!"

"Can't! The head's too far over! Loop won't catch! Fuck!"

The zombie lunged again, the Wranglers jumped back in perfect synchronicity, and then a black bolt appeared in the zombie's head as if by magic.

It collapsed forward over itself and crumbled onto the pavement.

Carl stopped fumbling for his pistol and stared open-mouthed. The Wranglers looked at each other, frozen, and then turned slowly to look behind them.

Dill stood ten feet away with her crossbow at shoulder level.

The Wranglers blinked at Dill, then blinked at Carl, and then turned their attention back to Dill.

"Thanks, Abby," the first Wrangler said, "but we're supposed to bring them back kickin'."

Dill's face, already very white, became whiter still. "Oh," she said and lowered her shaking bow. Her shoulders fell in dejection. "Well...*fuck*."

The Wranglers blinked at her again and then burst out laughing. "Don't you worry about it, Abby! Haw haw! Yer a good little Abby!"

"Better a dead deadie than a dead Wrangler! Haw!"

They clapped her on the shoulders, nearly flattening her, but Dill managed a grin. They hawed harder and commenced to slapping her on the back. She nearly went to her knees.

"Yer a good one, Abby! Yer a good assessment man!"

"You call us anytime, Abby! We're your wranglers!"

"Thanks–guys, thanks–oof, thanks, I–" She stepped away from their good-natured pounding. They continued to grin at her. "My name's Dill, though."

"Aw! Right you *are*, Abby!" the first Wrangler said and caught her up in a bear hug that took her breath away. "Grrr...yer a good man!"

"Jesus," Dill said, her voice a squeezed squeak, "put me down!"

The Wrangler dropped her all at once, and her teeth clicked together when her feet hit the pavement. The Wranglers leaned in, and once again, all traces of buffoonery had dropped from their features. Dell gazed into two pairs of brown eyes as warm and intense as any pit bull pup's had ever been. The first Wrangler said, "We mean it; anything you need–"

"–you call us first, Abby," the second Wrangler finished.

*

Dill and Carl watched from the SUV as the Wranglers sawed away at the zombie's neck in order to retrieve the unpopped collar. They laughed and yelled and occasionally gave the Assessment SUV either the finger or a thumbs-up and then broke up again, seemingly unaffected by their brush with death and unconcerned with the charges on the collar that hadn't fired. Of course, many Wranglers were missing fingers. It seemed a mark of honor among them.

"Weird. They're *so* weird!" Dill said and shook her head. Her voice was still shaky, and her face very white. Her wide eyes prismed with carefully unshed tears.

"You made a good impression, though," Carl said. His tone was halfway between admiration and irritation. "You seem to know how to handle yourself, especially considering you've just started. Most people aren't quite as confident their first time out."

Dill sighed and crossed her arms over her chest. "I'm not EA, if that's what you're wondering."

Carl glanced at her and away. "If you say so," he said and shrugged.

She turned to him. "I mean it. I'm not Employee Assessment. I promise I'm not."

Carl nodded, seemingly disinterested, and watched the Wranglers.

"I'm not, Carl, and anyway, it's company policy that I have to say I am if someone asks."

Carl snorted. "Who told you that?"

"I don't know, I mean, it's just something people say. It's just *known*."

"Dill, think about it–how could that possibly be a policy? How could they possibly *enforce* it?" He shook his head. "That's why I like being on the outside. Too much yapping and information cannibalism in the office."

The Wranglers had the zombie head removed, and the collar was in the truck. Now they stood at the sewer grate, where gore was flung across the road and sidewalk in wide arcs. They moved methodically, back to back, blinking and turning in quarter turns.

"What are they doing? Why are they blinking like that?" Dill asked.

"They're recording the scene. Wranglers have camera implants along with the scanner implants."

"Jeez," Dill breathed, "that's got to be expensive!" Her fingers went unconsciously to the call code scanner embedded near her eyelid, but she didn't touch it. It was smaller than half a grain of rice and activated by pressing. The laser scanned a series of squares and connected you to your party via the tiny phone implanted near your ear. The scanners and implant procedure weren't that expensive; it was the plans that really got you. Luckily, when she'd joined ZI, they took over her plan and deducted personal calls from her pay.

Camera eyes were usually only for richies like government workers.

"Company pays for it, obviously," Carl said. "Wranglers are far from rich. Same as the rest of us."

"Do you have an eye camera?"

"No way," Carl said. "No company plan combined scanner, either."

"How do you call anyone?" Dill asked. Her voice was almost breathless with befuddlement. He might as well have said he didn't have a brain.

"I have my personal," he indicated his left side, "*and* a company one," he indicated his right. "I won't have them controlling my plan."

"Why not, though? They make it so easy! They filter out all the personal calls and take it right from my check. I never have to pay a single thing."

He gazed at her, eyebrows raised. "You're paying," he said, "believe me, Dill. You're paying."

# TWO

## Zombie, Inc., Company Handbook
Employee Compensation, Sec. 8
After Death Benefit
Contribution and Payout
(*rev. 10/13/41*)

Zombie, Inc., (hereafter referred to as 'ZI') After Death Benefit employee contribution is MANDATORY and will be taken directly from employee's compensation at a rate of .05% of compensation per stated pay period. ZI matches employee contributions at 100%.

ZI will contain and dispose of your zombified remains solely at ZI's expense. Employee heirs and/or assigns will receive the employee's accumulated to DATE OF INCIDENT After Death Benefit (in accordance with 'Wales vs. The United Five-States' <*Mar. 27, 2033*> which states that After Death Benefits DO NOT pertain to the reanimated. Therefore, accumulation ends with first death.)

After Death Benefit will pay out at the following percentages based on the corresponding circumstances:

100% Benefit: Employee (heirs and/or assigns) will receive 100% After Death Benefit should employee incur a bite from the infected during the normal discharge of the duties and assigned tasks as related to their specific job title.

100% Benefit: Employee (heirs and/or assigns) will receive 100% After Death Benefit should employee incur a bite from the infected when participating in any STATED AS MANDATORY company functions, i.e., job training (also to include: weapons training, evasive maneuvers training, true death recognition training), annual grounds clean-up, trade shows, etc.

80% Benefit: Employee (heirs and/or assigns) will receive 80% After Death Benefit should employee incur a bite from the infected when participating in any STATED AS VOLUNTARY company functions, i.e., picnics, zombie shoots, booster events, etc.

50% Benefit: Employee (heirs and/or assigns) will receive 50% After Death Benefit should employee incur a bite from the infected when participating in ANY activity not related to their job and which occurs outside their stated shift.

— — —

"Take the death benefit scam, for example," Carl said. He tapped more information into the tablet laboriously, squinting. "Let's see, equipment failure, but there's no box for half-popped collars, and that's definitely a new one. We'll note it in comments. Two Wranglers, that's not too bad, but we did have a weapons discharge, and that's going to cause some–"

"What's the death benefit scam?" Dill asked. Her voice was languid, almost hypnotized. She was entranced by Carl's fumble-fingered tapping at the tablet. He was so agonizingly slow! She'd have that thing filled out in seconds. She tore her gaze away with an effort and scanned the mirrors and surrounding area. The Wranglers were gone, but the mess of twisted, broken, cut-up zombie remained. Gruesome. Her stomach rolled in a combination of guilt and delayed stress.

"Contribution is mandatory. You know they take it right out of your pay, right?" Carl tapped and tapped.

"Yes, but the company puts in, too."

"Sure. They match you 100%. But if you get bit at home or shopping or anything, they only *pay out* 50%."

"Well, that makes sense. If I'm responsible for half the money in there and ZI puts the other half in, then why should I get all of it if I do something stupid that gets me bit when I'm not working? ZI isn't responsible for what I do on my own time. I'll get back what I put in." Dill shrugged and scanned the area again. Carl was getting on her nerves a little. Her own dad had espoused a lot of weird conspiracy theories, too. Irritating.

"Scan for clean-up," Carl said. He glanced at the mess and then at the tablet again. "One Cleaner should do it."

Dill touched her eye, scanned the code on the visor under "Cleaners", and called in. Once she had disconnected, Carl started up again.

"Let's look at the numbers, okay? Say you put in ten a month for twelve months, that's one twenty a year. Over the course of ten years, it accumulates to twelve hundred, right?"

Dill nodded. She sighed internally. Here it comes, lecture time.

"Okay, so, who benefits from that money while ZI is holding it? Who gets the benefit of the investment?"

"ZI does, obviously," Dill said. She tried to keep the impatience from her voice, but it wasn't easy. She'd heard this and similar time and time again from people who'd been around before the plague. It was like they wanted the world just to run the way it had when they were younger. "But who cares? ZI has to make money to keep *employing* us. Don't you see that? We're lucky, Carl. Lots of people don't even *have* an after death benefit!" She crossed her arms over her chest and shook her head, but secretly she was almost enjoying the discussion and the fact that it distracted her from what she'd just done to that zombie. "Besides, your chances of first death on the job are really high. So, no worries."

"No worries, ha. That's a good one. Of course, your chances of first death on the job are good! We work seventy hours a week!"

Dill smiled. This was another thing she'd heard from her dad. The fabled forty-hour work week! She almost laughed. What the heck did everyone do with their extra time back then? Dad had talked about weird things like people being pumped for Fridays and getting gloomy on Mondays–back when the days of the week had names, in the olden days when the concept of 'week' even meant anything. Now a month was just the number of the days. *Every* day was a workday. So what? It was better than sitting in a two-bedroom apartment with the other five people that you needed to afford it in the first place!

"Whatever," Dill said, "I personally don't mind working. I'm not lazy like those welfare voucher whores who–"

A flat black station wagon with blacked-out windows and devoid of logos or ornamentation of any kind slid into sight.

"Don't be scared," Carl said, and his tone, flat and lacking emotion, chilled her because it indicated that he thought there was something she *should* be scared of.

"I'm not scared," she said, "they're just Cleaners. No big–" she swallowed as the station wagon door opened and a figure in a black suit emerged like a column of noxious dark smoke. "–no big deal."

"Uh huh," Carl said. The figure from the station wagon turned toward the Assessment car. His face was a featureless, white blank disk. Dill drew in a startled breath.

"Hey, where's his–"

"Don't worry, it's just a mask. They're around a lot of dirty shit. His hands are covered, too, see? From what I understand, it's an all-over white suit and the material is thin–measured in micrometers–but impenetrable. The black suit over it is for show, like our khakis. Morticians used to wear black."

"Impenetrable to a bite?"

"Jesus, if only," Carl said. "No, impenetrable to the bugs. Germs."

The man leaned back into the station wagon, and when he stood up again, a fedora as black as his suit sat snugly on his head, pulled low. To Dill, it seemed menacing, but she didn't know why. Either the tilt itself or the shadows it produced, but either way, he'd just become slightly more nightmarish.

He raised one white hand. Carl waved back.

"Wait here, and this time, I really want you to wait, okay?"

Dill nodded, unable to tear her eyes from the Cleaner. He'd swiveled his head toward the mess at the sewer grate. His head tilted, and his fingers tapped at his thigh.

"What's he doing?"

"Typing," Carl said.

"Typing? On his *leg*?"

"No, not exactly. There are sensors in his fingers, either in the gloves or..." Carl shook his head, eyebrows raised. "...or, you know, actually *in* his fingers. Either way, he's tied directly to a tablet in the station wagon. He's inputting the scene info without contaminating anything besides himself, his clothing. They never know what they're walking into." Carl's tone became admiring.

"Those guys have their typing down pat, that's for damn sure. Wait here."

The door clunked open, and he was gone.

The Cleaner continued tap tapping on his thigh, and the cloth beneath his fingertips shivered as if empty. Dill shivered, too.

*You're freaking yourself out*, she thought. *He's not a boogeyman. He's just a guy in a suit. Flesh and blood, same as anyone else. Relax.*

The Cleaner turned to face Carl as he got close, but to Dill, it looked as if the blank face was trained on her. She shivered again. Carl's head moved as he spoke, and he pointed to the house, the yard, the mess of a zombie. The Cleaner did not appear to speak, but he was too far away for Dill to see if the mask over his mouth moved with the breath of words.

Then Carl was headed back in a hurry.

The Cleaner had produced something that looked like a metal conductor's baton. Then it became two batons, and the Cleaner held one in each hand. They glinted in the overcast mid-morning light. The Cleaner's shoulders lifted and dropped, and then he raised his hands. A cord snaked back to the car. Whatever the things in his hands were, they were charged up.

Carl piled in next to her, his forehead lightly sheened with sweat, and slammed the passenger door unnecessarily hard.

"I'm glad it's just one," Carl said.

Dill opened her mouth to ask if he meant zombie or Cleaner, but all thoughts flew from her mind as the Cleaner bent to his work.

The batons in his hands were some sort of high speed, electric knives; had to be. He began at the zombie's legs and sliced first from kneecap to ankle, splitting the legs down the middle, exposing bone and rotted gristle and grayish meat. Then side to side, dicing the legs like large, soft carrots. Rancid bits dripped from the flashing knives and spattered onto the street, onto the Cleaner's mask and suit. He made his way up the thighs, again first splitting and then dicing. The coffee ground/blood clot substance began to accumulate like flotsam wherever the knives went. A large chunk of purplish meat landed on the Cleaner's shoulder and shivered wetly.

He went into the torso.

Dill looked away as her gorge rose, but the knife sound bore into her, seeming to bypass her ears to whine and vibrate directly into her brain. It was like a dentist's drill. She looked back in time to see the head get split, the eyes drifting apart, widening, and then split again. Quartered and then eighthed. The knives' whine cycled higher as they encountered the skull bones. Bits of white flew, landing on the Cleaner's black suit in a pattern of insanity.

Dill scrubbed her mouth with her hand.

"You okay? Getting sick?" Carl's voice was sympathetic but something else, too. As though he were looking for confirmation of something. Her weakness, perhaps.

"I'm fine," Dill said. She sat back and took a deep, slow soundless breath. Darned if she'd get sick. Darned if she would. She'd seen worse. Cripes, her boyfriend, Denny, played a game called 'Breeder' that was much more disgusting than what the Cleaner was doing.

The game had never made her stomach hot. Had never made her head feel spinny and light.

The knives cut off, and she sighed with relief. Not so bad. She could take it. She could do this job.

The Cleaner went to the station wagon and around it, to the back. He drew out a long black tube, corrugated and bendable, and stretched it from the car to the zombie salsa he'd just made. He clicked something, and the tube jumped. Dill recognized the deep, whooshing sound–the tube was a big vacuum. The Cleaner turned the nozzle on the zombie. Bits and chunks flew into the tube, bumping and thumping along its length. Bigger bits–a hand, a foot–began to crowd the nozzle, and the whoosh turned into a scream as the vacuum struggled to accommodate the load. The Cleaner kicked the tube and shook it, and the bigger pieces began to tumble one after another, disappearing into the back of the car.

Then a puff of gray smoke streamed from the top of the station wagon. A smell–a mix of barbecue, feces, cheese, and garbage–came to Dill like very bad news.

She gagged. Her eyes, wide and shocked, went to Carl.

His look was apologetic, but also slightly, very slightly, amused. "I forgot to tell you about the part where they cook it down."

The vacuum shrieked like a demon, and underneath it, somehow tangled with the smell, Dill thought she heard the Cleaner laughing. She leaned out the door and threw up, praying Carl was watching out for zombies.

*

"Better?" Carl asked as she pulled herself back in. He held a handkerchief under her nose.

She almost gagged again as she recoiled from it.

"It's clean, jeez," he said and shook it.

She pushed it away, but as she did, she caught the nostalgic scent of dryer sheet. He'd meant it when he said it was clean. She watched with regret as he stuffed it back in his pocket and then scrubbed her mouth with her shirt collar, which smelled only of dry cleaner's chemicals.

Her eyes drifted involuntarily to the Cleaner. He was still vacuuming, but a thin head attachment had been added to the end of the tube. He pushed it over the last bits of gore, sucking them up and away. He raised a hand, flicked the purple meat off his shoulder, and ran the vacuum over it. Dill's stomach tried to heave, and she breathed deeply and evenly.

"I should have warned you," Carl said.

She tipped her head back against the seat and rolled it side to side. "I don't think it would have mattered. I don't think you can be prepared for that." She glanced at Carl. He was looking from the Cleaner to the tablet on his lap, tapping things into it. "How come I didn't know?"

"Huh? Listen, I said I was sorry for not telling you."

"No, I know. I mean…how does *everyone* not know? About the cutting? The…the vacuum?"

Carl shrugged, glanced at the Cleaner, and tapped some more. "Probably because no one really *wants* to know. If you never come out here–" he nodded to indicate the neighborhood, "–you never know what's going on. Seeing things on the news or video games is *not* the same as seeing it in person. People's lives have become very clean compared to the pre-plague days." He shrugged again.

"Even the people who are out here don't want to see it. You think the homeowner was watching from his window? If this was the old days and someone was, say, cutting down a tree or something, he'd be watching. He'd be taking pictures to show his friends at work, but certain things…" Carl shook his head and tapped again, then turned his eyes to her. They were hard but not mean. "You don't want to watch the cleaning person scrub the toilet, right? You don't want to see what the plumber snakes outta the drain."

Dill didn't want to admit that she was too poor for a cleaning person, even though they were government subsidized: an initiative that put people back to work after so many businesses had failed. Someday she would have one, but for now, she was a paycheck away from being a cleaning person herself. At any rate, she scrubbed her own toilet.

She understood his point however.

"You're right. You hear about things, the especially gross things like limbers and zombieporn, and your mind just kind of skips over it," she said. "Like it's deciding on its own what you should and shouldn't know. Hey, I wonder if that's from an implant or something?"

"Ha! *Now* who's talking conspiracy theories?" Carl shook his head. "No. It's always been that way, believe me. It's like homeless people. By the early twenties, we'd stopped seeing them. There were whole communities of tent people, tunnel people, sewer people, and everyone just went around like 'ho hum, *what* homeless people?' as if there were no such thing. Even though it was worse than it had ever been."

"My dad used to talk about that," Dill said. She couldn't imagine not living in a zombie-proofed structure. 2027 was both the year of the plague and the year of her birth. At twenty-six, she had no recollection of any other world.

"Your dad still around?" Carl asked. His tone was light but cautious. The idea of an intact family had begun to disintegrate since the plague. It was very rare to hear of an entire nuclear unit that had made it through, and the years after the plague were not much better. As society had reformed, accidents, disease, and stupidity had all taken a smaller but more drawn out and agonizing toll.

"He was until I was fourteen. Then he wasn't." Her tone was matter of fact. "I fumbled around for two years and then joined ZI. That's when I moved to the inners."

"You still there?"

"Yes," she said, and her tone was clipped, ending the conversation. She didn't want to tell him about living cheek to jowl with five roommates, squeezing into two bedrooms and queuing for one bathroom. He probably lived in the outers in a townhouse, maybe even an actual house-house. Assessment Team employees made enough. It was one of the reasons she wanted Assessment, even beyond what Denny was asking her to do, and even though it came with its own raft of dangers.

The Cleaner was done with the vacuuming.

He unwound a hose from the car and sprayed the area with greenish foam.

"What's that?" Dill asked.

"The foam? An enzyme. It eats up any, you know, bits, and then it more or less eats itself and walla! The area is clean and sanitized. They call it bleach, even though it's not."

"Huh. That's gross. And cool."

"Yep. Like so many things nowadays."

# THREE

**Zombie, Inc., Company Handbook**
Dress Code: Assessment Team Attire
(*rev. 12/01/52*)

Zombie, Inc., (known hereafter as 'ZI') prides itself on the professionalism of its Employees, especially on any team which interfaces directly and physically with the public in general and ZI customers in the specific. With that in mind, ZI suggests the following MANDATORY dress code (all are to be purchased through the ZI corporate store or purchased online via an authorized ZI apparel dealer, such as Amazon):

Assessment Team FIELD Attire: ZI approved white Oxford button down, long sleeve or short depending on the season, with the ZI logo on the front left breast pocket. Tan Khakis, flat front, rolled and pressed cuffs. IMPORTANT ATTIRE CHANGE, PLEASE READ CAREFULLY: The former dress code requirement for tie-up or slip-on loafers has been changed. From the revision date of this notice and going forward, ALL ASSESSMENT TEAM PERSONNEL WILL WEAR ONLY AUTHORIZED STEEL TOE, HALF-CALF BOOTS. This is due to the incident in New Trenton on 09/27/47 where an Assessment team member lost his or her toes during a clean-up event.

Assessment Team NON-FIELD Attire: If Assessment Team Member will be scheduled for corporate ONLY days, such as job training (also to include: weapons training, evasive maneuvers training, true death recognition training), or similar, Assessment

Team Member attire is same as above with the exception of the steel toe, half-calf boot requirement.

Assessment Team PERSONAL TIME Attire: As an integral part of the ZI family, your personal appearance is as important as your professional one. We at ZI realize that personal time clothing restrictions are unpopular and have therefore decided NOT to restrict personal time attire EXCEPT AS PERTAINS to the following.

CLOTHING DEEMED NOT ACCEPTABLE UNDER ANY CIRCUMSTANCES:

Any attire that brings attention to your sexual parts or organs such as but not limited to: backless pants, crotchless pants, frontless shirts, backless skirts, see-through clothing of any kind, clothing that glows, blinks, beeps, twirls, or flashes in any way in the area of your sexual parts or organs. Shorts that are cut high to show your sexual parts or organs (including your rear end), shoes that change your height either up or down by more than one half inch, scarves or belts of ANY KIND, and flip-flops.

— — —

"Now what? Do we go back or do we wait out here for another call?" Dill asked.

Carl checked his watch–it was a nostalgic throwback from when he was a young man. The green foam had disappeared, and the street was clean of gore. The day had become warmer by about ten degrees as the sun rose to the middle of the sky. This time of year used to be known as 'fall', and it was true that leaves still fell from the trees in abundance, but without holidays, classifications like fall or spring had little meaning anymore. Carl couldn't help a small stirring of anticipation for old Thanksgiving–another nostalgic throwback. Although it was rumored some people still celebrated, it had been officially banned shortly before the plague in 2024 by President Clooney along with all the other holidays. They'd been deemed too offensive.

"We go back," Carl said. "Eat. See what sales have been up to. I want to get this report to R&D so they have it by the time the Wranglers drop the collar off."

"Don't they already have it? Once you input the info, can't you just send it?"

"Yeah, yeah, of course." Carl clicked his seatbelt into place. "If it's something odd or anomalous, you want to talk to someone face to face. You don't want it lost in the bureaucracy."

Dill pressed the steering wheel at the top, making the car glide forward. She curved widely around the area where the zombie had been, even though no trace of it remained. The three still in the yard tracked the car with eyes that seemed–to Dill–sorrowful, left behind.

"They *have* it, they have the report," Dill said. "I don't get why you want to talk to someone about it."

"Keep it under twenty-five, Andretti," Carl said. "Arrive alive."

"What? Who's Andretti?" Dill hated the cryptic way older people talked. Euphemisms, outdated references…it was embarrassing. She wasn't sure if she liked Carl or not, just yet, and in the long run, it probably didn't matter either way…but she didn't want to be embarrassed of him.

"Race car driver. Forget it. Listen," Carl said and then turned to look out his window, "you want to talk to someone face to face because some things are more important than others. I know that's a tough concept for you…for your generation. A collar that didn't pop, and a relatively new one at that–it needs looking into. They may have changed something, modified something that needs to be changed back. When you work in Assessment, you make the determination not only for what needs to be done at the moment, but what *will be done* going forth. Assessment has a lot of responsibility and culpability. Do you get that? People are, you know, precious. We can't squander them because we just want to sit back and let the *system* handle things."

He'd huffed and shifted at the word 'precious', and Dill wondered about the sentimentality of that word. It didn't sit well in Carl's mouth, and it seemed, in fact, to irritate him.

"Because they're customers?" All Dill's training had included rhetoric about the importance of putting the customer first.

"No! Jesus," Carl said. "Well, okay, yes that, too, but not *just* that."

He said no more after that. His silence seemed deliberate and angry. Maybe this was why Assessment had a reputation. This overabundance of emotion, but a lot of older people were like that.

It made Dill and her generation raise their eyebrows–why get so worked up? What was the big deal?

She piloted the SUV through barren streets of burned-out neighborhoods with the occasional unburned house scattered throughout like an island of reason. They all had security systems tagged with the ZI logo. Closer to New Trenton, they passed the small, gated communities that housed the mid-richies–people who weren't really *rich* rich, but had enough for a small house, a cleaning person, groceries. Some of the mid-richies even had marriages and children, or so Dill had heard. Weird to think there might be kids behind those gates, growing up with parents–their own, real parents. Growing up without the knowledge of hiding, of fighting. Being fed on a regular basis. Used to good hygiene. Almost no fear.

Dill couldn't imagine it.

They crossed into New Trenton.

From what Dill had been told, Old Trenton was the city, barely discernible, about ten miles west of New Trenton. New Trenton hadn't been New Trenton until Old Trenton had fallen along with all the other cities. Infestations had been bad in urban areas, all those people packed cheek to jowl. After the first year, the smell alone had kept anyone from going back. After ten years, as the old buildings had begun to crumble away, the cities had been completely uninhabitable. The real big cities like Old Philadelphia still had tall, tall skyscrapers that glinted in the sun, looking taller than ever as the smaller buildings and outlying areas had collapsed around them. Dill had never seen it, though, not anywhere up close. There were photographs, but the older people always said, "Oh, photos don't do it justice! It was the *atmosphere*!" Dill didn't know about that, either. She was shaken by the amount of lights in the nighttime pictures. How could they have wasted the energy like that?

If there were people in the cities now–which there were rumored to be–they lived outside the safety net of government and ZI protection. Why anyone would want to do that was beyond Dill's comprehension.

New Trenton was based around a planned community from the early twenties. Shops, eateries and commercial offices sat under a tall pile of apartments. The theory being (Dell guessed) that the people in the apartments above lived, ate, and worked in the one area. Hive-like. Insect-like. In the area to the west of the apartment and commercial building combination was a housing development. The first four streets were smaller, attached rows of houses once known as 'town' houses. Then came ten streets of 'ranch' houses and past them, four streets of the two-story 'colonials'. Within the community were also a school, tennis courts, fields, and a swimming pool, long emptied.

Survivors of the plague had colonized the apartment building first, drawn to each other and coalescing like gray and exhausted snowflakes once the worst of the slaughter had slowed. Then Zombie, Inc., had begun business in a large corporate structure less than a quarter mile away, and as ZI grew, they'd taken over the planned community, christened it "New Trenton" and walled it in. Some of the first zombie defense systems were still in operation at New Trenton's perimeter.

The bottom floor of the apartment/commercial building, the abandoned stores and offices, were leased back to what little government remained. The apartments and government offices were known as the 'inners' while the townhouses and houses were referred to as the 'outers'.

Dill lived in the apartments in the inners, and her rent was subtracted right from her paycheck, as was the rent of her five roommates, who all worked for ZI. Another convenience of working for the biggest, most successful post-plague company, in Dill's opinion. ZI was rumored to be more powerful, even, than the little bit of government that sat, squished, under the weight of all ZI's lowest level workers.

They drove past the gate, Carl nodding to the keeper. They passed the inners and outers on the way to the ZI building. It was five stories tall and sat surrounded by an empty, cracked parking lot and a wide open field. Very few people drove anymore. Even the employees were bussed in or walked. Dill had had to have special training on driving the electric Assessment Team SUV along with lessons on the Ze Cross when she'd been accepted as a trainee for the position.

She wheeled the vehicle carefully around the building and slowed to a crawl as they approached the gate to the underground garage. She stopped the car, and it hummed idly. She blipped the horn. In the dark, the gate's eye bloomed into red life and scanned the front of the SUV. There was a pause, and then the gate–metal mesh and complicatedly jointed–rolled up with a jingling like bells.

Dill pushed the top of the steering wheel again, and they glided into the semi-dark.

"Jingle bells, Batman smells...hm hmm hmmm, duh dum," Carl sang contemplatively.

Dill glanced at him, but his head was turned away. He was hunched into himself, and his eyes scanned the recesses of the garage.

"What's that?" she asked.

"What's what? The song? Oh, it's just...an old Christmas song. Kids used to sing it. Robin laid an egg; Bat Mobile lost its wheels? You've never heard it?"

"Before my time," Dill said. Old people loved their holiday talk. Get two of them together and they'd go on and on about Christmas, Easter, Holloway or whatever it had been called. All those things had revolved around food, it seemed to Dill. She steered into their assigned spot. Two other Assessment SUVs sat nearby. A handful of Wrangler trucks were further down. Cleaners' cars were nowhere to be seen. Probably, they kept them in a different part of the garage, or maybe out back where testing went on.

"We'll go to R&D first and then eat, okay with you?" Carl asked as he exited the car. He scanned the garage, hand on the pistol at his hip.

Dill exited the car and scanned, too, even squatting to survey the areas under the adjacent vehicles. Better safe than sorry. Carl had started off without waiting for her answer. Not needing it. She was the trainee, and she would follow his lead.

They took the stairs at the front of the building, closest to reception. No choice in it, elevators were considered energy wasters. Nobody wasted anything anymore. It was one of the things that made holiday talk so irritating. An entire holiday wrapped around gluttony? Another one that included sanctified begging for candy? Was there anything in the old days that didn't require excess?

*

The third floor housed the research teams. An iris scanner allowed Carl and Dill entry to a kind of waiting area as a soft voice stating Carl's name whispered and echoed down a long, nondescript corridor. Dill stood, unconcerned, but Carl was discomfited as usual by the voice. It was ethereal and ghostlike. He always had the brief fantasy that he'd died and now stood in some afterlife processing center.

"Yo, Carl! What's up?" Aaron's voice, warm and deep and always on the verge of laughter, broke apart the afterlife fantasy.

Carl hesitated, waiting for the voice-over instructions.

"Please speak naturally. Your responses will be tracked and relayed via Ze Listen/Speak System," the soft mechanical voice intoned.

"Aw, shut your head, Matilda!" Aaron's voice crowed and echoed off the blank walls. "What's up, Carl? Something troubling you?"

"Yeah, Aaron, I wanted to tell you about a problem with a collar this morning. Are you coming out?"

There was a brief hum. Then Aaron's voice came again. "I can't come out right now, buddy. We're in the midst. What's the case number?"

"Atlanta 1280," Carl said. Some odd compulsion always made him speak to the ceiling tiles when he was on R&D. The small holes, maybe, but whatever the reason, he always felt like a jackass when he realized he was doing it. Now, Dill was searching the ceiling uncertainly, confusion clouding her features as she tried to decipher what he was looking at. Carl lowered his chin and crossed his hands behind his back. "It was a new one, blue tag. Wranglers probably brought it in already."

Hum. "What seemed to be the defect?"

"Half-popped. Zombie kept his head even though he'd wandered out of the protected quadrant," Carl said. Now Dill was scanning the floor, following the direction of his gaze again. Carl jerked his head up and tried to stare into the middle distance. Ze Listen/Speak was a disconcerting pain in the ass.

Long pause. Hum. "Lasers checked out?"

"Yeah, there were three other yard zombies that weren't going anywhere."

Longer pause. Hum. "I'll check it out. Can't have only half the charges blowing on the collars, now, can we?" Another pause and a hum. "You going to be there on day eighteen?"

"Yep, yep. Ready to beat your ass, too," Carl said.

This time the hum was broken up by crackling laughter. "In your dreams, old man. Over."

Carl smiled. "Over and out."

He checked his watch as he steered Dill back out into the stairwell. "Okay. Time to eat."

"What's on day eighteen?" Dill asked. Her face was cautious as though she'd get in trouble for asking. Her tone was hushed as though she thought day eighteen some sort of code.

"Bowling," Carl said and almost laughed at the disappointment in her quickly lowered head. "We bowl on the eights, eighteens, and twenty-eights."

"Uh huh," Dill said. "That's great."

"You don't bowl, I take it," Carl said. He opened the door at the lobby level. This floor was reception and sales–the most attractive department–and then the cafeteria.

"Bowl? No," Dill said. "That's kind of, you know...older. An older thing to do."

"Well, what do you do for fun? You and *your* generation?"

They entered the caf and headed for the back. There was a long, buffet-style setup. Sandwiches. Carl sighed. Hot food days were better, but they were restricted to every other or every third day.

"For fun?" Dill said. She pulled a tray from the pile and grabbed the nearest sandwich without looking at it. Carl, who had scoured them to find his favorite, didn't understand that level of...non-pickiness. He put a dish of hummus and a bag of pita chips on his tray. Dill didn't. Wasn't she hungry?

"Yeah, you know. During your ample leisure time. Your whole four or five hours before you hit the hay," Carl watched to see if she took a dessert. She didn't, but she did grab a fruit juice. She considered it for a long minute and then set it back in the cooler.

She turned puzzled eyes on Carl. "You mean after work? What do I do?"

Carl nodded but something in her expression, unguarded and sad, coupled with the return of the probably too expensive drink made him feel bad for her. *No*, he thought to himself. *Don't get caught up. This is a dog eat dog world now. To each his or her own.*

He turned away and slid his tray up to the cashier. "Hey, Dee."

"Hey, Carl," she said. The lunch-lady was older, in her seventies at least. It amazed Carl to think that she had been at least in her mid-fifties when the plague had gone down. Had she fought? Had she had a family she tried to defend? Did any of them make it with her? Was she all alone?

"You doing okay today?" Carl asked.

Dee nodded. "Yes, I surely am. How about you, dear?" She was sitting on a stool, and she wore an old-fashioned white apron that covered her from chest to mid-shin and tied at her waist. Carl put his wrist under the laser next to the old-fashioned cash register. The laser beeped, but the register remained silent, unused. Neither the register nor Dee were part of the process, people just liked continuity from the old ways. Your chip kept track of pay and expenditures. Physical money had lost all meaning after the plague. It was all electronic, now.

"I'm doing well," Carl said and smiled. Dee smiled back, and the smile was genuine, but there was something disengaged in her eyes, something struck and numb. It had happened to a lot of people. The carnage had been too much, but some folks had the bad luck to just live on and on despite their traumatized brains. "You take care," Carl said and carried his tray to an open table. He felt eyes on him. Not as many as would be on a Wrangler or, worse, a Cleaner, but he was eyeballed nonetheless. Especially by the youngest ones who never ventured beyond New Trenton and the ZI compound walls. To them, he was a reckless superhero like someone from one of their video games. Or so he flattered himself, anyway.

Dill sat down across from him. She'd started eating her sandwich before her tray hit the table. She tore into it, barely pausing for breath. Carl considered her as she ate and then pushed the pita chips and hummus across the table. "Want these?" he asked.

Her chewing slowed, and her face flamed bright red. She shook her head, dropped her sandwich back onto her tray, and looked away from him. Her throat contracted as she swallowed with difficulty.

"Just take it," Carl said, embarrassed by the implications of what he'd just done–what she seemed to think he'd suggested. "It doesn't mean anything. I just don't want it."

He'd heard that there was a system in place among some of the people of the inners. Food for sex, that kind of thing. It had been worse ten years ago when food was still much more of a commodity. She would have been around an age to get caught up in it. Sitting there in her khakis and white shirt, though, it was hard to imagine. She looked like a pretty straight arrow.

She hesitated, her eyes going to his. Her glance was wary. He picked up his sandwich and ignored her. He was a little angry, with himself or her, he couldn't decide. When she pulled the food onto her tray, he felt some of the anger disperse.

"So, tell me. I'm interested," he said. "What do you do for fun over there at the inners?"

As the words left his mouth and her face began to close up, he realized he'd made another misstep. The inners had a bad connotation, even though half or more of the ZI workforce lived there. In that light, his words sounded lecherous, even to his own ears.

He cleared his throat, ready to change the subject, but then she answered.

"Nothing, really," she said and shrugged. "I was night shift until I started under you, so mostly I read during the day. There are six of us in the apartment, so it's really crowded. Some of the two-bedroom apartments have eight people in them, and that would be way, way worse. I'm lucky, too, that the roommates I live with are quiet and honest, at least. You hear horror stories."

Carl nodded even though she wasn't looking at him. He felt that tug again, that sympathy. This girl could be his daughter, she could be...no. Nope. Put that thought away. Done was done. He sat back and crossed his arms over his chest.

"I'll bet," he said, then dropped it. Her eyes scanned him again, seemingly confused by his sudden withdrawal, and he felt another tug but squashed it. "I'm going to sales to check the boards. You want to wait here or tag along?"

She stuffed the half-finished bag of chips into her khaki pocket as she stood. "I'm coming with you."

"You don't have to."

"I want to. I want to learn Assessment, every part of it, and the sooner, the better. It's..." She shook her head. "I've been on nights since I was sixteen–for ten *years*, Carl. I couldn't pay for any of the degrees for the other positions. It's important that I get this, okay?"

Carl raised his eyebrows and nodded. "Sure, Dill, no problem," he said. He had a terrible urge to pat her shoulder but controlled his hand at the last minute. The last place he wanted to visit was HR.

# FOUR

## Zombie, Inc., Company Handbook
Harassment
Sec. 18: Coworker contact: physical and eye
(*rev. 08/17/51*)

Zombie, Inc., (known hereafter as 'ZI') prohibits WITHOUT EXCEPTION the touching of employees by other employees. This includes, but is not limited, to: hugging, handshakes, kissing (even air varieties), putting of hands on necks, shoulders, arms, hands, knees, thighs, backs, or backsides, or patting of same. All employees are required to keep their hands to themselves at all times.

Employees should refrain from prolonged eye contact, which could be perceived as 'staring'. Although ZI couldn't possibly describe each and every instance where 'looking' at another employee becomes necessary, the following should be considered as a guideline:

1) Recreational (non-work related) conversational eye contact should be maintained for no longer than two to five seconds before taking a 'break'.*

2) Work conversation eye contact should be maintained for no longer than five to seven seconds before taking a 'break'.*

*During the eye contact 'break' periods noted in 1) and 2) above, it should be further noted that a break constitutes looking away from the coworker to an inanimate object in the near distance or far, such as, but not limited, to: walls, desks, tables, chairs, computer terminals, plants, etc., and UNDER NO*

*CIRCUMSTANCES during the break in eye contact should your eyes shift to your coworker's body.*

3) At no time should employees stare at coworkers with or without the coworker's knowledge. 'Watching' a coworker for longer than three seconds will constitute a hostile work environment and could be terms for immediate dismissal.

Please adhere to the above guidelines for inter-company staring and eye contact provisions. Refer to section 19 of "Harassment 'Visitor contact: physical and eye'" for ZI policies of behavior regarding visitors to ZI. Refer to section 20 of "Harassment 'Vendor contact: physical and eye'" for ZI policies on behavior regarding Vendors to ZI.

– – –

Dill tore her eyes from Candy's deep cleavage but found them going instead to the shiny, sticky pout of Candy's lips. Dill looked down only to have her eyes encounter Candy's legs, smooth and milky, crossed at the knee and bare almost to mid-thigh at one end, down to her feet pushed suggestively into stilettos at the other.

Dill forced her eyes to the floor. The move brought her to her own modest bosom, further camouflaged in white broadcloth, into view. Below that loomed her sexless khakis and thick, black, steel-toe boots. It was almost as though she and Candy were whole separate species.

Dill had started at Zombie, Inc., at sixteen in the Industrial Department night shift, which meant cleaning, mail delivery, grounds checks, general gophering–all in a spectacularly unattractive outfit of grayish coveralls and headscarf. She'd never been in the sales department when people were there–Sales didn't work a night shift–although she'd been entranced by the smell of it, spicy and sometimes flowery, the times she'd scuttled through in the semi-gloom.

She cast her gaze about again, trying not to let it get snagged on any one person. Even the walls in Sales, even the desks, the chairs, had an air of wealth, seduction, and rich indulgence. Voices murmured sexily, whispering and confidential, from the large cubicles. Well-groomed men and highly colored women comprised the very decorative ZI sales team.

"You might want to give him a call," Carl was saying. He seemed unmoved by Candy's obvious excess, but Dill didn't understand how. Candy was gorgeous, and she smelled like, well, like candy.

"Aaw...was he upset? My poor little man!" Candy's tone was a soft fur wrap, a sip of warm whiskey, silken sheets. She uncrossed and re-crossed her legs and leaned forward from her high-backed, deeply upholstered chair. She clasped her hands together lightly on her desk, tented thumbs seeming to point directly to the perfumed cave mouth between her breasts. "What about *you*, Carl? You escaped unscathed again, I see. So brave!"

Carl laughed, but it was a cynical bark, loud and harsh, out of place in the plush hush of the room. Well-coiffed heads appeared over cubicle walls and plucked eyebrows raised like thin crescent moons. Dill's face grew hot with embarrassment, but Candy's expression of admiring desire, eyes pinned to Carl, never changed.

"You know you oversold that guy," Carl said. "Four in the front? That's a little extreme. Even for you, Candy."

Candy's smile widened, showing her dimples. "Everyone has the right to feel safe, Carl. Everyone wants to be snug and secure...don't you? Don't *you* want to be snuggled, Carl?" Her eyelashes fluttered. At 'you' she'd lazily tilted a rosy-tipped index finger, pointing–not by coincidence–to the area of his groin.

Carl's eyes stayed on hers, half-lidded with disgust. Real or feigned, Dill couldn't tell.

"You don't need to waste your talents on me, Candy. I'm no richie."

The warmth in Candy's eyes chilled by more than a few degrees, replaced with disinterest. She turned away like a cat whose plaything had finally died. "I'll call him," she said as she flipped through an appointment book. A whiff of perfume wafted past Dill's face as the pages turned...was everything in Sales perfumed? Candy continued speaking without turning around. "Who's your little friend, Carl?"

"This is Dill, she's–"

"Dillalia!" Dill broke in, without realizing she was going to. Carl's eyes raked her, taken aback at either her tone or the interruption itself. "It's...my name is...it's Dillalia. My full name." She could almost feel Carl's eyes boring into the side of her face. "But everyone calls me Dill." For some reason, admitting to the nickname made her feel deflated and let down.

"–she's learning Assessment," Carl finished, still staring at Dill in puzzlement.

"As*sessment*? A pretty girl like *you*?" Candy had turned, and her eyes went round with incredulity. "Dilly, baby…what are you *thinking*?" Without taking her eyes from Dill she called, "Robert, Augustus, come here a minute. Look who Carl's trying to ruin now."

Two men, well-dressed and gorgeous, sauntered over. One man was sporty and clean cut, wearing slacks and a V-neck sweater with an additional sweater tied over his shoulders. The other was rugged with a neatly trimmed beard, wearing a spotless and obviously freshly pressed red and black check flannel over dark, new looking blue jeans. They both looked to be in their late twenties, just like Candy, but who could tell? They both wore thick foundation dusted with powder, same as Candy.

"What's going on, Candy-cane?" Sporto asked, and Candy raised her fingertips to her lips and giggled. Even her giggle came out like a cat's purr.

"This is Dilly, and *isn't* she, though?" Candy said and indicated Dill with a small nod. "Carl's training her in Assessment. With *his* reputation; can you *imagine*?"

Rugged eyed Dill up and down, making her take a step back. She was unused to scrutiny of any kind…the handbook expressly forbid it. Sales must play by another set of rules entirely.

"Yum, she *is* a dilly!" Sporto said. He gazed into Dill's eyes, and his gaze was so intense, so narrow and focused, it nearly took her breath away. Denny never once looked at her like that. Even during the brief times they found to get naked together. "Have we met before? You seem so familiar to me." He smiled, and the fine lines at the corners of his eyes looked like cat's whiskers. Dill felt her own mouth wanting to smile back, but his attention was overwhelming.

Rugged grasped her upper arm, further confusing her. *No touching!* her panicked mind squeaked, but his hand was warm, almost hot, as he massaged her.

"You're too pretty to be out on the streets, beautiful," he said, and the deep grumble of his voice caused a shiver of reaction down her spine. His fingers traced down to her elbow, but the sexy effect was ruined by the hard cotton of her sleeve.

"Yeah, only uggos and old folks should put themselves in harm's way," Carl said and barked his ugly laugh again, as if to underline the statement.

Dill blinked, shocked out of the reverie the men had caused in her.

Sporto looked to Rugged with uncertainty clouding his beautiful eyes, but Rugged nodded with confident assent. "Well, yes, of course, Carl," he said as if that much need not be stated–as though it were simply too obvious. "Those of us blessed with good genes should be in Sales. It's for the betterment of everyone in the company. Same as the really brave guys, the straight shooters, strong, smart, resourceful–like yourself–are best utilized in Assessment. It's the hardest job going." Now Rugged grasped Carl's arm and squeezed, staring him dead in the eye. The contact was different from the contact he'd made with Dill, manlier, earnest. "We *need* you guys out there, Carl. *You're* the heroes. Without you, we'd be nothing."

Dill held her breath. So much touching and staring, so much inappropriateness, but so flattering. Would Carl be flattered? How could he not? Carl shook Rugged off with another laugh.

"Save it, Robert," Carl said. "Save it for your customers. You don't want anything from me, and quit pawing me. Dill shouldn't be seeing that; she's by the book. She'll turn you in, Robert."

Rugged Robert turned sad, hurt eyes from Carl to Dill. "You wouldn't do that, would you? No, I can tell you wouldn't." He smiled. "You're one of us, Dilly. You're sales all the way."

Dill felt herself sinking forward, hypnotized, magnetized by his tone and his beard and his manly eyes.

Above and around them, a Klaxon blared. Red emergency lights spun into dizzying life.

"Five seconds," Candy snapped, all pretense of flirtation leached from her clipped tone. She produced a machete from her desk drawer. A pistol appeared in Rugged Robert's hand as if by magic, and Sporto was suddenly holding a knife. A very large knife. Dill was shocked by the amount of weaponry suddenly in view. Overnight teams were strenuously encouraged not to bring weapons of any kind to work. "Carl, get her out of here. Gate's gonna close. Four seconds."

Carl's hand was rough on Dill's bicep. "Come on," he said and turned to one of the department entrances. A mechanical groan came from the ceiling, deeper than the alarm horn, rumbling under it. The leading edge of a stainless-steel gate–like the ones used for security on storefronts in the old days–began to descend from the ceiling.

"Three seconds!" Candy said. Her face was pale and tight. She and Robert put their backs together as the other man, the sporty one, faced the falling gate. Up and down the department, the Sales team had turned to face the falling gates.

"No breach, no breach," Sporto said almost in a chant. "We're clean so far. We're clean. Gate's almost down. Almost there."

Carl and Dill exited Sales as the gate rolled down behind them. Dill looked back at the last second. The red lights flashed from the ceiling, rotating, nauseating. The languid, laid-back members of the sales department had changed completely in the four seconds since the alarm rang out–they'd become sharp-eyed, grave, weapon-wielding soldiers. Candy gave Dill a small, serious nod and then disappeared as a second gate–this one solid–sunk into the floor between them.

"What is it?" Dill asked, yelling to be heard over the alarm. Carl had pulled her into a jog back toward the cafeteria.

"Maybe nothing, maybe just a drill," he said. He glanced at his hand on her arm, blinked, and dropped his hand. "Sorry about that. Habit."

They trotted past reception, where three attractive girls stood in military stance, their backs together as they looked in every direction.

"Is it a drill?" Carl yelled as he and Dill hurried past.

The girl facing them cut her eyes to Carl and away. "We don't know," she said, her voice threaded with controlled panic. "We weren't told, if it is."

Carl nodded acknowledgment and then picked up his pace as he slipped the gun from the holster at his side. Dill's stomach tightened in a knot. Why didn't she have a gun? Or at least a knife. She needed a knife. She suddenly missed Carl's hand on her arm. There'd been a rough comfort to it, regardless of the inappropriateness.

"What is it?" Dill said. "What set off the alarms?" This had never happened at night. She'd never even heard of it. They came to the cafeteria's one big entrance, and Carl slid to a halt, putting his arm out to stop her too. "Carl? What's going on?"

His eyes scanned the cafeteria. Everyone who'd been eating stood facing the entrance, even Dee. The bottom edge of her apron trembled.

"Anything?" he yelled into the room. Heads shook, but no one relaxed. Carl turned to glare down the hallway that led to the stairs.

"Carl?" Dill said and couldn't keep the panic from her voice. Her stomach seemed to be turning over on itself like a coiling snake. "Please." She placed her hand on his forearm. It felt strange for her to do so, but she didn't know how else to get his attention. His eyes came to hers and held.

"That alarm is for an inside breach. You'd never hear it at night because they don't usually run the drills at night–not enough people in to make it worthwhile, I guess." He reached up, patted her hand, and gave her a one-sided grin although his eyes stayed grave. "It's probably–*probably*–just a drill. They run them at random. But you can't be sure, so you have to be ready." He scanned her and apprehension darkened his eyes. "Where's your weapon? Your crossbow?"

She looked down, as if she might find it on her person, but of course, it wasn't there. She'd left it in the SUV. She looked back at Carl, her mouth hanging open. His lips tightened, and he shook his head.

"What the *fuck*, Dill? That's rookie shit," he said. "What are you thinking? You *never* leave your weapon behind!"

The anger in his voice made tears sting her eyes, but she wouldn't let them fall.

"I *am* a rookie!" she said and swallowed. The alarm blared and blared, drilling into her brain. "This never happened in Maintenance! You're supposed to *say*!" She stomped on the word

'say', she couldn't help herself. She was acting like she was nine–
she *felt* like she was six or seven.

"You're gonna have to stay here in the caf. I'll come get you
when it's the all-clear." He started to turn away but then turned
back. His lips tightened again. He leaned closer so she could hear
him without yelling. "You're right, I'm sorry. I wasn't paying
enough attention. I will from now on."

She gripped his arms, panicked. "Let me come with you!"

"Stay here in the caf. Get to the back where the exits are. Fuck
what anyone says to you about it, okay? Get behind the line; stay
away from *everyone*. Give yourself room to react if something
goes wrong…" He shook his head. He laughed, startling her. "If
something goes wrong, we're all fucked." He gave her a light
shove. "Go!"

Carl turned and trotted down the main hall, pistol up and ready.
A few people joined him, but they all kept a good distance from
each other. Dill turned back to the cafeteria. The people in there
were the same way, huddled in groups of no more than three with
wide, empty areas between the groups. It looked both random and
deliberate. She glanced over her shoulder, but Carl was gone. She
went into the cafeteria.

*

Carl strode past the bank of unused elevators, turned a corner,
and faced the blank door to the stairwell. It was solid steel with a
mesh-laced glass rectangle at eye level. The people who'd
followed him down the hall stopped short. He glanced over his
shoulder. They were fifteen feet back, at least. Good. That gave
them room to react should something go wrong.

He put his face to the glass and scanned the stairwell. He craned
his neck to see up the stairs but the sightline was only for eight
steps before the stairwell doubled back on itself. Each level was
comprised of a split stairwell.

There was no movement, only the dizzying red light. Carl
barely heard the alarm anymore; he'd pushed it to the back of his
mind. He glanced up again, straining to see through the small
window, and then pushed the door open.

"Should we let him go in there alone?" came from behind him. As the door swung shut, he heard, "He's Assessment. He can take care of–" The door closed with a soft, hissing thunk.

The stairwell was a little quieter than the outer hall, and there were no pulsing red lights. Carl looked up the stairs. No movement. He checked his watch. The alarm had started forty seconds ago. If it went past a minute, then there was no way this was a drill.

He ran up the first set of stairs and then the second. He went to the door and scanned the second-floor hallway. Nothing looked amiss, no bodies, no gunshots, but the red lights continued to twirl their hazard. Carl checked down the stairs, then up to the next floor. He listened and then ran up the next set of stairs to three.

Research. If there was a problem, it was most likely on this floor.

He checked through the rectangle of glass and then pushed the door open to be greeted by the long, blank hallway. The inner door scanner scanned his eye. The white walls had taken on a pinkish, bleeding hue, and the alarm was loud again.

"Aaron!" Carl said, bellowing to be heard over the alarm. The voice announcement wouldn't work as long as the alarm was on. "Aaron, you guys okay up here?"

They would all be tucked securely in their rooms. Should be. This was the most dangerous floor because in Research, as Aaron always said, they played with zombies, and sometimes they played rough.

"Aaron!" Carl said again then listened. Nothing. Nothing but that long, stained-pink hallway. "Shit," he muttered to himself. "I'm coming in!" he said and started down the hall.

The alarm stopped. The red lights slowed and then blinked out.

"Carl? It's Aaron. We're okay." His voice was thin through the ZE Listen/Speak. "Hold on, I'm coming out."

A door halfway down the corridor opened up. A man in a white overall suit hurried toward Carl. "Hey, man," he called out, with a small wave, "we're good. We had a small incident. A minor escape."

"An escape? Jesus, Aaron," Carl said and lowered the gun, "what the hell are you nuts doing up here?"

Aaron smiled and shook his head. He was still forty feet down the hall but closing the distance. His face broke into a raft of good-natured wrinkles when he laughed. "Yeah, one of the techs must have fucked up when we–"

A door between Aaron and Carl slammed open. Another man, small and compact in his white coverall, smashed shoulder first into the wall across from the door. His eyes were wide behind thick glasses. He put his hand up toward Aaron, palm out in a stop gesture. His coverall was stained red from collar to groin, and the stain was spreading. "Aaron, no!" the man cried out. "Get back in the–" Behind him, the door slammed open again and disgorged a nightmare.

A zombie, nearly seven feet tall, stood in the hall, swaying. It was naked. Carl's first, confused thought was that it was wearing a corset, but then he realized that the 'corset' was the circlet of muscle and tendon on its midsection…its torso had been flayed. One of its arms was gone from the elbow down and a rough metal armature had been strapped over the stump. Wires that had been embedded into its shaved head swung and shivered. The dirt/coffee ground substance had caked and dried around the end of each wire. Its eyes had been braced open with metal springs, and its ears removed. It moaned, and the hair on Carl's arms stood up. The zombie swayed, looming over the small man, who cowered with his hands over his head. Aaron stood open-mouthed, watching.

"Aaron! Move!" Carl yelled down the hall. He couldn't get a bead on the zombie with Aaron standing behind it like a stunned lamb. "Drop! Drop, Aaron! On your knees!"

Aaron dropped. Carl shot. A hole appeared in the zombie's head, and then bone, brain, wires, and dark granules appeared on the wall in a spray of modern art. It collapsed as though it were an electrical appliance come unplugged. Beside it, the small man in the white coat shook and whined, his hands still over his head. His glasses had tumbled to the carpeted hallway floor. They hadn't broken.

Carl walked closer. "Head up, buddy," Carl said to the shaking man in the lab coat. His voice was neutral, his features calm but watchful, his gun held discreetly out of sight next to his thigh. At his feet, the man's quivering hands parted. He looked up at Carl, and tears like pearls ran from his eyes, leaving shiny trails. His face looked naked without the thick glasses. His irises had already begun to fade to the washed-out gray of the undead.

The man said, "Hey, hey don't–"

Carl shot him.

*

"What happened?" Carl asked Aaron, who'd bent over the small man. Carl's tone was still calm, controlled. He had not holstered his gun.

"You shot him," Aaron said and looked at Carl with spacey, fear-filled eyes. "You shot Randy. You shot him."

"What *happened*, Aaron? Why did you turn the alarm off when that zombie was still mobile?"

Aaron swallowed and looked down. His hands fluttered over Randy as if he could conjure the tech back from the dead. "Matilda!" he said, his voice urgent. "Matilda!"

The hidden overhead speaker of the ZE Listen/Speak hummed briefly. "Yes, Aaron? How may I assist you?" The voice was feminine but only on the surface, only due to the pitch. It was a series of sounds that simulated words, with a slight slurring as the sounds were strung together. Inflection was random and occasionally maddening. If the pitch were lowered, the voice would become masculine. Carl didn't know the psychology behind the AI voice; he only knew that something in the human brain objected to it. At least, his did.

"Matilda, we need a gurney for Randy. Contact Dr. Patel. Contact Dr. Morris. We'll meet in the–"

"Aaron," Carl broke in. It seemed the speaker above hummed with disapproval. "You don't need doctors; he's dead. *Dead*, dead. He's not getting back up. I put the bullet right in his brain."

Aaron looked at Carl, his mouth working. "I...I know. I know that, Carl." Aaron swallowed. "They're his friends. They'll want to...to help. We're all...we're all friends up here."

"Okay. Okay, sorry," Carl said and leaned against the corridor wall. He holstered his gun and scrubbed his hands over his face. "Sorry, buddy. Go ahead."

Two techs in white coveralls had already appeared with a gurney, and Aaron helped them load Randy onto it. "Take him to C," Aaron said. "Patel and Morris should be there already. Tell them," Aaron glanced at Carl and then away, "tell them I'll be there in a minute."

The techs nodded and wheeled the covered gurney back down the long corridor.

"Matilda," Aaron said, "we need a Cleaner and the bleach." A panel popped open, revealing something like an old-fashioned fire extinguisher. Aaron pulled it from the wall, his movements slow and despairing. He trained the nozzle to where Randy's body had lain, and he squeezed the trigger. Green foam shot out in a flat spray, and Aaron methodically covered the bloodstain on the floor and the wall, being careful not to spray too near the zombie. The foam crackled and spit as it began to eat.

"The Cleaner would have handled that," Carl said. His voice had hardened again. Something seemed odd, off.

Aaron turned to Carl with exasperation. His eyes were still shocky and sad. He looked to be on the verge of tears. "He was our *friend*, Carl. We take care of each other up here. I don't want his DNA mixed with the zombie's, okay? Is that reason enough for you?" His face was inches from Carl's as he yelled. "We're not like Assessment with their lone fucking wolf mentality. We *help* each other. We *care* about what happens to our coworkers. Okay? Is that okay with you?"

Carl tented his fingers on Aaron's chest and pushed, lightly but firmly. Aaron stepped back, and his eyes dropped.

"Sorry, Carl. I'm just…you know." He gestured behind him. "Randy was a good tech and a good friend. A nice guy," he said and looked up again. "Even *you* would have liked him."

"Maybe so," Carl said. A flush of anger and shame had colored his features as Aaron yelled. That lone wolf line had hit a little too close to home considering his last two trainees, but now his calm returned like a shield. "At least it was only one death for the guy, and he'll get full bennies. No worries for his family, if he had any," Carl surveyed the zombie again, "but it's gonna be a shit-ton of paperwork for me."

Anger flashed in Aaron's eyes and then disappeared. His shoulders dropped, and he sank back against the wall. "Jesus, Carl," he said, his voice almost a whisper.

A Cleaner appeared from the stairwell door. He opened double doors opposite and rolled out a machine roughly the size of a hotel maid's cart from the old days. This Cleaner had the white suit that covered him from head to toe, completely concealing features or identity, but not the black suit or hat. He (or she) was in the grayish coverall of Maintenance. Most street Cleaners came up from Maintenance. The Cleaner nodded without speaking when Aaron pointed to the metal prosthetic on the zombie's arm and gave instructions that Carl couldn't hear.

"Let's get out of here," Aaron said. "I don't want to see this right now. I'm going on break."

Carl nodded and followed Aaron out the exit but glanced back as the door began to close. He braced it open with his foot.

The Cleaner flicked a switch on the big machine, and it grumbled to life. He drew forth a reciprocating saw and turned to the zombie.

The zombie faced Carl, and its eyes were filmed white with cataracts. The electrodes still embedded in its shaved head trailed gaily-colored wires–a nightmare, tribal headdress. As the Cleaner bent to work, sawing the arm from the shoulder, the zombie's head jerked and rocked and the wires waved merrily. An eye-brace popped out, and its eye slid closed in a lecherous wink.

Carl let the door swing closed.

*

Dill was standing just outside the cafeteria, her bow hanging forgotten in her hand. Her face was tight with worry. Carl came into view from the stairwell corridor, and she took a few tripping steps toward him, her breath rushing out and a smile surfacing.

"What happened?" she called out just as Carl said, "When did you get your bow? I told you to stay in the back of the cafeteria."

Dill's smile faded, and she glanced at her bow as though surprised to see it. "After the...when the alarm stopped," she said and shrugged. "Everything was all-clear, wasn't it?"

Carl shook his head and walked past her. The man following him shot her a sympathetic glance and motioned for her to follow. She fell in next to him as Carl marched determinedly on.

"You're Dillalia, right? Carl's new trainee? I'm Aaron. I talked to you guys right before the alarms went off, when you came up to R&D." He pulled out a chair for her at the round table where Carl had seated himself. Annoyance crossed Carl's features at Aaron's gesture.

"Oh, yeah, I remember," Dill said. "You cursed Matilda."

Although Aaron and Carl were probably around the same age, Carl's rough, weathered exterior was in sharp contrast to the soft, white, almost lineless face of Aaron. He looked more like the people of Dill's generation and after. Most never saw the sun for any great duration. Besides being dangerous, there was simply nothing to do outside.

"That's right, I did. That voice is…" Aaron shook his head and shuddered, and his small smile fell away. He stared at the tabletop for a distracted minute. Then he shook himself and smiled at her. "Anyway, how do you like it so far? Are you getting along all right? What department did you come from?"

Dill answered the easiest question, her eyes cutting to Carl, who glowered opposite her. "I was in Maintenance. Overnight shift."

"Aah. So you know this place well, don't you?"

"What do you mean?"

"Well, just that you get to see almost every department; most people only see their own desks! Maintenance does the tasks that allow everyone else to do their specific little jobs. They're the backbone of the company. The lifeline of it." Aaron's tone was admiring.

She smiled uncertainly. "I guess, yeah."

"Yeah," Carl snorted. "The trash emptiers are a rare and noble breed. How about you grab us coffees since you're our oh-so-vital *lifeline*?"

Dill's face flushed a deep, embarrassed red. She pushed her chair back without looking at the men and dropped her bow onto the table.

"Take it with you," Carl said and poked the table for emphasis. "*Learn*, Dill. Try to learn as you go along."

After she was safely distant in the line, Aaron turned to Carl. "Why were you so mean to her? What's got into you?"

"Got into me? Nothing! She has to learn, that's all," Carl said. He crossed his arms over his chest and blew out an agitated breath. "Ah, fuck."

"What?"

Carl glanced back to see where Dill stood in line. She had hitched her bow over her shoulder and was talking with the young man behind her. She seemed recovered. Carl turned back and shook his head.

"What, Carl?" Aaron asked. "Are you afraid about your rec allotment?"

"No, Jesus. They're not going to cut me off for losing the last two."

"Two in a *row*, though."

"So what? So what if they were in a row?" Carl said. "It's only numbers that count, not order. I haven't lost that many if you total it. Especially not for Assessment!"

"Assessment is tough. Very dangerous," Aaron agreed. "So, what, then? Why are you reacting so strongly to her?" An idea dawned across his features, and he leaned closer to Carl and dropped his voice. "You think she's EA? You always hear rumors."

Carl shrugged. "For a second I did. She seemed pretty self-contained out in the field. For the first little bit, anyway, but then she fell apart. Started getting scared." He grew quiet for a long moment, and then looked at Aaron. "She killed a zombie that the Wranglers were having trouble with."

"*What?*" Aaron said. "Are you *kidding* me?"

Carl shook his head and laughed. "I shit you not, man. The thing was tripping and flinging itself all around, and it got hold of one of 'em–nothing major, you knew the Wranglers had it covered–but then up she pops and creams the sucker with an arrow!"

"An *arrow*?" Aaron's tone had gone past amazement to outright disbelief.

"Yeah, buddy, I'm *telling* you." Carl started to laugh. "She almost took out the Wranglers, too."

Aaron laughed, his hand over his mouth and shoulders shaking. "Oh, geez…how'd they react to *that*? Did they try to kill her?"

"No, that was the best," Carl said. "They manhandled the poor girl, loved her up and down, and pledged their undying allegiance. Big damn dogs that they are, you know?" He wiped his eyes. "It was a sight."

"I can't even begin to imagine," Aaron said, getting himself under control. "So but then…why?"

"Why what?" Carl said and glanced to where Dill was running her wrist under the reader to pay for the coffees. He felt a stab of guilt–he knew she probably didn't have enough to cover it. He'd pick up her lunch tomorrow.

"Why were you being so hard on her?" Aaron asked. He'd sobered completely, and his tone held real curiosity.

Carl shrugged. "I guess I just don't want anything to happen to her, and when I saw she'd gone to the garage by herself…I got pissed. Now shut the hell up about it; here she comes."

Carl could feel Aaron's eyes on him as Dill put the coffees on the table.

"So," Dill said into the silence, "what happened? Was it just a drill?"

"Nope, not a drill," Carl said. "That's why you shouldn't have gone to the garage before you knew what was going on." He talked into his coffee cup. "The garage is dangerous. Too dark and too confined."

This time, Dill didn't point out that the alarm had stopped *before* she made the garage run; she merely nodded, but her earlier protestation made him remember the all-clear. He turned to Aaron, who was stirring his coffee slowly.

"Why *did* the alarm stop? Did you shut it off?" Carl asked.

Without looking up, Aaron raised his eyebrows. His hand hitched and then returned to stirring. "I did, I'm afraid to say. I thought we had it under control." He grimaced. "I know you'll have to put it in your report, Carl, but I don't think it would have changed anything had the alarm been left to whoop. Randy would still have been bit."

"What happened?" Carl asked. "How did it get free?"

"I'm sure I don't know; I wasn't there. Of course, I'll start digging into it once I get back on three, but for right now, I'm going to sit and drink coffee. My nerves are shot," Aaron shuddered lightly, "and I don't want to see the clean-up."

"You're telling me you're squeamish? Come on, Aaron," Carl said and smiled. "You guys see and do that stuff all the time if zapped is to be believed."

"Ugh, those people. They are the bane of my existence," Aaron said. "I'd like to get some of them up on three."

Carl and Aaron laughed, but Dill just looked down into her still-full coffee cup.

# FIVE

## Z.A.P.T.
## !!ZOMBIES ARE PEOPLE TOO!!
Mission Statement

Zombies Are People Too (Z.A.P.T.) was founded in 2047 by a small group of citizens incensed by the mistreatment and exploitation of our Zombie family and friends. Z.A.P.T. has grown to many members and is quickly becoming a force in bringing about new legislation to protect our Zombie brothers and sisters.

Z.A.P.T. has chosen to work primarily to stop:

1) The brutal vivisectionism practiced by corporations such as **Zombie, Inc.**, and the practices, experiments, goods, and services they provide, which harm our Zombie compadres and detracts from their dignity and rights as citizens.

2) Zombies as entertainment as practiced by media outlets such as **First Death Fun Corp.**, which produces the video lines titled *MenZie: Fights!* and the even more reprehensible *WomZies: Fresh Enuff to Stuff!*, which harm our Zombie companions and detracts from their dignity and rights as citizens.

3) Second Death Laws. **Z.A.P.T.** is working tirelessly to get legislation on the books making it a CRIME to kill a Zombie.

Always remember: ***ZOMBIES ARE PEOPLE TOO!!***

NEVER FORGET THAT ***YOU*** COULD BE ***NEXT!!*** DO YOU WANT YOUR RIGHTS AS A CITIZEN ***DENIED*** SIMPLY BECAUSE YOU HAVE DIED AND RESURRECTED?!? MORE RESEARCH NEEDS TO BE DONE AND MORE STUDIES MADE!! **Z.A.P.T.** STANDS WITH OUR ZOMBIE BROTHERS

AND SISTERS!! WE WILL NEVER STOP *FIGHTING* FOR **YOUR** RIGHTS!!

"Assholes," Carl said and crumpled the flyer. "They don't even know they dropped a comma. Sloppy." He dropped it into the bowl and flushed.

The Z.A.P.T. flyers appeared now and again in the bathrooms of Zombie, Inc., taped to the insides of the stall doors. Probably because it was the only area not policed by cameras. The group and their supporters were young and idealistic. Too young to remember the plague itself, too young even to remember the handful of years after, when it was still so dangerous that there were more people dying than being born. By at least ten to one.

Little shits. Like to see them stuck in a small room with one of their "Zombie friends"; see how fast they'd reach for a weapon. Or maybe they wouldn't. Jesus, who knows? Carl sighed and moved to the sink. As he washed his hands, he studied himself in the mirror. Old. No question he was getting old. He didn't understand the post-plague generation any more than his own old man had understood Carl's generation. Carl–who'd been born in 2000–hadn't understood them much, himself. He'd sided with his dad on the issue.

Excess. That had been the problem for Carl's generation: too much of everything. Food, entertainment, communication–everything so accessible. By the time Carl had reached his late teens, cancer had been cured, diabetes, heart disease, anything congenital. No one got sick. It seemed like hardly anyone died, and the world was an unending steam of information. Instant, invasive, impossible to ignore but also impossible to assimilate or to…what? Impossible to prioritize, that was it. Everything was so urgent that everything cancelled everything else out.

What a shock when it had all crashed.

How many had simply killed themselves in light of the atrocities occurring? Carl turned away from the mirror and left the bathroom. He didn't want to be reminded of his age and bitterness, didn't want to see the hurt that lurked, always, in his eyes.

Dill was still at the table, but Aaron had left.

"What now?" Dill asked. "Do we go back to sales again?"

Carl looked at his watch without sitting back down. It seemed the day had gone on forever, but it was only just past two. "I have to write up what went on upstairs. I had to shoot an employee of R&D. It's going to take some time to get it all down."

Dill's eyes had dropped to her coffee cup when he mentioned shooting Randy. Did she know him or something? How could she have?

"You okay?" he asked.

She shrugged. "I guess." Her voice hitched, and she dropped her head so he couldn't see her face. Was she crying? Shit.

"Well...what the hell? What's wrong?"

"Nothing, I just," she looked up, and to his relief, her eyes were clear of tears. "I don't know if I could do it."

Carl pulled out his chair and sat back down. "You did it this morning. That zombie out in the suburbs. You did great!"

Dill shook her head dismissively, her mouth tucking in on one side. "That was a zombie, though. I don't know if I could shoot a person."

"What do you think that zombie was? He was a person at one time, just changed. Still the same thing on some level, if you look at it a certain way." Carl cleared his throat and changed tacks–he was beginning to sound like one of those zapped assholes. "Besides, one person resurrecting in the building would be an absolute nightmare, even with all the security measures. The people on three know that, and they know the risks. They do unsafe work, and  that's why they're so tightly controlled by security measures. For the other departments, like sales, it's all about defense with those security gates. For R&D, we play offense. Nobody gets in or out without notice, alarms or no."

"Because that's where they do the experiments. On the zombies," Dill said. Her head tilted.

Carl felt irritated by Dill's tone; it didn't seem entirely based in curiosity. Maybe she was the one who'd been putting flyers in the bathroom. Maybe she was a follower or even worse, an infiltrator from Z.A.P.T., coming in with an agenda. But then again, she *had* shot that zombie. A Z.A.P.T. believer, a *true* believer, couldn't have done that.

"Everything they do up there and out back is what keeps us in jobs," Carl said. "The new technology, all the new products...it all comes from R&D. Take the yard zombies, for instance; Zombie, Inc., came up with the idea of using zombies for home defense. That was back when looting had become so common. When people were ready to take their homes back, it wasn't unusual that someone would be, say, sitting eating dinner and in would come a looter. There were all kinds of messes."

"The burning put an end to that, not the yard zombies. Or at least, not *primarily* the yard zombies. Once the reoccupiers got onto the idea of burning down the empty houses, the looting stopped."

Carl pursed his lips, considering her words. She seemed to know a lot about stuff that happened almost before her time. She would have been just a kid, maybe five or six. She couldn't have been so aware of it. "You're right, the random looting stopped, but burglaries–real burglaries–started in earnest. Lot of people beat up and even killed," Carl said. Then he had a thought. "Where did you grow up, Dill? You said you were with your dad until you were fourteen?"

"In the suburbs. Like the one we were at today, but it was...when we were there, I was little, and it was...different than it is now."

Carl nodded. It would have had to been. The time frame she was talking about was not very long after the initial plague, not in terms of progress, at least. At that time, the suburbs were a lawless wasteland. Cities had emptied out. Government was struggling to regain control. Hysteria was still the name of the game back then. Lots of humans had been killed by crime, accidents, sickness...the desiccated medical community hadn't had a hope of keeping up. It had been a frightening, disorderly time–not like now, when it was richies in control of those sprawling suburbs.

Carl couldn't imagine what the world had seemed like to a little girl in her position. Monstrous, unsafe, but she'd had her dad, and that must have given her some security, some hope. Many children had lost both parents.

Many parents had lost children, too. It was a hard life, so?

Dill looked up, and her eyes were wide and vulnerable. She opened her mouth to speak, but Carl wasn't ready for a heart-to-heart. He cut her off.

"Anyway," he said and pushed the chair back. He ignored the hurt on the girl's face. Why should he get involved? *Because you said you would,* his mind whispered, *you said you would look out for her...pay better attention.* Carl shook his head once, a rough shake. He had meant he'd make sure she carried her weapon, did her job right. He wasn't in charge of her mental well-being; he wasn't her father. "Let's get up to two and get this stuff entered. It's going to take a while."

*

She didn't understand him. He was so moody–indifferent to her one minute, kind the next, angry after that. If the first day was an indication of things to come, she wasn't sure if she could do this, no matter how much Denny wanted her to. Dill pulled her jacket closed as she walked. There was a fair amount of people on the road that led from Zombie, Inc., to the inners. Shift change. Dill didn't know anyone because she was used to the night-shift crowd. Maintenance didn't start until eight o'clock and worked to six in the morning. All the other departments–the professional groups like Accounts, Sales, and R&D–worked eight in the morning until six at night. There was no overlap in the shifts. Although Assessment, Wranglers and Cleaners were on call as necessary.

She dropped her head to watch her feet scuffing along, feeling lonelier than she'd ever felt walking this same road in the other direction at night.

"Dill! Hey, Dill! Wait up!"

Denny. Dill turned, smiling, as he jogged up to her. Denny was younger than her by three years. They'd met in Maintenance and become friends and then more than friends. He smiled, too, and put his arm around her in a one-armed hug. At six three, he was almost a foot taller than her. His face was lean and earnest, and usually serious. When he smiled, which was rare, Dill's insides warmed.

There *had* been a time when she'd been just as lonely walking the other way–back when she didn't know Denny yet. Back when she'd still been on her own and missing her dad. When everything was still too fresh.

She leaned into Denny's heat and shivered as they bumped along together.

"How was it today? How'd you do?" he asked. He squeezed her again as she shrugged.

"Not great," she said. She wished she could snuggle into his coat and they could both just *not* talk about this.

"Not great in what way?" His voice held a note of caution, and his arm loosened. Chilled air slipped between them.

"Just...not great. The guy is kind of moody. He's hard to get a read on," she said. She pulled on Denny's hand, making his arm tighten around her again. "It's nothing major. Nothing I can't handle. Just first-day stuff. Don't worry." She squeezed his hand. "How about you? Any progress with the invoices?"

He was quiet for a long minute, and Dill thought he wasn't going to speak or, worse, that he'd keep pressing her about Carl and Assessment. They were almost to the inners, and the walkers had closed in, cramming onto the sidewalk that traversed the entire complex.

Denny glanced around and shook his head in warning. "Later," he said, whispering from the corner of his mouth.

Dill smiled, but stifled a laugh. The secret agent stuff struck her as juvenile, very make-believe, but everyone else in the group took it seriously. She should, too.

Why didn't she?

She and Denny fell into step with the crowd as people started to funnel into the four sets of double doors at the front of the apartment building part of the complex. Dill's eyes skated over the warmly lit windows of the ground-floor government offices. When she'd been on night shift, these offices were always dark.

They looked like scenes from old movies. People in suits, dresses, pant suits. Scarves, nice hairdos–but not like the overblown sexpots in the ZI sales department–these women and men just looked...normal? Was that the word that came to mind? "How would I even know what was normal?" Dill said, unaware that she spoke out loud. It must be from the things her dad used to tell her, the stories he told her at night to calm her and turn her mind from the scary time they'd been living in.

In the window, a middle-aged woman at a desk laughed up at an older man who was gesticulating and smiling. In his suit and pulled-askew tie, he was like a spruced-up version of Carl, or her dad.

Dill nearly stumbled with sudden, heavy depression.

"What?" Denny asked as they passed through the doors and into the gloom of the echoey, marble-floored lobby. "Did you say something?"

She glanced at him, his taut features turned gray and watchful by the cold light. She wondered if she, too, looked that sickly. Of course she did. The woman in the government office slipped into her mind, smiling and normal, warm. Old fashioned.

"No," Dill said, "I didn't say anything."

He considered her for a moment more, quiet and cautious. She hated that look. That 'can Dill be trusted or is she just way too emotional?' look of his.

"I *didn't*," she said, insisting. "Come on." She pulled his hand, tugging him back into the flow of residents. "Let's get upstairs."

He nodded and allowed himself to be dragged away, but the caution didn't leave his eyes.

There was an elevator, but it didn't run. People took the stairs. The crowd thinned at each level as people peeled off. Dill and Denny left the stairwell at the third floor. Denny ran his wrist over the automatic door lock. It blipped, but the door didn't open. Dill ran her own wrist over the laser. The door buzzed, and she pushed it open. "Your account still messed up?" she asked as she went to the living room light. She clicked it into life. The yellow glow brought the government office briefly to mind again. She looked at her hand–her skin had returned to its normal, warm tone.

"Yeah," Denny said and clicked on the light in the little efficiency kitchen. A row of upper cabinets over a row of lowers with a sink on one side; a stove and wide shelves where a refrigerator used to go on the other. "They missed a pay when I switched departments last month, and they can't seem to find it in the system. My chip still says I'm flat broke." He glanced at Dill almost shyly. "Hey, this is our first time together since I switched over, and we have the place to ourselves while everyone is working." He smiled and gathered her to him. She nestled her head under his chin and sighed. She *had* missed him over the last handful of weeks. He must have missed her, too.

He squeezed her again. "Let's play a few rounds of Breeder before we get started on the new pamphlets, okay? I've been dying to play but haven't been able to." He tapped his wrist to indicate the finance chip embedded there.

Dill's lips tightened, but she merely nodded. It was too cold in here for anything else, anyway. Even though it was a rarity to have the apartment to themselves. She turned on the game console and ran her wrist over it as Denny pulled two controllers from the drawer in the coffee table. He collapsed back onto the couch and held a controller out to Dill. He wiggled it. "Come on, hurry. It's starting!" His eyes had already begun to glaze as the mechanized squeals and grunts poured forth from the surround-sound speakers. She glanced into the small dining area, feeling slightly guilty. The table was covered in Z.A.P.T. pamphlets that still needed folding, but if he wanted to play first, then, okay. She was feeling ambivalent, anyway. More ambivalent than seemed the accepted norm.

It hadn't been very hard to kill that zombie today; what did that say about her? It went against everything Denny believed in, and everything that Z.A.P.T. was working for.

She accepted the controller and sank down next to him. His weight and heat were comforting even though his eyes were glued to the screen. She selected her avatar and joined the game.

*

A mile or so distant, Carl drove the ZI Assessment SUV into the garage of his ranch house in the outers. He glanced at the big inners building as the garage door closed and wondered briefly which light might be Dill's. He hoped she had made it home without incident, but of course she had. What could happen to her in the ZI compound? Nothing. Everything was safe.

He flipped on small lights as he walked through the living room to the kitchen. The kitchen was his favorite spot. He'd been the first to occupy this particular house since the plague and he'd left all the original family accoutrements on the fridge. Doctors' appointments, soccer games, gymnastics, dinner invitations, play date invitations–a busy family had lived here. Their chaos, captured in stasis, made Carl feel more at home. Surrounded by their arrested energy.

"Hi, honey," Carl said, "I'm home."

He blew a kiss, seemingly to a snapshot on the fridge of a pretty blonde smiling poolside. She wasn't a member of the nuclear family that had lived here–he had the other scattered pictures to tell him that. This woman, the blonde, had probably been a sister to the husband or wife. A *younger* sister, a fun and rambunctious aunt to the three kids. Long dead, of course. Even if not, she'd be Carl's age now, or maybe even older, but she was most likely dead. Along with the mom and dad and their three towheads. All dead.

Carl stepped closer to the fridge, to the collage taped and magneted there, nearly covering one entire side. Everything belonged to the original family save one small snapshot. Eye level and partially covered–just where Carl had placed it when he moved in–it showed a young woman in profile, smiling shyly and holding her small round of belly. Annie…the one he'd really been blowing the kiss to.

Carl touched one shaking fingertip to her face, lifting a class schedule to do so. He'd camouflaged this picture, his only one of Annie, so that he could look at it when he wanted and ignore it when he had to.

"I missed you today," he said. He kissed the picture gently, his lips barely touching the surface. Then he let the schedule fall back over it, obscuring Annie and the baby. The picture was from 2027. Year of the plague.

Carl poured a whiskey and sat in the living room. The computer was functional but off. There were no televisions like the ones from his youth. Everyone had switched to computers and media streaming long before the plague. Satellites still existed, so cell phones and satellite programming still existed. Once the electricity had become stable again, anyway.

By then, Carl had lost interest. He never even watched the old movies, and he sure as hell didn't have a game system.

He drank the whiskey fast and poured another from the bottle at his side. The first was working on his head before he finished the second–softening, easing. Muddling the past and the present. He poured a third. His eyelids began to get heavy and then heavier. He poured a fourth.

He gazed out the picture window at the inners tower. The baby had been born the year of the plague, just like Dill. Dillalia. Stupid name, who had named her that? She'd been lucky, stupid name or not. She'd had her dad.

So. Her dad had been lucky, too.

Carl ran a hand over his face, and it came away wet. Crying? Already? Usually he was well into his sixth before that happened. He poured a fifth drink, his hand shaking. The crying was bad. He had to get out from under it. There was only one way, one place of dark refuge.

He poured a sixth. The room swam around him. Black fuzz was sneaking in from the edges of his vision, like sooty wool. Ah, better. That's better. *Bring it on*! his tired and aching mind cried out. He grinned through tears, the darkness prisming the light from the small lamp. He reached for the bottle and missed.

He passed out.

# SIX

## Zombie, Inc., Company Handbook
Sec. 6: Paid Time Off (PTO) Policy
*(rev. 06/27/41)*

Zombie, Inc., (known hereafter as 'ZI') takes a generous and democratic approach to employee time* off. Number of days is commensurate with tenure. One consecutive year of employment entitles employee to four (4) PTO (Paid Time Off) days to be used at employee's discretion.** Two consecutive years entitle employee to six (6) PTO days to be used at employee's discretion.** Three consecutive years of employment entitles employee to eight (8) PTO days to be used at employee's discretion.** Each year of consecutive employment thereafter entitles employee to one (1) additional day per year up to fourteen (14) days off. PTO is capped at fourteen days (14) regardless of tenure. PTO resets at employee's anniversary and time not taken does not carry forward. TIME DOES NOT ACCRUE AFTER FIRST DEATH NOR IS IT AWARDABLE MONETARILY NOR CAN IT BE WILLED POSTHUMOUSLY.

PTO is calculated and awarded PER SPECIFIC EMPLOYEE and cannot be sold or reassigned.

*Employee PTO time is limited to not more than two (2) consecutive days at any given time with prior written consent of immediate supervisor and departmental HR representative.*** PTO is to be taken at the employee's discretion, but an immediate supervisor can, at will, revoke scheduled days as deemed necessary by the supervisor.**** In the case of serious illness and/or incapacitation due to accident, consent can be obtained once the employee has returned to his or her duties, but more than five (5) consecutive days off constitutes a reset of tenure.

**Days may not be taken without prior written consent of immediate supervisor filed three weeks (minimum) in advance of the time to be taken. In the case of an emergency time off requirement (defined in Section B), consent can be obtained once the employee has returned to his or her duties, but more than five (5) consecutive days off constitutes a reset of tenure.

***In case of pregnancy, see Sec. 18 of the Zombie, Inc., Employee Handbook, titled 'Pregnancy'.

****Employees can appeal immediate supervisor's decisions regarding revocation of scheduled time off by contacting their HR representative. HR decisions regarding revoked time are resolved within five to eleven days.

– – –

Carl groaned and sat up, righting himself in the chair. He shielded his eyes against the sun shining through the plate-glass window and cursed. His stomach heaved, and he scrambled to the small half bath off the hallway and vomited until nothing came up but bile. He pushed himself away from the bowl and sank back against the wall.

From his position on the floor, he reached over and turned on the shower. It was tempting to think about calling out but then what? What would he do with the day? Spend it thinking?

Fuck. That.

Steam billowed around the shower curtain, and Carl lurched to his feet and struggled out of his clothes. He belched as his stomach began to turn over on itself, marinating in an acid bath. He belched again as he stepped into the shower. More bile came up, hot and stinging, filling his throat. He yawked it onto the floor of the shower, near the drain. He leaned into the spray and closed his eyes.

Fuck.

He had to stop drinking at night.

He should just call out. His hand hovered near his ear, ready to tap, but then he hesitated. Today was only Dill's second day. If he didn't go in, they might send her to another department for the day, maybe sales, and then who knew…maybe she'd decide not to keep trying for Assessment. Maybe she'd decide he was too big of an asshole and the job too dangerous.

*Was* the job too dangerous?

Well, it wasn't the safest job at ZI, but R&D was probably worse. Those guys played with zombies all day long.

His ear buzzed, startling him. His fingers, already so close, poked the call through even though he'd have preferred to let it go to the message bank that he could have accessed after the shower. The voice, automated, began after a short buzz of adjustment. "Hello…Carl…this is Assessment Central Messaging. Your inbox contains…one…message marked…vital. Play your message now…Carl?"

"Yes."

The line buzzed again and then smoothed out. "Hey, Carl, it's Aaron. Listen…" An empty pause went on so long that Carl thought that maybe he'd dropped the call. He raised his hand to touch his ear, but then Aaron's voice started up again. "I found something weird from yesterday. Something on the surveillance. Come see me when you get in, okay?"

The mechanized voice cut back in. "Replay message, call back, or disconnect?"

"Disconnect," Carl said and reached to turn off the water. He felt marginally better, and his stomach wasn't looping the loop anymore, but he'd need to eat, and he didn't relish going to R&D first thing, either. The whole floor smelled bad.

Like rot.

*

He drove slowly past the lines of people walking from the inners. He scanned their backs but didn't recognize Dill among them. Everyone was hunched into their coats against the wind. The day was gray and even colder than yesterday.

His eyes went beyond the pedestrians to the brown, wind-blown fields that surrounded the ZI building right up to the cracked and crumbling parking lot. Everything outside looked plain and desolate. Landscaping wasn't really a consideration anymore. Little attention was paid to the exterior of most buildings unless it involved security.

He spotted Dill and began to ease the steering wheel back, slowing the SUV. He'd stop and offer her a ride, but only because Aaron had sounded urgent (kind of urgent), and Carl didn't want to have to wait for Dill to walk the whole way.

Just then, she turned to the person next to her–a tall young man, Carl couldn't see his face beyond the upturned collar of his coat– and smiled. The man encircled her shoulders and pulled her close.

Carl allowed his hand to tilt the steering wheel forward, and he accelerated slowly past the pair. His eyes went to the side mirror, and he scrutinized the guy with his arm around Dill, but now the guy had turned his face to Dill's, and Carl still couldn't make out his features. Was he a good guy? What did he do at ZI? Was Dill serious about him? He sped up. He'd have to ask her about him.

He was only interested because he didn't want to get too invested in Dill if she weren't planning on being around. If she weren't really invested in Assessment. His concern was really more for himself and his time than it was for her.

*Oh, is that right?* his mind whispered, and he jerked the wheel into the ZI lot. He ignored the pedestrians who yelled in indignation, startled by his sudden, sharp turn.

*

Dill looked up as a handful of people yelled and wheels squealed on the old tarmac. It was an Assessment SUV, but she didn't catch the LIC# on the side and back. Could that have been Carl driving like a madman? After calling her 'Andrea' or whatever he had called her over her driving yesterday? She shook her head and snorted. "Hypocrite," she said under her breath.

"What?" Denny said, but his voice was distracted as he felt around the inside pockets of his long coat. "Shit, I *know* I put those papers in here somewhere."

She patted the lowest pocket, the one that rode against his knee. "Down here," she said, "the inside pocket."

"Thanks," he said, "that would have been a major disaster. I'm going to–" he looked around furtively, and then continued, "–I'm going to plaster the fourth-floor bathrooms today. Tomorrow the fifth. Keep pounding the message home."

"Mm hmm," Dill said. She had pulled her bow around from her side and twanged the bow string. Weird that the little arrows were called bolts. They were made of carbon fiber: short, tough, wickedly sharp, and effective. She'd seen that yesterday. A small grin surfaced on her face as she remembered.

"It's important we hit it hard once we roll into a new campaign," Denny said. His voice held a note of reproach. "It's dangerous, but it's important–too important to stop. You hear me, Dill?"

"Yep."

They were halfway across the parking lot, and the tight line of pedestrians had fanned out. They were well out of earshot of the other employees.

"Dill, seriously. This is important. You know that, don't you? You know how much I'm putting on the line just by putting up these flyers?"

She glanced up at him. "What floor did you say you were on yesterday? Which bathrooms?"

"The lobby," he said and swallowed. He glanced away from her and then back. "I did it at lunch time. Why? Did you hear something about it?"

She shook her head and kept walking. She'd thought for a second…just a brief second…that maybe he'd been on three yesterday. Maybe he'd seen what went wrong up there when the alarms sounded, but he'd have told her already.

She wished she could tell him about her experiences yesterday, about how she had saved the lives of those two Wranglers–well, maybe not *saved* exactly, but she'd helped them out, they'd told her so–but Denny's expression as he looked at the bow was one of distaste.

"I wish you didn't have to carry that thing around with you. It's a symbol of the death hierarchy. A display of our misinformed sense of superiority over our zombie brethren," he said, his chin rising. He seemed to be eyeing her fingers as they caressed the string. "I know you must hate it, too."

"Oh…yeah. I totally do," she said and let it drop back into place at her side. No. She definitely wouldn't be able to tell him about killing the zombie. She glanced up at him again, his tightened lips and the righteous tilt of his chin. Had he ever been confronted by a zombie? Had he ever *really* been in danger?

She began to wonder if people her age didn't have as good a grasp on the zombies as they thought they did. For her part, she didn't even remember the years right after the plague–the worst years, according to older people. She'd been a baby. So had Denny. So had most of the people in Z.A.P.T. In fact, many of them were even younger, born way after the real crisis had already passed. Dill had only been outside the ZI compound walls for one day on her new job, but already she felt a little changed by it. When had Denny last been outside the compound? The younger people in the group, had they ever been out? It was unlikely.

Killing the zombie yesterday hadn't been like killing a person. It was just a bag of animated bones and slowly rotting flesh. Its eyes, the little she'd seen, were empty. Not just devoid of feelings, either–its eyes held *no humanity*.

For the first time since she'd been taken in by Z.A.P.T. at seventeen, she felt an inkling of discord with the goals of the group. But if she lost them, then what did she have? She'd be on her own again.

They neared the doors, and Denny gave her another squeezing, half-armed hug. "Call me if you think we could meet for lunch, okay?" He split off for the stairwell, to four, where Accounts was housed.

Dill stood in the lobby and watched as he disappeared through the doors. He loved her. She was pretty sure he did. They didn't see anyone else. (*You barely 'see' each other*, her mind whispered, but she hushed it.)

The group was like a family or what she imagined a family used to be. In the old days.

So was Carl, in a weird way.

The thought of Carl brought her dad to mind.

Her dad–what had happened to him–was the real reason she'd joined Z.A.P.T.

\*

"We have to go further out today. We have a non-emergency complaint from a client south of here." Carl spoke without looking up. His designated section of the second floor–like the others in Assessment–was wide open and filled with a myriad of equipment: tablets, folders, books, monitors, weapons. It was a study in controlled chaos. "I think we'll drag a Wrangler along with us. They like this client." He paused, considering, and then looked up from the tablet in his hand. "Dill? You listening?"

Her eyes had gone to the window, but now they came back to Carl.

"Yeah...complaint, going south, Wranglers," she said.

"We have to go up to three first and see Aaron. He's got his panties in a bunch over something with a surveillance tape from yesterday."

"What about it?"

"I don't know; that's what we're going to find out," he said and looked at her hard. Her face looked white again, but his own thoughts were muzzy. "You okay?"

She nodded and hitched her bow, shifting it. She seemed nervous. Probably worried about going south. It was woodsy down there and wild in a truer sense than she'd meant when she called the suburbs wild yesterday.

"You worried?" he asked.

"About the surveillance video?"

"Jesus Christ, Dill, no. I don't mean the damn video. Get your shit together." He rubbed his forehead and then his eyes. "Sorry, look. I'm just...I have a bad headache, and today isn't going to be easy." He looked at her, and his vision had gone blurry. He blinked, trying to bring it back. "You want to stay here? You could do some cleaning or whatever." He gestured around the space.

"No!" Dill said, and her voice cut into his head. He winced. "Sorry," she said. "Do you want something? A pill or something for it? I'll get you one from five."

Medical was on five, along with Archives and Marketing.

"No, I just need water. Let's get up to three and then get on the road." He rubbed his forehead again. "Thanks, though."

"Yeah, sure," she said.

Did she sound sad? He was being a dick again. Why did she irritate him so much, especially after all his good resolve from yesterday?

"Listen, we'll get the same Wranglers from yesterday to tag along if they're free, okay?"

"The ones that think my name is Abby."

Carl snorted as they entered the stairwell. It echoed up and down. "They call everyone Abby. Even me, and they all call each other Floyd." He shook his head and rubbed his eyes again. He didn't worry about having bloodshot eyes. The retina scanner didn't care. "Nobody knows why. Except them, and they ain't tellin'."

He could swear he felt a pulse of heat every time his retina was scanned even though he knew intellectually that the technology carried no heat. The door to three slid open. The voice of Ze Listen/Speak system said, "Welcome to Zombie, Inc., Research and Development. Please state the name of the person you are trying to reach."

"Aaron Carmichael," Carl said and spoke to the ceiling out of habit. There was no actual operator of ZE Listen/Speak, just a kind of centralized brain. Aaron's name would trigger an alert to him wherever he was in the building.

"Carl!" Aaron's voice, echoing after a delay. "Give me five. I'm out back."

Carl slumped against the wall and crossed his arms over his chest. Five minutes was probably actually going to be more like fifteen. 'Out back' referred to the large outdoor area behind the building, past what used to be a multi-level parking garage. R&D was the only group with access to the garage and the outdoor area behind it. The windows facing the back of the building had been blacked out for secrecy. Once during bowling, when they'd both been drunk, Aaron had told Carl that the height of the levels of the garage came in handy. Carl hadn't asked for what.

They waited in silence. Carl was glad that Dill wasn't fidgety, wasn't a yapper. He cracked his eyelids a couple times to see how she was taking the wait, and each time he looked, she was standing stock-still, staring down the hall. Her jaw clenched and unclenched, but that was it.

She had the patience to do Assessment. That was a mark in her favor.

"Carl, come on back to door six." Aaron's voice again.

Carl pushed himself off the wall, and Dill fell in just behind him. She had good instincts, soldier instincts. Carl appreciated that. Plus, there was something that felt right about having her behind his shoulder.

The door buzzed, and a click indicated a lock sliding free. Carl pushed it open, and the door sighed on its hydraulic springs. Cold air wafted over them as they entered a blue-lit room.

Dill put her hand over her mouth and nose and took a sharp step back. "What the hell?" she said. She sounded offended, as though someone had played an inappropriate and unfunny joke on her.

"You get used to it," Aaron said, appearing from behind a large column. "I don't even notice it anymore! Although," he said and held up the lapels of his white coveralls. "I have a suspicion it sinks into the uniforms. Thank goodness for on-site dry cleaners."

Dill looked around, wide-eyed. The room was large, and the walls were lined with big plastic tubes, each seven feet tall and banded at the top and bottom with heavy, gray plastic. The tubes themselves were clear, or *almost* clear, and also plastic. They lined each wall and were stacked back to back throughout, like old-timey grocery shelves. There had to be at least a hundred.

About a quarter of the tubes contained zombies.

Some shuffled in place, bumping their noses over and over, leaving streaks of gore and the coffee ground crumbles on the plastic. Some had slumped over and become jammed in their tubes and struggled to right themselves. One–the one nearest them–stomped endlessly through its own guts. The large rotted hole in its midsection still contained stringy bits of entrails, but most of its organs were part of the mash at its feet. The noise was like that of someone walking through thick, sucking mud.

A low chorus of moans ran like an undercurrent throughout the space.

Dill pulled her shirt up over her nose. She heaved as though she were going to vomit.

"Take it easy, Dill," Aaron said. "Turn away. Don't look at them. It makes it easier. Feel that slight breeze? That's fresh, cold air. Just try to relax." Aaron shot Carl a look of disgust. "You didn't warn her?"

Carl shrugged. "I didn't think about it," Carl said. "You okay, Dill?"

Dill's gorge rose again. She realized she was listening to the moaning. She closed her eyes and turned her face more fully into the stream of cold air from the nearest vent. She wished she could climb into that vent and right out of here. Think about something else, she told herself. Don't think about the smell.

The smell of rot. Of decay. Festering.

"Here give me the—"

Carl's voice. Almost disembodied as she struggled with her stomach. Bile filled her mouth, hot and sour. She swallowed it back down. She wouldn't vomit in front of them. Wouldn't.

She heaved again, convulsing.

Then Carl's hand was on the back of her neck, frightening in its suddenness, its strength and heat; her hand was brushed away from her mouth and something cold was swiped across her upper lip. Gummy. Like mucous. Her stomach began to roll again, and then she smelled menthol.

She took a breath. Another. The smell of rot was fading, disappearing under the menthol. Another breath.

Carl's hand squeezed her neck, steadying her, and then disappeared. "Dill? You gonna make it?" His voice quiet, not teasing, not putting her down. Just honest concern.

She nodded. She opened her eyes but stayed facing the blank wall. "I'm okay. I'm fine. Thanks. Can we keep going?"

"Hell yes, we can," Aaron said and turned. "Follow me. My office is at the back." He glanced back at Dill, and she met his eyes with a small smile. "Better? Yes? With the menthol?"

Dill glanced at Carl's back and then smiled shakily at Aaron. "Yep."

He smiled and led them on. She put her finger lightly to her lip. She wanted to see if it had color, if she looked like a fool with a green upper lip, but it was colorless. Now she could look at the zombies without her stomach turning. Denny would die if he saw this. He'd die from horror.

She could still feel the weight and heat of Carl's hand on the back of her neck, and she missed the comfort of it.

She followed them through another door with pebbled glass with Aaron's name on it.

"They sent this to me for review this morning. HR did." Aaron fussed with a monitor on the desk. The monitor bloomed into life. Aaron tapped at the screen. "They think it's just routine stuff, well, not routine exactly. We don't have zombies breaking loose every day." Aaron laughed, and it was a strained huff. "Okay, here. Watch."

Suddenly, Dill was watching Carl from behind in the hallway they'd just come down. A small man in a white, blood-streaked coverall was at Carl's feet, and a zombie was lying in a heap just past the man. Aaron kneeled further down, facing the camera. His hand was over his mouth, and his eyes were shocked and distressed.

There was no audio.

Carl bent closer to the smaller man, and Dill saw the gun concealed at Carl's side. The smaller man looked up at Carl; his face was only partially blocked by Carl's body. The small man shook his head; his hands began to rise, palms up, defensive. His lips moved as he spoke. Carl moved so quickly and economically that Dill barely caught the movement. A hole appeared between the small man's eyes. Carl stepped back as Aaron stepped forward. It looked almost choreographed.

Aaron stopped the recording.

Carl looked up, eyebrows raised expectantly. "What about it?"

"There was a face. In the bathroom doorway. Watch again."

The scene replayed, but this time, as Carl was shooting the unlucky tech, Dill kept her eyes trained where Aaron indicated. After the man was shot, a face appeared in the doorway just beyond Aaron.

Carl shrugged. "Okay. Guy's takin' a leak and hears the commotion. What's the big deal?"

"He's not from R&D," Aaron said, and Carl's eyebrows shot up even higher. Aaron nodded. "Someone turned that zombie loose and got Randy killed. That might be the person that did it."

"Zapped, you think? You think that's the angle?"

Aaron nodded again.

Dill turned and felt behind her for a chair. She sat abruptly.

Carl turned to her. "Feel sick again?"

"No. Or I don't know, just a little, maybe." She tried to smile, and it felt odd on her face. More like an exercise, a stretch.

Carl turned back around and hit play again. The scene repeated itself.

Denny's face appeared in the bathroom doorway.

*

"Those assholes," Carl said. His voice–a rough grumble–cut into her chaotic thoughts.

"Huh? Who?"

Carl nodded to the rearview. "Your buddies back there. Floyd and Floyd."

Dill looked at her side mirror. The Wrangler truck was so close to the Assessment SUV that all she could see was grill and the heavy cowcatcher mounted on the front of the truck. The wheels chirped as the truck braked abruptly, and the two Wranglers came into view. They were laughing and giving the SUV the finger, slapping each other on the shoulder. Then the truck roared up on their bumper again.

The road was deserted as expected, but the woods that lined it–leafless but dense with washed-out gray underbrush–gave it an extra dimension of desolation. Dill didn't like it. She felt too far from the ZI compound, too far from safety.

"Well," she said, "at least they'll help if something goes wrong." Doubt as gray and lifeless as the woods surrounding them hung over her words.

"Maybe, maybe not."

Dill looked at Carl's profile to see if he was teasing. He seemed intent on the road ahead, and his eyes swept the mirrors at regular intervals. It didn't look like he was joking around.

"What do you mean?" Dill asked. She kept her tone even, but another swell of uneasiness tried to flip her stomach.

"You hear things," Carl said. "Stories, rumors. About them." He nodded to the mirror again. "They're clannish. Unpredictable."

"*How* unpredictable? Like 'kill us out in these woods' unpredictable?" She grinned, but Carl's expression stayed the same. The grin tumbled off her face. "Carl?"

He shifted, and his eyes swept the mirrors. "No. No, I don't think so."

"You don't *think* so?" Her gaze went to the side mirror again. The Wrangler truck had dropped back, but even at this distance, she could see that their heads were together, conspiratorial. Not laughing anymore.

"I mean, I don't think they'd kill us; I don't think they'd kill an Assessment Team member. We work too closely with them, but…"

"But what?"

"Well, '*not killing you*' is not a whole lot different than '*letting you get killed*'," he said. "You know what I mean?"

She did and she didn't but decided abruptly that she didn't want to know any more. She sank back in the seat and took her eyes off the mirror. "So. What do you think Aaron is going to do?"

"Do? About the security tape? Nothing."

Hope bloomed in her stomach. "Nothing? You mean it isn't that big a deal?"

"Ha! No, I don't mean that!" Carl barked out a laugh and shook his head. "It's a *very* big deal. Whoever that was might have caused that zombie to get loose and caused that tech to get killed. Especially if it was one of those zapped assholes." Carl shook his head again. "Aaron isn't going to do anything because it's not his job."

"Whose job is it?"

Carl glanced across the cab of the SUV, and his eyes were half lidded. "Ours–Assessment's–but only obliquely."

"Why wouldn't security handle it?"

"Dill, have you ever met anyone in security?"

"Sure. They used to patrol the building at night."

"What did you think of them?"

Dill shrugged. "Not much, I guess. They were kind of…" She dropped her chin into her hand, thinking how to phrase it. "They asked for your hand for a scan every time they saw you, even if you saw them three or four times in a shift. I guess they're sticklers."

"Well, that's one word for it. Here's another: unimaginative. The internal security people are fodder, you know what that means?" Dill shook her head, and he continued. "They fill space, they do the job they're told to do, *as* they're told to do it. They're automatons. They're expendable. That's why they do the outside checks. The best minds in ZI are in two places, R&D and Assessment."

"How did I qualify, then?" Dill asked. There was no fishing in her tone, just honest bewilderment.

"The tests," Carl said, "you did well on them. That's why you were picked."

Dill nodded, but she was surprised. The tests had been a year ago when she'd first applied for Assessment. A lot of other people had taken the tests, too. A lot.

She turned to him. "Why would–" she began, but Carl spun the wheel and sent her into the passenger door, hard.

He cursed and wrestled with the steering wheel as the SUV hit the soft dirt shoulder. The gas engine of the Wrangler truck roared behind them. Then came a sound almost like a giant clapping his hands, one hard, meaty slap.

Whatever Carl had swerved to miss, the Wranglers had hit.

Carl eased the steering wheel back, slowing the SUV, and parked on the shoulder. Dill reached shakily for her door handle.

"Don't get out," Carl said. "First rule of Assessment, and you better learn it good, Dill: *assess*. Always assess first. Know what you're getting into."

By now Dill's eyes were on Carl. His hands shook a little, too, but his eyes were glued to the mirror. Dill turned to look out the back window.

The Wrangler truck was turned sideways on the road and rocking. A zombie was half on the grill and half under the truck. It struggled like an oversized bug. After a minute, the truck's passenger-side door opened.

Carl's door thunked open. "Okay, Dill, hop out. We've got to keep an eye out while they unstick the thing. Climb up on the roof." He leaned back in as she was exiting. "Take your *bow*."

Dill blushed and reached back for it, then scrambled from the hood to the roof, her boots thumping and squeaking. The woods were unrelentingly gray. Carl had gone a distance from the SUV in order to be able to see beyond the Wrangler truck. Everything was quiet save the gurgling, moaning zombie. Its arms and half its head were stuck in the grill. Above it, the rack of bullhorns had lost one of its zombie head decorations. Dill scanned and saw it lying smashed on the road. Must have flown off when they braked hard. It dragged a tail of gore and the blood clot, coffee ground crumbles. Must have been a pretty ripe head. Dill's gorge tried to rise, and she tore her eyes from the head and scanned the woods instead.

The Wrangler had gone to the back of the truck and now came back with a long pry bar. He glanced at the SUV as if to make sure they were on guard. He jabbed the sharp end of the bar through the zombie's head with a short, businesslike thrust, and the zombie ceased to struggle. Then he wriggled the bar between the zombie and the grill and began to pry.

Dill tried to keep her eyes on the woods and not on the gruesome process going on at the Wranglers' truck, but with each screech of metal on metal, her eyes were pulled back. It was almost as though the zombie were screaming in pain. The Z.A.P.T. manifesto went through her mind. It was horribly undignified, being pried from someone's cattle-catcher grill, but was it wrong?

The zombie finally fell free with a thick, sucking sound, like a boot pulling from mud. Dill looked back again in time to see the Wrangler wrestle an arm from the grill. He turned and threw it into the woods.

Then the Wrangler stood looking at the zombie, hands fisted on his hips. He looked to the cab of the truck.

"Fresh one, Floyd, pretty fresh. Good for the truck?"

"Jesus, guys, *no*. Let's get going," Carl said from his spot twenty feet away. He scanned past them and behind. "You don't fucking need a–"

"Come on, Abby!" the Wrangler said. "Don't be a cunt! It'll only be a minute. Get in your pussy-mobile if'n yer scared!"

"Fuck you," Carl said, his voice wavered between annoyed and amused. "Just hurry it up."

The Wrangler grinned and gave a thumbs-up to the cab of the truck. The truck rocked and rough laughter drifted up to Dill. The Wrangler drew a long, serrated blade from a sheath on his leg. He bent over the zombie. He glanced up at Dill and grinned, and his teeth were black with tobacco and rot. He began to saw at the zombie's neck.

Dill looked away and swallowed. In the still morning, the gradual ripping and tearing of flesh was the loudest sound. She glanced back, unable to stop herself. The zombie's head was shaking violently left to right as if in negation. With each tear of the knife, a rolling jerk made the coagulated blood blop in clots onto the pavement. Strings of skin and white tendons caught and stretched on the teeth of the blade and flung like rubber bands. When the Wrangler reached bone, Dill looked away again.

She concentrated on the woods as the sound went on and on. Oh yeah, it was wrong. Could it be any more wrong than this? That was someone's son under the Wrangler's boot, maybe someone's dad. Tears burned in her eyes, and her throat tightened. The Wrangler slammed the head onto the tip of the bullhorn, and anger whipped into her system like hot adrenalin.

A hand grabbed her ankle and yanked.

She belly-flopped hard, teeth clacking together and breath shoved roughly from her body. Her bow popped out of her hands and clattered down the side of the SUV. She pulled in a screaming, burning lungful of air and kicked back. Her boot connected with something hard and yielding, but the pressure on her ankle remained. Carl turned, his eyes filled with sudden alarm. She screamed again, and her hands scrabbled at the window, seeking purchase on the slippery surface.

"Abby, no!" the Wrangler shouted. It was a bear's angry roar, and the other Wrangler sprang from the driver's side of the truck.

"Kick, Abby! Kick the fucker!" the second Wrangler shouted. She kicked back and gripped the very edge of the window, her fingertips white and aching. Time slowed down, as pulling and elastic as a zombie tendon. When she kicked again, her boot sank into nothing. She closed her eyes, screamed, and waited for teeth to sink into her leg. Running feet pounded around the SUV. It tilted and rocked, and the springs groaned under new weight. Another zombie, it must be, climbed onto the roof of the SUV. Time stopped. She could almost feel a cold mouth on the back of her neck. The hard teeth sinking in. Her life leaving her in gush after hot gush.

A hand slapped her ass.

"Fucker's done, Abby. Get up now." The Wrangler's voice was a soft growl in her ear. He was kneeling next to her on the roof. Dill rolled over and scrambled onto her knees, her breath a whistling gasp. The Wrangler's arm was heavy around her shoulders. "Don't fall off the roof, now, Abby." He laughed and squeezed her.

Carl stood at the driver's side, his knife in his hand. A chunky spray of black blood decorated his white shirt and khakis. He stared at her, his eyes intent and unwavering.

"You okay, Dill?" he asked. "Not bit?"

She swallowed hard and shook her head. Carl looked past her and nodded slightly. She glanced behind her just in time to see the other Wrangler lowering a pistol. He grinned at her, but he'd been ready to put her down if she'd been bit.

"You're a lucky man, Abby. That was just a little'un and couldn't reach past yer boot with its dirty fuckin' mouth."

Dill tore her eyes from him and leaned forward to look over the side. A child zombie, a kidzie, maybe nine or ten, lay crumpled by the driver's side door. He was very fresh, with clothes barely soiled or torn. His skin, although pasty white, was still free of the red and purple rot that developed as zombies 'aged'. His feet were small and bare and dirty. Her eyes drifted with reluctance to her khakis. At her ankle, where the heavy boot protected her, the cloth was damp where the zombie's mouth had been.

He had almost killed her.

Clouds crowded around her peripheral vision, and she fell forward. She put her hand out to steady herself but encountered only air. She was too close to the edge. She was going to fall.

She grayed out.

*

Carl barely caught the girl as she fell forward. Good thing the Wrangler had a grip on the back of her pants or she'd have gone face-first into the zombie at Carl's feet. He got his arms around her and hefted her weight across his shoulder. She was heavier than she looked, and he huffed as he struggled to the front of the SUV. He stood her on her feet and leaned her against the hood.

She swayed, and her eyes rolled back in her head.

"Dill," Carl said. He shook her lightly, and her head snapped forward. "Dill, come back."

"What...what...happened, did I...am I..." she said, and her voice sank away as her eyes fluttered.

"You're fine," Carl said and gave her another small shake. "Lean against the SUV. Sit on the bumper and put your head between your knees. You hear me, Dill?"

She must have, because she sank down onto the bumper and leaned over. He put his hand on her neck to steady her. Her neck was thin but corded and strong. Despite the cold, she was sweating.

"Aw, Abby's okay, Abby," the first Wrangler said, addressing Carl. He slapped Carl on the shoulder. "Don't you cry none, Abby, my girl."

"Get the fuck off me," Carl said, but his voice was distracted. "Clean up your mess, and let's get the hell out of here. Who knows how many more are in these godforsaken woods."

"Right you are, Abby," the Wrangler said, and his eyes scanned the trees as he adjusted the black bandanna on his head. His tone was soft and serious. "'Bout as godforsaken as they come. God left this land behind long since." The Wrangler squeezed Carl's shoulder and then trotted away. "Hey, Floyd! Time to get going, cunt! Time to fly!"

"Fuck you, Floyd," the second Wrangler said as he climbed into the driver's side of the truck. "Straighten that head, and climb the fuck up."

Carl shook Dill's shoulder. "Come on, Dill. Time to go."

She struggled into the passenger side, and Carl picked up her bow and tossed it in after her. By the time he got around to the driver's door, she'd come around fully. She scrubbed her face with her hands as he started the electric engine. The Wrangler truck roared to life behind them.

"Doing okay?" he asked and scanned the mirrors by habit. He glanced at her when she didn't answer. "Dill?" He pulled out onto the road.

"I fucked up pretty bad," she said, and her voice was quiet but not self-pitying. "Am I done?"

"Done for the day?" Carl asked, annoyed. "We still have a half hour just to get there. Unless you wanted to walk back on your own." He tried to shoot her a grin, but she had dropped her head into her hands.

"No, I mean...are you going to fire me? Or demote me or whatever?"

He could see she fully expected to be told she was not cut out for Assessment. He laughed, and she looked at him in surprise. Her brows came together in confusion.

"Listen, Dill," he said and paused. When he started speaking again, he kept his eyes on the road. "When I was in my twenties—younger than you are now—and the plague hit, I was almost killed every day. Sometimes three and four times a day. I wasn't, you know, equipped. Few of us were." He glanced back at the Wranglers' truck, then at the girl again. She was watching him in that steady way she had. "I don't know what it was like for you when you were a kid, I don't know if you were in danger a lot, but my feeling is that people your age...you had someone looking out for you. You had to have had, otherwise you wouldn't have made it. Do you remember much of it? The first ten years, the really hard ones?"

"I mostly remember being hungry a lot," she said, "and running. We were always running." Her voice and expression were still and neutral. "I have...flashes. Things I saw my dad doing. They weren't..." She swallowed, and her careful neutrality slipped as her voice dropped. "They weren't nice things."

"No," Carl said. "There weren't a lot of nice things going on back then." He hoped she understood what he was trying to convey in his tone: acceptance, understanding. "Your dad must have been pretty well equipped to survive if he was able to bring you along, too. Most kids didn't make it." He felt her eyes on him. His voice hadn't broken, but something in his tone must have alerted her.

"Carl, did you—" she said.

"So, listen," he said, cutting her off. He didn't want to have that conversation. Not today, not ever. "What I'm saying is that being out here takes practice. It's been a long time since danger was an everyday occurrence, and for lots of kids—your generation and the one after who mostly have always lived behind the ZI walls or in some other kind of safety–it's not an issue anymore. You haven't internalized the dangers." He glanced at her again. "Either you'll learn or you'll get killed."

She swallowed. "You had someone die, right? Your last trainee? That's the rumor."

"Yep," Carl said. He could feel her eyes again, but she didn't press him. She was a fast learner. "Here we are."

He turned the SUV off the highway, and the trees closed in, tight and claustrophobic. The day darkened. Even the Wranglers' truck behind them took on a more muffled, subdued note. Twenty feet in, the pavement ended, and the SUV bounced along the ruts in the hard dirt.

"Is this the Pine Barrens?" Dill asked.

"Yep. Nice, huh?"

Dill shivered. "Who would want to live out here? It's so...it's just so..."

"Barren?"

"Yeah."

Carl glanced in the rearview mirror. The Wranglers bounced like angry wraiths behind the reflection of trees in their windshield, their twin expressions of anger pulling their features into knots. They were jabbering at each other and, seemingly, at the trees around them. Wranglers took a lot of things in stride, but branches scratching and itching at their black paint did not turn them on at all. There was a reason they'd agreed to come out here. One that made them happier than a scratched truck made them mad.

"Some people want to stay isolated," Carl said, answering Dill's question. "They believe they're safer." A clearing and house flashed in and out between the trees. "I want you to stick right by me and keep your eyes open. If they're having trouble with their field, then we have to be especially alert."

Carl put his finger to his eye and scanned the Wrangler tag on the visor. He spoke to the automated system and glanced at the rearview in time to see the driver Wrangler touch his ear as his call went through. "Stay in the truck until we get the escort. They still have the old Ze Fences up all over the place."

He disconnected as they rolled from the woods into a wide-open clearing surrounded on all sides by the gray/green pines. The underbrush was not high, only ankle height in most places and patchy as hell. The ground was black. The house, sitting dead center on the lot, was a log cabin, big but dark. Sooty looking. Smoke drifted from four chimneys.

"Why's everything all black?" Dill asked. "It's like something from a bad dream."

"They burn the land surrounding the house. To keep an open sightline. Smell it?"

Dill nodded, then froze, head tilted, listening. "What's that?"

"You mean the barking? The dogs?"

She looked at him, wide eyed. "They have *dogs*?"

"Yeah, they're our escort. They know where the fences are and aren't." Carl grinned and pointed. "Look."

A roiling pack of animals, brown, black, tan, tongues, teeth, feet and tails raced toward them across the nightmare landscape. As they got closer, they resolved into five separate dogs so big that Carl would bet they each weighed more than Dill. They barked, bayed, and leapt over each other in their struggle to get to the trucks. Carl looked out the back window. The Wranglers' guffaws came dimly through the glass.

Then the dogs were upon them.

They jumped at the windows, their feet leaving large black smears, their mouths red and strung with white ropes of slobber. They barked ferociously, and Dill put her hands over her ears. "Geez, they're *huge*! They're gonna *kill* us! These are *dogs*?" Her eyes were wide with disbelief.

"They're Rottweilers," he said and cracked his door open. The barking became louder, and he snaked an arm out the door. "Put your hand out to them!" He had to yell to be heard over the din that filled the cab.

"Are you *crazy*? They'll rip my arm off!"

Carl laughed, in part at her expression and in part from the slobbering reception his arm was receiving. He opened the door and stepped out. One dog leapt to put his paws on Carl's shoulders, and Carl was slammed back into the SUV, laughing as a hot tongue lapped across his face like a soaked towel. He was engulfed in the hot stink of fish and rotten meat.

The Wranglers rolled with three of the rotties, dust and soot flying up around them like puffs of smoke. Dogs and men wore identical expressions of mutual love. Carl laughed again as the Wranglers began howling along with the rotties in an ear-splitting chorus of excitement.

# SEVEN

**Ze Fence!®**

Are you overrun by the living dead? Zombie, Inc., introduces the newest in home security with Ze Fence!® line of defensive home security. Keep zombies at bay with a system of underground wires delivering shocks guaranteed to short-circuit the brain of any animated corpse. Special anniversary pricing coupled with the new federal rebate program* makes this system ideal for every income level.

Check with your ZI rep for multi-property discounts.**

***You'll sleep in comfort when you have the Zombie, Inc., Ze Fence!® system securing your property and life!***

*\*The ZI five-year anniversary price will be good through the end of 2032. Please contact a Zombie, Inc., representative for details regarding the federal rebate program. Federal rebates are not guaranteed by ZI and are subject to change if the government should fail.*

*\*\*Landlords and landholders can get the multi-property discount based on title and deed ownership. (Properties obtained illegally may still be eligible through the POP [Perceived Ownership Program].)*

Dill watched it all from the safety of the SUV. She'd heard of dogs and seen the old pictures, but she'd never seen one in person before. These behemoths were not what she was expecting. Carl's back was firmly planted against the driver's side window, and it seemed the dog he wrestled might be trying to eat his face. The

Wranglers were by now nearly indistinguishable from the dogs they rolled in the dirt with. Dill tore her eyes from them and looked out her side window. Another dog sat there; one slightly smaller than the others. Its mouth was open in what looked like a wide grin, and its tongue hung off to the side like a thick, red rag.

"Dill, come on," Carl shouted with impatience. "Let her smell that you're alive, and then stick close; she'll make sure you don't hit a fence." He was ten feet down the track with a dog at his side, and the Wranglers were even further, running as dogs leapt around them.

She looked again at the dog outside her window. It was in the same position. Waiting patiently for her to come out. So it could eat her, no doubt. She glanced back in Carl's direction, intending to tell him she would wait in the truck, but Carl was too far away.

Shoot. She was gonna have to get out.

She eased the door open, and at the sound, the dog stood, startling her. She paused and then opened the door just enough to get her hand out. It was immediately engulfed in hot dog slobber as the rottie first snuffled and then licked her hand. The dog's entire body shook from end to end, and its fur gleamed in the sun. It looked up at Dill through the glass, and it seemed to be laughing at her unease.

Dill opened the door the rest of the way and stepped out, breath held. The dog stepped politely back and sat. It panted and gazed after Carl and the others.

"Hello," Dill said, unsure what else to do. Her voice seemed to galvanize the dog. It wriggled and whined, and Dill smiled, unable to help herself. She put her hand out, cautiously, and patted the dog's bowling ball head–it felt like a thin layer of silk over rock. "Good, um…good dog."

The dog barked, and Dill pulled her hand back.

"Dill! Move it!" Carl called across the field. He was halfway to the log cabin.

The dog trotted in the direction Carl had gone and then turned to bark at Dill over its shoulder. Dill got that message clear enough.

*

"I don't know if anyone even repairs Ze Fences anymore, Paul," Carl said. "We don't have anyone at ZI. I can see if the Wranglers want to take a look; they're usually pretty mechanical. Other than that, though." He shrugged.

"'Buy a new system'...is that what you're telling me?" Paul looked askance at Carl but grinned. He was older than Carl by at least ten years, and he looked weathered tough. Like cowboys from the old, old movies.

They stood on the porch that looked over the back half of the property. Dill stood on the far side of Carl, listening. Behind them, the log cabin radiated warmth, and it wasn't just from the fireplaces going inside.

The Wranglers ran past, chased by four of the five dogs. The dogs jumped and bit at the Wranglers' flailing elbows and caught their ankles, tripping them as the Wranglers laughed uproariously. Dogs and men both were filthy with the sooty black dirt of the yard.

The fifth dog, the smaller one, stood at Dill's side.

"Well, I'm not in sales," Carl said, "but I could have someone contact you."

Paul laughed and put a hand on Carl's shoulder. "Let's wait and see what Mary has to say about that. She's in charge of security."

The door creaked behind them. A tall woman with long gray hair pulled back in a neat horsetail carried out a tray with six steaming mugs.

"Are you talking about me behind my back?" she asked and set the tray on a table between two rocking chairs.

"Yes, we are, my dear," Paul said. He took her hand. "Now we'll talk about you in front of your front." He twinkled a smile at her, and she smiled back. Then she turned to address Carl and Dill.

"Have a coffee, Carl. Do you drink coffee, Dill? Maybelline certainly has fallen in love with you, little girl!"

Dill's face was a confusion between pleased and chagrined. *Probably not used to being called 'little girl' and not sure how to take it*, Carl thought. She'd see that Mary and Paul meant no harm.

"Call those two boys up here, would you, Paul? I don't want their coffee to get cold." She sighed and sat in a rocker and patted the one next to her. "Well, Carl? Can you get someone out here to fix the fences?"

Carl sat and grabbed the mug. Mary's coffee was better than anything you could get in the cafeteria at ZI. Richer and more flavorful. He didn't know where she found beans, but she did.

"I can have the Wranglers take a look, Mary," he said, "but no. No one can officially see to them anymore. They're too far out of date."

Mary snorted. "Like me!" She laughed.

"Don't say that, Mary," Paul said from the railing, where he was handing mugs to the panting Wranglers.

"Thanks, Abby," one Wrangler said, and the other seconded the thanks, both with their eyes on Mary. Their voices were little-boy bashful. Carl almost laughed and would have done if he hadn't already been aware of the effect Mary–and the dogs–had on Wranglers.

"Drink up and then have another lap with the pack. They'll sleep good tonight," Mary said. At the sound of her voice, the dogs' heads tilted one way and another. One of them began to climb the porch steps, but Mary waved it off.

"Go on, Duke, stay out there," she said. "Don't you drag your sooty self up here onto my clean porch."

The dog turned obediently and rejoined the other three.

"They really listen to you," Dill said, her voice marveling as though she couldn't believe a mere human could command such beasts.

"You've worked a charm on one of them yourself, Dill," Mary said. "It's just consistency and training. Keeps good dogs good. Of course, the hardest thing was to keep them from trying to eat the dead people. Dogs do enjoy a bit of rotten meat."

"I can imagine," Dill said, but her voice was faint. Carl thought maybe she was imagining with a little too much clarity.

"So," Paul said. He sat on the other side of Mary and addressed Carl. "What's the next best thing, then? What came after the fences?"

"Well, the rake system, but that failed pretty quickly. You really want Ze Poppers in conjunction with the new style Ze Fences."

"Do Ze Poppers keep the dead people out of the yard?" Mary looked at Carl closely. He began to have the feeling she already knew her options, and she didn't like them.

"No, not exactly. And Ze Fences are completely different now, too," Carl said.

"Now they keep the dead people *in* the yard, isn't that right?" Mary asked.

Carl nodded and shrugged. "People aren't having as many problems with zombies anymore. The bigger problem has become other people. Zombies are a good deterrent. Nobody in their right mind would approach yard zombies."

"And the Ze Popper...that blows their heads off? Is that the idea?"

"Well, not exactly, no. It severs their heads at the neck with a series of small charges embedded in the collar."

"Does it always work?"

"We've had one that didn't work, but that's the first time since the system's been out. The first problem I've seen, and I think it was a fluke, Mary; I really do."

"Why not just have something that kills the brain?" Mary asked. She watched Carl over the rim of her mug as she sipped her coffee. Dill shifted, hands going to her hips.

"Yeah, that makes better sense," Dill said. She looked at Carl in confusion. "Why don't they do that? That's a good idea!"

Carl rolled his shoulders and dropped his head. Then he looked into Mary's wryly smiling face.

"She's too new to know, isn't she?" Mary said. The wry smile never left her face, but her eyes had gone hard. "Don't keep the girl in suspense, Carl."

"They use the heads," Carl said. His voice was flat and blunt. She may as well know; all Assessment teams knew. "R&D uses them. The bodies sometimes, too, but not as much."

"Gross," Dill said. "That's really, like, *gross*."

Carl shrugged, but he was annoyed. "How do you think they develop all the new systems? All the deterrents and things that keep everyone safe? They use *zombies*, Dill. You know that."

"Yeah, I guess, but..." Dill shrugged again. Her hand had gone unconsciously to the dog at her side, and she fumbled with Maybelline's velvety ears.

"Seems wrong somehow, doesn't it?" Mary said, addressing Dill. "Something about the process twangs an instinct."

Dill nodded, and Carl felt another surge of annoyance. "Well, it's the way it is, Dill. You'll have to think long and hard about Assessment if you object to it."

Dill dropped her eyes, and Maybelline whined uneasily, nosing the girl's hand.

"Carl, for Christ's sake," Mary said. Her tone was less scolding than it was despairing. "Give the girl a break. We're not all born killers, are we?" Her tone had taken on a slightly teasing note.

Carl rolled his eyes, and Paul laughed. Everyone had had close calls, and Carl had known Mary and Paul long enough to know that they'd struggled as much as he had. In the beginning, the killing hadn't come easy. Not if you were a feeling person.

"No, I guess you're right," Carl said. He was tired of debating this with Mary, but he also wondered how much of his irritation was born from thinking she might be right...at least about some of it.

"Are you guys part of Z.A.P.T.?" Dill asked. Carl wanted to laugh at her question, but the shaky quality of her voice made him feel bad. He cupped a hand over his mouth to hide his smile.

Paul laughed, and Mary snorted.

"No, Dill," Mary said, "Z.A.P.T. is a bunch of misguided children and or assholes with no clear idea of the state of the world we currently live in."

Dill looked taken aback; at the language or the statement itself, Carl couldn't be sure. He felt even worse for her, and his smile evaporated. She was just a kid, really.

"I thought...from what you said..." Dill said.

"I don't think the dead people are our *friends*, Dill," Mary said. She sat forward in her rocker. "The walking dead will kill you given even a sliver of a chance. There's no humanity left in them. They are merely reanimated corpses."

"Then why...?"

"I'm not concerned with ZI using the dead people for experiments or research or whatever they want to call it. They aren't being hurt, their dignity isn't being derided...they have neither of those things. The problem is the same problem that you have using dead people as security in your yard–it puts you in the same proximity as them." Mary leaned forward and pinned Dill with her eyes, but Carl knew she was speaking to him, too. "Any system that depends on having the walking dead around undead people will result in catastrophic failure." She glanced at Carl as she sat back. "It's inevitable. That's why we'll never use your so called 'yard zombies' out here."

There was an extended silence, and finally Paul was the one to break it.

"You're too hard on Z.A.P.T., Mary," he said. "Yes, they're misguided, but I would bet they are mostly younger people. The ones who don't remember. We were idealistic once, too."

"Yes, but not about *dead* people!" Mary said. "We fought against corporate greed and the poor working conditions in Texas after they had seceded. We fought for scientists' rights after the Clergy Party gained a foothold in Congress. What we did was *noble*. We had integrity behind us, Paul. We had *morality* on our side." Her eyes were bright with fervor and anger. Carl could see plainly that she must have been a force in her day...she still was. "We had reason and actual facts that we worked with...not cotton-headed conjecture."

"Well," Paul said, "that didn't serve us very well at the Chance Hearings, did it?"

Mary looked shocked for one second, and then she laughed, Paul and Carl joining her. They laughed as children laugh at a dirty joke, as though they wouldn't want to get caught in their hilarity. As though to be caught would bring punishment and shame.

"What are the Chance Hearings?" Dill asked, obviously mystified. Her hand had gone to Maybelline's solid head as if for support.

Carl coughed into his hand, trying to control his laughter. Paul wiped his eyes, and Mary sat back with a hand on her lower belly.

"Before your time, Dill," Carl said. "They were in 2025."

"The year before the plague," Dill said, and Carl nodded.

He didn't want to get into it in front of Mary and Paul, especially since the protests might have been a contributing factor to what eventually happened. Science run amok, the prosecution said, but many had defended those scientists.

They might laugh about it now as though it was black comedy, an unfunny joke on them, but he figured that they still wrestled with their own freight of guilt. He looked at his watch and brought the subject back around to the original topic.

"We only have a few hours. I'll set the Wranglers loose if you cut the grid. Dill and I can keep an eye on the east and west if you watch north and south." He stood and stretched.

"We haven't seen any in quite some time," Mary said and gathered up the mugs. "Their population is dwindling; I'm sure of that."

"We saw two on the way here," Dill said. "The Wranglers hit one, and the other one, a kid, bit my leg right at my boot."

Mary set the tray down too hard, and the mugs jingled nervously. She turned to Dill.

"A kid? A boy?" Mary said, and Dill shrank back a little at her intensity. Maybelline whined and put herself between the women. Mary ignored the dog. "What did he look like? What was he wearing?"

Carl cut in, "It wasn't your grandson, Mary. I'd have recognized him."

She turned to him, and it was his turn to step back.

"How?" she asked. "How would you know it was him? You've never met him."

Paul had put a hand on her arm, turning her to face him. "From the pictures, Mary," he said, and his voice was soothing. "Carl has seen a dozen pictures of Robert." He smiled, and there was pain in the smile. "You showed him the pictures, remember?"

Mary sank into herself, deflating. She reached up and put a hand on Paul's cheek, and Carl turned away, uncomfortable at the sad vulnerability in her face. He preferred the fiery Mary, the fierce fighter. Grief sagged and aged her. Carl didn't need a reminder of the transformative powers of sorrow.

"Come on, Dill," Carl said. "I want you on the east side of the house. Keep an eye on the tree line, but don't get hypnotized by it." He turned halfway back to the couple but kept his eyes averted. He also didn't want to see their love for each other although Dill seemed to be watching them as though there would be a test on it later. "Let me know when the grid's off."

"Of course, Carl," Paul said. "Give me two minutes."

Carl grabbed Dill by the upper arm, forgetting the ZI rules of harassment, and led her away.

*

The Wranglers had dug a box out of the blackened ground. They huddled together over it, but were too far away for Dill to see what, exactly, they were doing. The dogs, all except one, stood near the Wranglers, tails waving as they waited for attention, but the Wranglers were intent on their task.

Dill ran her eyes over the gray woods again. Same nothing. She shifted her bow to her other hand and stretched. She was tired of standing but wouldn't take a chance on sitting down. If she screwed up again, Carl might not be so forgiving, and the Wranglers were counting on her to watch out for them.

It felt odd to have those two burly beasts depending on her. For some reason, it made her think of Denny. She and Denny had a good relationship, but it was…

Dill frowned and reached for Maybelline's ears as she thought. The big dog's eyes closed, and she rested her bulk against Dill's leg, sighing her contentment.

Dill pictured the way Paul and Mary had looked at each other. They really *knew* each other. Of course they did, they had *grandchildren*…they'd been together a long time. Maybe when she and Denny had been together for as long, they'd have the same connection.

The thought of staying with Denny that long seemed almost comical. Certainly far-fetched, but why? Why did their relationship seem so immature? So juvenile?

Because they never looked at each other the way Mary and Paul did, and face it, they never would. When you got right down to it, she didn't even like him that much sometimes. Why was she realizing this now, and was it even true?

She felt stupid about the Z.A.P.T. stuff, too. Mary was right; even Carl was right. Or so she was starting to think. What did it

93

mean if she was so ready to throw over her convictions? Either she was weak or those convictions hadn't really been hers in the first place.

Which was it?

"Dill?" Mary's voice pulled Dill out of her confused reverie. "Can I offer you a coffee or a water?" She had put on a sweater knitted from soft, seawater green yarn. Her hair was out of its ponytail, and it hung past her shoulders. In the overcast light, she looked thirty years younger. Maybe more. Dill found she couldn't answer.

"Are you worried about my part of the watch? Don't worry," Mary said. "My grandson took my post."

Dill blinked, confused, and Mary laughed wryly, shaking her head. "My *other* grandson. My 'not dead' grandson." She joined Dill at the railing, her eyes on the Wranglers. "I didn't mean to upset you earlier."

"I wasn't upset," Dill said. Her protest was almost a squeak, and she swallowed before she continued. "You thought it might have been your grandson we saw. I understand you being, um, abrupt about it."

Mary looked sideways at Dill, and her smile was still there but smaller.

"I meant what I said about Z.A.P.T...but I admit I was a little harsh on the subject," Mary said. "You're a part of them, aren't you?"

Mary's voice held no accusation, no derision, but Dill colored and shifted her feet. Her hand went unconsciously to Maybelline, and she dropped her eyes. She didn't say anything. Couldn't.

"You don't have to tell me," Mary said and bumped Dill's shoulder lightly with her own. "I wouldn't rat you out, though. Just so you know." She bumped Dill's shoulder again, a little harder. "It's because of a boy, right? Can you tell me that much?" Her tone was teasing, but not mean. It was kind and playful. Knowing.

Dill's face grew hot, and she smiled without raising her eyes.

"I knew it!" Mary said. She leaned her elbows on the railing and clapped her hands lightly. "Oh my goodness, the things we do for love."

Dill cleared her throat, and the smile melted away. "Well, it's...it's complicated."

"I see," Mary said. She was quiet for a long minute as they watched the Wranglers work. They were reburying the box, and their curses and laughter sailed thinly across the field. "I can't imagine what it's like for young people today, and I won't pretend any different, but I think there are probably a few constants. Like, how being a girl feels different from being a woman. How girlish things seem so important until you look back on them from further down the road." She grew quiet again, and Dill could feel her eyes like warm search beams. "I think you might have gone a little further down the road today, Dill...am I right?"

Dill shrugged but then nodded. It sounded right, and it felt right. Maybe that's why Denny and especially Z.A.P.T.–the meetings and proclamations–seemed juvenile. Something had changed in the last two days. Something that seemed now to have been waiting to happen. Destined to happen.

All at once, Denny felt like a too-small shirt. A shirt depicting a much-loved cartoon character that held no real sway in her life anymore. A shirt you're ashamed to wear in public because it speaks so absolutely to one aspect of your life that should have been given over long since.

"Mary, can I ask you something?" Dill said and let her eyes meet Mary's.

"Of course you can, sweetheart," Mary said. She put an arm around Dill's shoulders and gave a small squeeze. Dill's throat contracted. Is this what having a mom felt like?

"Hey, Dill! Wranglers are wrapped up," Carl said, coming around the far side of the porch. "Get your shit together, and let's–" He stopped short. "Am I interrupting?"

Dill stepped out from under Mary's arm, feeling vaguely ashamed. Maybelline whimpered, and Dill glanced at her and then away, averting her gaze from the dog's worried brown eyes.

"No," Dill said. "I'm ready to go when you are."

"Well...come on, then," Carl said. "Mary, Paul is with the Wranglers, but I don't know if he understands what they're telling him. Can you come translate?"

Mary smiled. "Sure thing, Carl. I speak Wrangler. Dill?"

Dill turned. "Yeah?"

"You come back any time you want, okay? Maybelline is going to miss you."

"Thanks," Dill said. She met Mary's eyes with her own and had that feeling again: cared for, warm. She smiled. "I'll remember."

*

"Mary's a good person. Her and Paul both," Carl said. "The dogs are something else, huh?" They'd been on the road for an hour. The coffee Mary had put in a thermos for him was still hot, and he sipped it periodically, reluctant to drink it all away because he might not get it again any time soon. The SUV hummed along in silence, and behind them, even the Wranglers' gas engine monstrosity seemed to growl with a lot less vigor. It had been a long day. "Do you know they used to cut off dogs' tails? Seems weird now. Barbaric. I'm glad that stopped. They look good with their tails, right?"

Dill pulled her booted feet from the dash and sat up, running a hand over her eyes. She'd been very quiet since they left the cabin, and the gray light of late afternoon had drained away all her color.

"Yeah," Dill said. She blinked through the front windshield and ran her hand over her eyes again. She took in a breath as though to say something more, but slumped back without speaking. She fiddled aimlessly with the bow in her lap.

*What was wrong with her? Did she miss the dog, or what?* Carl wondered but didn't ask. It was her business. He should just leave her to sort herself out. He nodded to himself–one curt nod–at a decision well made.

Then Dill sighed.

"What the hell, Dill?" Carl said. "What's your problem?" The words came out more annoyed than he felt. He swallowed and tried again. "Are you okay?"

He caught her nod in his peripheral vision, but he glanced her way anyway. Her head was down. She didn't look okay. "Was it the kid that almost bit you? You still bothered by that?"

"No," she said, "I'm just thinking." Then she shook herself, like a dog coming out of water as if trying to rid herself of something. She sat straighter. "Where does ZI get all the zombies, Carl?"

"Where? Well…" He shrugged and indicated the outside with a wave of his hand. "Everywhere. The Wranglers catch them and bring them back. Why?"

"I was just wondering about what Mary said."

Carl thought back to the conversation. Mary had said a lot about not having 'dead people', as she called them, around–not as security, not for experiments–but he didn't remember anything along the lines of what Dill was saying.

"Did she say something about that when you two were on the porch?"

"No, that was…we were talking about something else." Dill's cheeks flushed. "From earlier, I meant, when she was saying how it used to be all about keeping the zombies out, and how you said that now it's about keeping the people out, but hardly anyone sees zombies anymore," she said and turned to Carl. "I bet most of the really young people, especially the ones that grew up in the ZI compound, have never even seen one in person."

"Jesus, Dill, did you forget we were attacked by two on our way here? The one almost bit your leg!" Carl shifted uneasily and glanced back at the Wrangler truck that growled sedately behind them. The Wranglers sat calm in the cab, no horsing around. They seemed to be watching the SUV.

Carl didn't know why Dill's words made him uneasy, but they did. There was something almost blasphemous about them although Carl didn't think of himself as spiritual at all.

"But is two a lot?" Dill asked. "For the time we've been out? We didn't see *any* while we were at the cabin, so it's not like the woods are full of them." She fell silent, her gaze remote as though she didn't expect an answer.

Carl thought back to the last time, prior to today, that he'd seen a zombie in the wild. You couldn't count the one in the sewer grate–that was a ZI zombie, same as the ones in the yard.

No. When had he seen one *truly* in the wild, completely unrelated to ZI? The Miller job? Could that have been it? That was at least three months ago. Maybe four.

Four months? Carl shook his head and sat straighter. "Well, that's good, though," he said and wasn't sure for a second if he was responding to her or his own internal dialogue. Didn't matter…same answer either way. "That means the zombie population is dwindling. That's a *good* thing, Dill," he said. His tone implied that she thought otherwise, and he assumed he'd probably get a rise out of her. She slumped against the window, her chin sunk into her hand, and didn't even look at him as she mumbled her response.

"What?" he asked. Ahead of them, the ZI compound outer gates came into view. Carl slowed the SUV in anticipation of the checkpoint. "What did you say?"

"I said," she said without taking her eyes from the long, wooden Zombie, Inc., sign planted firmly just outside the first gate. Two zombies were chained at each side, and they swayed and shuffled at the length of the tethers. The ground beneath them had been ground low, like the area under a much-loved child's swing. Or the spot the junkyard dog's body makes just outside his dilapidated doghouse. "What happens when there are *no more* zombies?"

*

Carl stared out the window at the dimly lit inners apartment building. The living room was dark and quiet. He finished his third whiskey and put the glass neatly on the side table next to the chair. He wasn't feeling the effects of the alcohol even though he had no food in his stomach. That was probably a bad sign.

He wondered which window was Dill's. One of the lit ones? Hopefully. He didn't want to picture her sitting in the dark. Like he was doing.

Younger people had so much to live for. Didn't they?

He pushed himself forward, intending to get up and get something to eat when the alcohol hit. Hard. His head swam, and he tipped forward as the brown shag carpeting rose to meet him.

He yurked, and the whiskey, followed by Mary's good coffee, left him in one harsh, hot stream. He huddled on hands and knees, stomach contracting. He heaved again and another coffee/whiskey mixture came up. *Still smells pretty good*, he thought, and then his stomach clenched again, and he brought up bile.

He collapsed onto his side, careful to roll away from the brown puddle on the brown carpet. At least it would blend in. He chuckled and then rolled onto his back. Tears slid from the corners of his eyes, down across his temples and into his ears. He tilted his head back until he found the window again. From this angle, he couldn't see the apartment building, but he knew it was still there. He hoped Dill was in her boyfriend's arms.

Nobody should be alone.

His eyes closed and then opened to vertigo.

Closed again.

He slept.

He dreamed about Annie. Her face a red fist as she clenched and pushed, the house burning around them. He had to get her out, but she had become so heavy. She was as immovable as a boulder half-buried in clay.

She cried out, throwing her head back. Then she clenched again, clamped down, pushed. Her eyes, savage and full of miserable determination, met his. "You have to save the baby!"

"No! I'm not leaving you, Annie!" Dry air baked his throat, and he wanted to cough. In the dream, he could feel the heat on his face, see it on hers, but he didn't hear it. There was no crackle of fire, only he and Annie in a soundless bubble. Annie groaned and clenched, her eyes narrowed. Then a different cry. A new sound. He looked at the red, slimy thing that seemed to have appeared by magic in his hands.

"Please," Annie said. Her voice was pale, exhausted. Her eyes were closed now. Yellow and orange light leapt and flicked across her skin. "Save the baby, Carl. Save the baby."

"I'm going to save *you*, Annie," Carl said. "I'm going to save you."

He laid his hot bundle across her still-distended belly and sat back on his heels. He scanned the beam that held her pinned to the floor. It had fallen on her, first knocking her to the ground, then rolling her over, crushing her arm and her shoulder right up to her neck.

He would have to do something about her arm, his panicked and addled mind said.

Do? What can I do? What can I…?

*Amputation*, his mind whispered back as though keeping it a secret from Annie.

Carl's eyes went to Annie's. Her eyes were slitted open. Her good arm had gone to the baby. She smiled. Blood glowed darkly in her teeth. It darkened her tongue. "It's a girl, Carl." Tears shone on her cheeks as she smiled. "We have a little girl. Sarah…Sarah."

"Annie, save your…save your strength," Carl said. "You have to save your strength for when…for when we get out of here…please, Annie. Please." He wiped viciously at the tears in his own eyes. He knew she was dying. He knew he couldn't stop it from happening.

But he had to stop it anyway.

She sighed, and in the bubble of silence created by his dream, her sigh was the loudest sound. She took in a short breath and then sighed again, the breath going out and out. Her hand sagged away from the baby. More blood pooled beneath her, under her legs. A trill of it ran from the corner of her mouth. It was red at first, and then it blackened, became thick. Then it became even thicker and then began to crumble. The tell-tale sign of the start of a new existence–that of an undead monster.

The firelight jittered in her open, glazing eyes.

"Annie?" He ran a hand down her cheek. "Annie? Can you hear me? Can you hear me?"

As if in answer to his question, the baby whimpered. Horrified, Carl tore his gaze from Annie's dead but animated eyes and gaped at the baby. She struggled on Annie's belly, the umbilical cord shining and slimed with blue and red clots of blood. The umbilical cord blackened where it came from Annie's body. The black was headed up the cord, toward the struggling infant. Annie's baby. His baby.

Sarah.

He hated her.

Oh, how he hated this baby that had caused them to hole up in this house. Had caused them to be slowed down. Had caused Annie to die.

He reached for her and–

–woke up on his back in another family's living room, his neck strained. Dawn had cracked a bleary eye over the horizon and lit the room in a sickly pinkish orange. He rolled onto his side, and his stiff neck screamed in misery. He hissed and put a hand on the part that hurt the worst; the sharp smell of last night's sick drifted up and into his nostrils.

He curled around himself and cried; each sob jerked from him, each jerk tearing across his neck like fire. He cried until the tears had wrung him dry, until his eyes were gritty with salt. He cried until his breath left him in gasps and came back in shudders. He cried until a spike of pain planted itself firmly from the middle of his brain down the back of his throat.

He wished he would die.

When he didn't, he struggled up and sighed, rolling his shoulders over his chest. He hugged himself and sighed again, waiting for the cobwebs of the dream to fall away.

# EIGHT

**Zombie, Inc., Company Handbook**
Sec. 2: Code of Conduct;
Deportment on Scheduled Work Time
(*rev. 03/14/29*)

Zombie, Inc., (known hereafter as 'ZI') has a vested interest in our employees' roles as representatives of the ZI brand name. It is to that end that we must demand the full cooperation of every member of the ZI team in regards to deportment in the discharge of their respective positions.

A ZI employee will, during all scheduled work times, wear the proper uniform (or type of dress) indicative of their job title. Uniforms (or type of dress) will be well cared for, cleaned and pressed at regular intervals. Due to water shortage considerations, ZI would suggest that team members use the services of the ZI dry cleaning team located in the ZI main building.*

A ZI employee will, AT ALL TIMES, be courteous and congenial to other ZI employees (including the maintenance department) regardless of conflicts which may arise. Please report all conflict to a direct supervisor.**

A ZI employee will, at all times, conduct themselves in a manner becoming to a member of the largest and most successful post-apocalypse company in the United Five-State Republic.

**TAKE PRIDE IN YOUR COMPANY AND YOUR COMPANY WILL TAKE PRIDE IN YOU!!**

*The dry cleaning service is available to both shifts, and employees will enjoy an efficient, 48-hour turnaround time. *(For* *employees' convenience, a nominal fee will be deducted directly from your pay. Dry cleaning bags will be purchased at the employee's expense twice per year on the first day of April and the first day of September.)*

**If a conflict is with a direct supervisor, the direct supervisor will bring it to the attention of the HR representative assigned to your department.

--- --- ---

Carl ran a dribble of water over the white Oxford and scrubbed at the brownish stain with a bar of soap. The soap was old and deeply creviced, but still held a faint scent of citrus, and it turned his stomach.

"Fuck," he said and sighed at the stain. He'd have to take the shirt in. He hated using the dry cleaning service. It was almost impossible to read the monthly pay statements when it came to the 'services' portion. He had a suspicion, a gut feeling that ZI was overcharging. At least he didn't use their phone plan. Although his rent did come directly from his pay and was equally as confusing. Taxes and user fees changed month to month. Something to do with the constantly changing policies of the politicians housed under the apartments. Who were also at the mercy of ZI.

Indentured servitude was what it came down to.

The resentment that underscored most of his thoughts flowed with an especially strong current today. He was clear-headed this morning since he'd sicked up most of the whiskey last night—it was harder to fool yourself about the nature of your existence when you weren't drunk or hung-over.

He gave up on the stain and bundled the shirt into the ZI-approved dry cleaning laundry bag. The bag had come from his pay, too.

*"What happens when there are no more zombies?"*

Dill's words from last night came back to him as he stared at the ZI logo emblazoned across the bag. Twice a year he 'purchased' a new bag–every employee 'purchased' two a year. The handbook addendum had stated it was for the health and safety of the employees, but the bags were canvas…why not just clean the bags, too? It's not as though they wore out in six months' time. They wouldn't wear out in six *years'* time.

"What happens when there are no more zombies, huh?" Carl said softly and ran his thumb over the ZI logo. "What becomes of ZI, then?" He looked through the kitchen doorway to the living room picture window that perfectly framed the inners. "What becomes of everyone?"

*

Dill was walking alone, bundled into a thin coat, arms crossed over her chest and head down. Carl swerved the SUV to the shoulder. Her face appeared, wary and tired, in the window. She stared at him for a long minute before opening the door and clambering onto the seat. Her eyes were circled in exhausted brown.

Carl pulled away from the curb. ZI wasn't far, but as he caught sight of her shivering, he was glad he'd picked her up. She looked terrible. Probably trouble with the boyfriend. The thought made him angry, but he cautioned himself that he didn't know her...he didn't have any rights to her life or how she ran it.

He could ask, though.

"Where's the boyfriend?" he asked, keeping his tone offhand.

She shrugged and turned her face to the window. "He's running late today."

"Huh," Carl said. He waited.

"And," she said with another shrug, "I guess he's not my boyfriend anymore."

"Did you have a fight?"

She shrugged again, and Carl found it maddening, but he held his impatience. She still gazed steadily out her window, but by now they were bumping through the ZI parking lot, and what was there to look at but cracked blacktop?

"Dill, did he, uh...did he hurt you?" His face reddened in a mixture of anger and embarrassment, but to his surprise, she laughed.

She turned to him as they passed into the dark garage, and he saw the laugh was not a happy one, but also not entirely unhappy. Her skin yellowed in the dim overhead lights, and her eyes darkened as a shadow fell across her face.

"It was pretty mutual," she said.

He pulled the SUV into the spot and kept his eyes on his hands as they clenched on the wheel. He searched his mind for something to say, some kind of comfort or advice, but it was like searching a dark, cobweb-filled attic with a Bic lighter. He'd lost Annie so long ago, and they hadn't been married long enough to dislike each other, yet.

"Listen, Dill, if you want, I could–"

"Everything is fine; I'm fine. I guess it was bound to happen, but I just didn't know it until yesterday." She had a hand on the door handle but hadn't made a move to exit the SUV, so Carl kept still, listening. "We're not compatible. He has…ideas…that I used to agree with or, at least, *thought* I did. Now, I wonder if it wasn't mostly because I was just really young and really lonely when I got here. After my dad…after I lost my dad, I didn't have anyone. This place, the inners, seemed like a dream come true. Not in every way, of course. There wasn't enough food, and there was a lot of fighting going on back then, residents stealing from each other and everything. People doing whatever they could to keep themselves fed. It could be pretty tough at times. Pretty unsavory. Then things got better as ZI grew and grew, and everyone was employed, and everything became more regulated. It got better but I was still lonely. I was safe and fed, but I was just so, you know, by myself, and then I met Denny and his…his friends."

The silence drew out so long that Carl wondered if he should say something, but he wasn't sure what to say. Her story was not so different from a hundred others. The standard lines of comfort had lost their reassurance long ago. Or so they had for him.

Then Dill continued, and her voice was so quiet she could almost have been talking to herself.

"It's hard because they all seem like family, but they won't want to have anything to do with me now."

"Just because you broke up? Dill, they'll still be your friends. You've known them as long as you've known Denny…they'll stick by you."

She turned to face him, and she was smiling, but her eyes were still shadowed. She pushed down on the door handle, and the door clunked open. She shrugged. "It doesn't matter. When I was a kid, it mattered…but now it doesn't. I'm okay on my own."

She smiled again, and the sadness and tired bravado of it made Carl's heart ache. Why would anyone choose to be alone in this lonely world? Then he realized it was not dissimilar to how he'd arranged his own life, and the ache in his heart intensified.

*

*"Did you ever believe? Or was it bullshit all along for you?"*

Denny's face–incredulous, disgusted–hovered in her mind, his voice an angry echo as she followed Carl up the stairs. It hadn't been easy last night. He'd been angry about everything, but he seemed most upset that along with breaking it off with him, she was withdrawing from Z.A.P.T.

*"Don't forget what they did to your dad, Dill,"* he'd said. *"Don't forget that part as you decide it's okay for everyone to kill zombies. Let me ask you something–"*

Denny's voice had been contemptuous as he threw the things she'd confided in him back at her. It wasn't anything new, but she was seeing it with new eyes. She had decided to let him have his say; maybe it would be easier for him to let go if he got all the anger out of his system. There seemed no end to his derision.

*"Let me ask you this...what if they had your dad in a tube? What if they were cutting his arms off at the elbow, removing his skin, and putting electrodes in* his *head? Still sound okay to you, Dill? Still on board with it?"*

She'd felt the tears hot and stinging in her throat but hadn't let them fall. If he'd been sad or even if the anger had been more about the breakup than about her leaving Z.A.P.T., then she might have cried–but not when he was being mean for the pure satisfaction of it.

*"You never supported us all the way; you always held back,"* he'd gone on, and his tone had dwindled away into petulance. *"You always think you're smarter than everyone else, don't you? You think you're above us."*

He'd pursed his lips as he'd considered her, and Dill had readied herself. She knew the look in his eye, and what he'd said next *had* been hurtful to her, but probably not as much as he'd hoped.

*"Your dad would never have quit like this,"* he'd said, and Dill had briefly seen red, but it was less for what he'd said than how

he'd watched her afterwards as though any pain she displayed would somehow fulfill him.

Then her rage had drained away all at once, leaving her oddly neutral.

*"You don't know anything about it,"* she'd said, and she'd meant it: he didn't know anything about her father, or how it had been, or how she felt even now. He didn't *know* her.

*"I suppose* Carl *knows all about it, though, huh?"* he'd said, and she'd turned out of the room, shocked by his jealousy. She hadn't expected that. He'd continued to berate her through the door. *"All those Assessment people have mental problems, you know! Is that what you want to do with your life, Dill? They're all psychotic loners!"* His sudden laugh was bitter. *"Come to think of it...you'll fit right in!"*

She'd climbed into her bunk and drawn her pillow over her head. Then she'd dug into the secret hole in the mattress and pulled out a little crystal horse. She'd cupped it lovingly in one hand at the level of her eyes. It sparkled, and rainbows had appeared in faint splashes on the walls. His ranting had become muffled and distant, unimportant. She would get reassigned to another apartment and get her stuff out tomorrow.

Then she'd figure out what to do with the rest of her life.

"Fucking meetings," Carl said, pulling Dill from her reverie. He was reading a memo taped to the glass of the stairwell door. "If it's about benefits, then they can cram it up their...huh."

"What is it?" Dill asked.

"It's about those zapped assholes," Carl said and glanced at her. "Probably because of what happened in R&D. The company is finally taking it seriously. I'm surprised, though."

"About what?"

"That it hasn't been turned over to Assessment," Carl said and pushed through the door, checking his watch. "It's usually kept pretty quiet. ZI doesn't want any bad publicity. Listen, we've only got ten minutes before the meeting starts. Go grab us seats, and I'll get coffee."

She made her way to the first-floor auditorium. A crowd was filtering through the double doors, and she allowed herself to be pulled along with them.

The auditorium was spacious, capable of holding just over four hundred people. Stadium seating curved in a semi-circle around a shallow stage, where a podium sat dead center flanked by black curtains.

The noise level was high as employees took their seats. Dill heard her name called across the din.

"Dill, baby! Over here, Dilly! Come sit with us!" It was Candy from Sales. She was flanked by the two good-looking men Dill had met previously, Augustus and Robert. They gazed at her with lust. The rugged man, Robert, stood and called to her where she stood fifteen feet up in the aisle.

"Dill, my darling!" he said. He put a hand to his heart and flung his opposite arm dramatically in her direction. "Join us, and make my life worth living!"

Dill's face burned as people turned to stare. She smiled weakly at Robert, ducked her head, and moved toward him. She was better off, she figured, just doing as he asked before he made more of a scene. It wasn't that she *wanted* to sit next to him. It wasn't that she was at all *dazzled* by him, Candy, and Augustus.

He made a show of holding the back of her seat as you'd pull out a chair for a lady at a table. The move was ridiculous–all the seats were firmly attached to the floor–and Dill found herself mortified but also flattered. It was hard not to feel flattered by the warm glow of Robert's attention.

When she sat, he gave her a half-bow and took his seat next to her. He grabbed her knee and squeezed, and her face grew hot again as the HR rules on 'no touching' ran through her mind. She flashed him an awkward grin and then looked around the auditorium. Something was odd about the crowd, but she couldn't put her finger on it.

"Where's your fearless leader, Dilly?" Candy asked as she leaned across Robert. Her voice was a rumbling purr, and her breasts pressed heavily into the deep V of her blouse. "Or has Carl decided he can't slum with the rest of the humans?" Her tone was not derisive but rich with held-in laughter–teasing and confiding all at once.

"He's on his way," Dill said and tried to smile. It was hard not to look at the dark valley in Candy's shirt. "He stopped for coffees." She turned her gaze to the crowd again. What was wrong? Something was definitely off. Something was–

Then she saw it and realized it wasn't the crowd that was throwing her. It was a large, cylindrical shape in the shadows behind the curtains on the stage. It looked like one of the tubes from R&D, the ones they kept the zombies in. Her stomach turned. "Hey, did they bring a–"

"There you are!" Candy's voiced sailed over hers, and Dill turned to see Carl standing at the end of the row, coffees in hand. His gaze was on the stage, and his posture was one of tense watchfulness.

"Carl!" Candy called again, as though Carl was just too far away to hear her. She stood and leaned across Robert and Dill, and Dill struggled to rise as Candy's body loomed over hers. "Carl, baby…we've got your little Dilly over here!" Candy's hand came down on her shoulder and gripped it with harpy strength. Dill wondered briefly if she hadn't somehow becomes this Sales clique's hostage.

Carl gazed at the stage for a few seconds more–stubbornly, it seemed to Dill–then his eyes went straight to hers.

"You see what's up there?" he asked her.

Dill nodded and swallowed. Candy's hand squeezed again.

"Carl, just come sit down. You're making a fool of yourself in front of all these people," Candy said, and her voice had become a throaty drawl. She nodded and winked at the employees who were watching her, putting on a show. Then Candy's eyes cut back to Carl, and there was a flash of something naked there, some fleeting vulnerability, and Dill realized that Candy actually *liked* Carl. Like, *liked* liked him. Huh.

Carl settled next to Dill with a huff and handed her the coffee.

"I never saw that kind of visual aid at a meeting before," he said, still ignoring Candy. Candy shook her head, shrugged in an exaggerated way, and took her seat. Carl went on, "Doesn't seem like a good idea." He glanced around Dill. "Got your bow?"

The question put a heavy pit in her stomach. He wasn't joking. She patted the bow at her side and nodded, feeling suddenly very alert.

"I wish we were closer to an exit, but…" He twisted in his seat to look around. "At least we're on the aisle. That gives us some maneuverability. You see the exits?"

Dill followed his gaze and noted the exits nearest them. She also noted the other employees talking and laughing, complaining, drinking coffee, eating and in general being oblivious to their surroundings.

For the first time, she began truly to feel like Assessment, and to understand the 'outsiderness' of the job.

"Would you head for the main exit? Or–" Dill said but shook her head as she considered and reconsidered her own words even as she said them. She glanced around again, and her eyes fixed on an exit behind the last row of seats. "I guess it might be better to…"

He half-smiled at her. "That's the right instinct. If something were to go wrong, you'd want the least accessed exit. The crowd will pile up at the main doors, you'd never get through, but no one is going to want to backtrack *toward* the danger. That's where you would have at least a few seconds of advantage. If you consider–"

"Carl, my gawd, would you please talk about something else for five minutes?" Candy said and mock-laughed. "Let that poor little Dillybean have a *rest*!"

Augustus laughed, too, and Robert squeezed Dill's knee with a conspiratorial chuckle. Distractedly, Dill pulled her knee out of his grip. Robert's charms diminished as long as she wasn't looking directly at him.

"Why would they bring one here? Why take the chance?" she asked, her attention focused on Carl.

Carl shrugged. "I guess–if there *is* one in there–someone is trying to make a point, but to say that it is not well thought out would be an understatement."

Dill liked Carl like this. Calm and rational but still watchful.

A woman dressed in a smart two-piece suit walked onstage. Dill didn't recognize her as one of the higher-ups in HR. The crowd quieted by degrees as the woman waited, neutral faced and still. Then she bent slightly toward the mic.

"My name is Rosalind Sparks, and I am the Vice President of Human Resources for Zombie, Inc." She glanced up with eyebrows raised as though anticipating applause–or anticipating the need to squelch it. The crowd remained quiet. She nodded once and continued.

"Our purpose here today is not a happy one. We won't be discussing the wonderful benefits package or the record sales of the last three quarters. No. Unfortunately, our discussion today will be about–"

Her eyebrows raised again as her eyes swept the crowd. Her face was grim and almost disapproving.

"–treachery."

A sigh of whispered conversation swept through the employees, and Rosalind waited patiently, arms crossed at her waist and eyes downcast. Then she leaned back into the mic.

"For those not familiar, there is a terroristic organization that is trying to undermine everything that ZI has done and will do for the betterment of our society. This group would make the streets more dangerous, jeopardize jobs and lives, and plunge us back into the terror we all experienced in the first few years after the plague…and all for the sake of a romanticized, dangerously soft-hearted view of what *they* think a zombie is."

Rosalind's eyes scanned the crowd again as she shook her head.

"This group of young, misinformed children would have it so zombies and humans coexist peaceably. They would have you believe that zombies are still the loving, rule-following, sensitive, living, breathing human beings they once were. This group values the *zombies* existence *equally* to yours–" her arm swept up and across, indicating the audience, "–and they would populate our fragile world with these *monsters*, allowing them to roam unchecked and unguarded so that *you*–the *living, breathing, actual humans*–would have to once again scrabble for safety, food, light, comfort…"

Rosalind stepped back and raised her chin as though the thought were too much to bear. She regarded her audience and nodded. She leaned back in. "ZI has tried to let this group pass, to let them fritter about with their flyers and their manifesto, so-called. We've tried to ignore their petty vandalizing of company property and their attempts in the past to convert the loyal employees of ZI. We can't give them a pass any longer.

"This group–known to themselves as Z.A.P.T.–has been born of an *excess* of safety..." Rosalind raised her eyebrows and scanned the crowd, nodding. "That's exactly right...there is *not enough danger* in our world today. The children who are the muddled brains behind Z.A.P.T.–the very children who might be in this audience *right now*–are the product of a generation enjoying the freedoms that the rest of us have fought for! That we have *died* for!" Rosalind's arm shot into the air as she made her point.

The crowd murmured, and heads turned as Dill tried to find Denny among the other employees. Her stomach heaved with fear and uncertainty. Were Denny and the rest of the group about to be called out in front of everyone? Would she be called out with them? She glanced with almost unconscious apprehension at Carl. What would he think of her?

"Many people have begun to question the rigorous safeguards that ZI has in place. There are whispers and rumors that the zombie population is not only very decimated, but now *controllable*." Rosalind shook her head and spread her hands at the folly of the thought. "Although the immediate and daily danger of zombies seems to have passed and we all enjoy the safety and security of a relatively zombie-free environment..." Rosalind continued, her voice low, "...the escalation of attacks by members of Z.A.P.T. have forced ZI not only to *acknowledge* the existence of this terroristic group, but to try and impress upon *everyone...*" her eyes raked the crowd, "...the gravely serious situation that will become the *immediate* and *mortal* concern of every man, woman and child alive today if the zombie outbreaks begin again in earnest.

"I stated earlier that the members of Z.A.P.T. are most likely children with little or no real memory of what the world used to be like, or what the rest of us struggled through in order to bring them to this safe haven, and like spoiled children...they are ungrateful." Rosalind looked up, and her smile was patient and tolerant but sad. "We've done our job too well, it seems." The overhead lights seemed to catch a glint of tears at the outer edges of her eyes. She smiled tightly.

"But since, too, the problem is that most or all have little to no experience with actual zombies, we have decided to give *each* and *every* employee here today a good, long look at what Z.A.P.T. would have you believe is a being capable of rational thought, good decisions and even, yes, love." Rosalind's face was grim as she gestured to the crowd. "Please begin a line at the furthest edge of the stage stairs, starting with the first row. It's time for everyone to meet a *real* zombie."

At the word 'real', the cylinder was wheeled from behind the curtain and into the harsh overhead lights at the front of the stage. Two Wranglers stood at either side of the cylinder, weapons raised and ready. The addition of the Wranglers seemed largely for theatrics–the leather-jacketed and heavy-booted men were nearly as frightening to the timid office personnel as the monstrosity encased in the cylinder.

It was a menzie–formerly a human man–and beside Dill, Carl murmured derisively, "Oh, of course," but she barely heard him, as her eyes were trained on the zombie. It was naked, and its skin was the trademark gray of the undead. Its head had a mangy look from the patches of hair interspersed with patches of brownish, rotting skin where chunks of hair had either fallen or been pulled out. It stepped forward and stepped forward again, never gaining ground, bumping over and over into the heavy plastic. As Rosalind waved the employees across the stage, the zombie's arms flailed as it reached for each person filtering past. Its hands left streaks of brownish-blackish gore everywhere they struck. Its jaws yawned open, showing the black cavern of its toothless, ruined mouth.

The crowd chattered distractedly as the rows rose one by one, but that didn't block out the wailing moans of the trapped zombie. The top of the tube–three feet above its head–was open, and the zombie's leaden cries were picked up and amplified throughout the auditorium. By squinting into the dark area above the curtains, Dill could just make out the microphone that had been placed above the cylinder. More theatrics.

Rosalind watched with tight patience as two more rows passed the zombie. No one lingered or drew too near the cylinder. Some averted their eyes. The zombie moaned and wailed, its movements becoming more frenzied and a meaty *thump, thump, thump* was also picked up by the microphone.

The fifth row was crossing the stage when a young woman in the white coat and clunky clogs of the food prep department stopped short. She stepped closer to the cylinder. A tall, fluted white hat she'd been holding fell to the stage as her hands went to her mouth. The Wranglers on either side of the cylinder watched her with neutral, but cautious, expressions.

The woman screamed. It was muffled behind her hands, but the mic above the zombie picked it up anyway. The crowd in the auditorium went silent for three seconds and then burst into whispered conversation.

"Assholes," Carl said.

Dill turned to him, but his gaze was trained on the stage. He was shaking his head with mild disgust.

"Who? Who're the assholes?" Dill asked. "The Wranglers? The employees?"

He glanced at her and then back to the stage.

"She knows him," Carl said. Dill's stomach sank, and her eyes went to the woman. She'd fallen to her knees as she stared at the cylinder. It was obvious she was crying from the way her shoulders shook. The Wranglers still watched her, but they were also cutting their eyes uncomfortably to Rosalind as if looking for instruction. Rosalind stood next to the podium and watched the woman with nervousness, seeming completely at a loss as to what to do.

Their row rose, but Carl didn't stand, and when Dill began to, he bumped her with his elbow and shook his head. His meaning was clear: stay in your seat.

The Sales clique brushed past, practically *dragging* their bodies across them–pushing and brushing in a sexualized way. People looked but then quickly averted their eyes. No one would report Sales for inappropriate behavior, as they were expected to act that way.

Once the rest of the row had finally gone past, Carl scrunched down in his seat and tented his hands almost at eye level. Dill, who thought he'd been preparing her for something by not letting her join the other employees, looked impatiently from the stage to Carl and back to the stage. The woman was still crying in front of the cylinder.

"What are we doing?" Dill asked Carl in a harsh whisper.

Carl glanced at her in surprise. "We're sitting in a meeting...what's wrong with you?"

"No, I mean, why did you stop us from going up there? Is something going to happen?"

"I hope not."

"Then...why? Why are we staying back here?"

He glanced at her again. This time he shrugged. "Did you *want* to go see the zombie? I thought you'd have had enough of them from the last two days."

Dill sat back and ran a hand over her face. "No, I...I just thought...I dunno, I guess I thought *you* thought there was going to be some kind of trouble. That's all."

"Look, I don't have a sixth sense or anything," Carl said, "but it doesn't take a psychic to realize that it's a bad idea to bring a zombie into a crowd of people in a space with limited traffic flow." He sat straighter as Candy and the men from sales slid past, retaking their seats. He didn't take his eyes from Dill. "I sure don't need a close-up look at a zombie. I've seen plenty of them. I'm not the one who needs a reminder."

Dill looked away from him, feeling accused. Did he know? Her eyes scanned the crowd again, looking for Denny–he should be in the audience, but she couldn't locate him.

"You looking for that boyfriend of yours?" Carl asked.

"He's not my boyfriend, Carl, remember?"

"Yeah, I remember, but do you?"

"What's *that* supposed to mean?" Dill nearly hissed with agitation.

"I just hope that *you* remember that you broke up with him. Don't get back together with him. That's what I meant."

She turned to him, furious, knowing half her anger was exacerbated by guilt and a cold dash of the fear that she'd be tagged as part of Z.A.P.T.

"You don't know *anything* about it," she said, "and stop butting into my life. You're not my dad." She crossed her arms and threw herself back into her seat. Candy laughed, but Dill couldn't tell if the woman was laughing at her or not.

Her face burned with angry, embarrassed heat. She was afraid, too, that Carl would now explode on her and tell her she could kiss Assessment goodbye. In fact, she was sure it was coming.

He leaned close to her, and she could feel his heat and weight at her side. She cringed internally while keeping her face stony on the outside. She wouldn't cry. Even if she had to go back to Maintenance, she wouldn't cry.

"I'm not your dad, but I'm the closest thing you've got to it," he said, his voice low enough that Robert on her opposite side wouldn't be able to hear. "Dads give advice that their kids don't want to hear...that's what dads do. If you're going to keep working for me, you better get used to it."

He sat back, and her side cooled instantly. She should be angry. She *would* get angry in a second–but the anger didn't come. Instead, a feeling of deep satisfaction warmed her, and she relaxed, her arms uncrossing.

On the stage, the last row had shuffled past, and the crying woman had finally gained her feet. She stumbled away from the cylinder, shoulders still shaking, and the Wranglers watched as she navigated the vacant aisle to her seat. Her seatmates leaned away from her, avoiding her shaking hands as she sat. Her shoulders curled in dejectedly, and her hands curled together, one into the other, as though she was holding her own hand for comfort.

Dill sighed and caught Carl's gaze. She nodded. *Okay*, the nod said. *We're in it together.*

He half-smiled and then returned his gaze to the woman, sobering as he watched her cry alone.

# NINE

## **2041 FIRST ANNUAL ZOMBIE, INC., EMPLOYMENT FAIR**
**********

• Are YOU tired of scrambling for food, money, and safety? •
Then !!JOIN US!! as Zombie, Inc., Celebrates Ten Years in Business!!
*Armed personnel will be in attendance, and refreshments will be served*
**********

The 2041 First Annual ZI Employment Fair will be held on March 13 at ZI Headquarters, located at 100 ZI Boulevard. Industry professionals and Human Resources personnel will be on hand to interview YOU for a position with the ZI family!!
*Positions to be filled include:*
• Assessment
• Accounts Payable and Receivable
• Collections (Virtual and Physical* Divisions)
• Sales
• Maintenance and General Laborers
*...and many, many more...!*

Zombie, Inc.–the industry leader in zombie defense and home security–has !!THE BEST!! benefits package available to citizens of the United Five-State Republic! Join us on March 13 at ZI Headquarters, located at 100 ZI Boulevard, and discover an avenue

to safety the world hasn't seen since 2026! Included in the MANY perks of employment with ZI:**
- Comprehensive After Death Benefit
- The SAFEST environment in the United Five-State Republic
- Generous Paid Time Off
- Access to company discounted phone plans and implant procedures
- Complementary Dry Cleaning!***

*...just to name a few...!*

Bring a resume (handwritten is acceptable!) and dress to impress as Zombie, Inc., searches for the people that will make the BEST TEAM MEMBERS at the BEST COMPANY in the United Five-State Republic!!!!

**********

*\*Physical Collections requires a pre-employment agility test that will include: running, firing a weapon, hand-to-hand combat, courage assessment, and pain tolerance testing. It is suggested that applicants interested in Physical Collections wear sneakers and bring a change of clothes to the employment fair.*

*\*\*Benefits shown may not be available for all ZI employees. Benefits are commensurate with physical attractiveness, intelligence, agility (mental and physical), and age.*

*\*\*\*Dry cleaning is a "complement" to looking your best! There will be a small fee for dry cleaning.*

--- 

Dill sat through the rest of the meeting but heard none of it. She was aware of Carl as a solid presence beside her, an advocate, a comrade. Like a dad, kind of, sure...but like her dad had been? She shifted and settled again.

She'd been fourteen when her dad had gone to the ZI employment fair. They hadn't given him a job. She hadn't understood. She'd been so sure that he'd come back and tell her that their worries were over–that they could stay in one place, eat every day, feel safe.

He'd come back to 'their' house–an easily defensible rancher where they'd been for just under a month–in a neighboring suburb after being gone for the better part of two days, and told her how it was.

"There were twenty dogs there for every bone," he said and chuckled as he dropped an armload of wood to the tatty living room floor. "Want to walk, Dillalia? You must be pretty stir-crazy by now." He put a hand on her head and ruffled her hair. She'd been torn between relief at having him home and anger that the place he'd gone to hadn't hired him, and something else, too, a feeling so complicated that her fourteen-year-old self had had no reference for it and, therefore, no name, but her gut had burned. Disappointment, shame, anger...all had coalesced to create a mire of bad feeling. She didn't want to feel that way about her dad, didn't want to feel as though he wasn't capable of taking care of her.

"Yeah, let's walk," she said, "I need air."

She wasn't allowed out on her own, and she didn't leave the house at all when he wasn't there. She stayed 'holed-up' as he called it. Even though she knew how to fight and how to shoot, the world was too dangerous for a young girl.

"Okay, grab your bag," he said. You never went out without a scavenging bag–there was no telling what you might find–and she didn't need reminding, but she didn't resent it. Not after she hadn't seen him for two days. On another day, if they'd been cooped up together for too long, she might have snapped, but not today.

Today she was just happy to see him, and she swallowed her disappointment that he hadn't gotten a job.

The day had been very cold and very gray, but even that weak light had been a balm to her. She felt as though her skin were drinking in the light as she tilted her face up to the sky. The smell of burning was thick in the air, and you never knew if it was someone's cooking fire or another house being burned down. Not that it mattered...but it was best to avoid someone else's cooking fire. Tempers were short, and nerves frayed.

Dark bits of ash floated in the air like anti-snow, and Dillalia had no urge to run her tongue out and catch the flakes. Her dad's face was already turning dark gray with the powdery hitchhikers. Hers must be, too.

"Let's go west today and see about some of those other roads. We haven't gone down Amontillado or Ligeia Way yet," he said.

They walked in the middle of the street. The sidewalks were clear, but the trees there made her dad wary. Better to be in the wide open where you'd have some advanced notice of an attack than have a walking corpse step into your path from behind a tree.

He told her about the contest for the collections job, the one he'd thought his best possibility. He wasn't an office-type person and never had been. Things like accounts and sales were unknown quantities and therefore out of his realm. He'd been a retail manager pre-plague. He'd joked with Dillalia that being in retail had prepared him well for the apocalypse. She never fully understood what he meant, but she'd always laughed along with him—you couldn't help laughing along with him. He was that kind of person.

"When they were sticking everyone with little knives to test pain tolerance, I really thought I'd be a shoe-in," he said and bent to peer into a car that sat on four flats at the side of the road. It was obvious that the car had been stripped of necessities—the trunk was up and the windows smashed in—but better safe than sorry, he always said. Only takes a second to check so you might as well do it. He straightened and continued, "Everyone has a high pain tolerance, now. Everyone. There was even a few women trying for the collections jobs, and they sat through the knives, too. One of them cried, but so did two of the guys, so."

He rubbed his arm in an unconscious way, and Dillalia wondered just what had been done with the knives. How deep had they been stuck in? Did he have to have a bandage? What had he gone through, really? Her stomach burned and burned with the unnamable feeling.

He remained as even tempered as he'd always been. "Not that the ladies aren't tough; I don't mean that at all. I guess it's just a hangover of sorts."

"What does that mean?"

"It means that I see stuff like that in terms of your mom, I guess. It would kill me to see her…you know, going through something like that. It's worse when it's ladies. It just is." His tone had been slightly defensive but mostly just tired.

Dillalia didn't remember her mom, as she'd only been three when her mom had passed away. A throat infection had killed her.

Of all things, her dad had often said, strep was what did her in. In the old days, it wouldn't have been anything. A doctor's visit and you'd be good as new after two days of antibiotics. There hadn't been a doctor around, and that year–2030–was the year that had been the height of the zombie population. You couldn't sit still for a minute, much less have a lengthy and debilitating illness. He'd never mentioned how he'd kept her and himself alive in the days and weeks after her mom's death. He must have been working purely on adrenalin. She couldn't imagine it.

He scuffed his boot through a small pile of junk and bent with a cry. "Look at this!"

Dillalia trotted to him, trying to quell her alarm, but his face was glad and open.

"What? What is it?" she asked.

He straightened, and his hand was even with her chest, curled under. He grinned. "Open your hand."

She reached out without hesitation and splayed her hand flat under his. He looked into her eyes and opened his fingers. A tiny, clear animal tumbled into her hand. It was multi-faceted and seemed to amplify the poor light of the day into something extraordinary, and Dillalia wondered immediately how it would look in real sunlight.

It would be beautiful.

"What is it?"

"It's a horse. Cut crystal, I'm pretty sure. Stores used to sell them."

She looked up at him, but then her eyes had been dragged back to the horse. Its ears and hooves were gold. It looked like magic.

"This has to be someone's," she said, and the thought made her feel almost faint with envy. She'd never wanted something as badly as she wanted the little horse.

"It *is* someone's," her dad said, and her stomach had sunk to the pebble-strewn road. His hand found her head again, and his hand cupped the nape of her neck. "It's yours, Dillalia."

She looked at him, wide eyed and wanting to believe.

He nodded. "It's yours if you want it. Finders keepers, right?"

Another term she'd been unfamiliar with but understood at once. She hugged him, being very careful not to let the horse drop.

*Cut crystal*, her mind whispered. The words seemed magical in their own right.

"I'm going to name her Crystal," she said into her dad's shoulder. She felt the quaking as he chuckled.

"That's a good name," he said and squeezed her again. "I think you should–"

Then he'd stiffened.

A mild sound, nothing more than a faint shuffle-step, came from behind him. He turned and pushed her back with one gesture, saving her...but it was too late for him...the zombie was upon him...it was too late, it was...

"Time to go, Dill," Carl said and stood. He stretched. People packed the aisle. Dill blinked several times, trying to pull herself from the thoughts that wanted to suck her down like thick and gritty mud. She pressed her fingertips to her eyelids to cool the sting of tears.

"Wake up, Dilly, my dear," Robert said. His tone was bluff and oblivious. He glanced at Candy and Augustus with one perfectly groomed eyebrow raised. "You know she's dreaming about me!"

Candy's laugh was a witchy cackle that overrode Augustus' forced-sounding chuckle.

"Shut up, you asshole," Carl said. He waved Dill up, his eyes dark with concern.

Candy's mouth closed with a snap, and Robert gave Carl a look of confused dismay–why would anyone call *him* an asshole?

"What did I do?" Robert asked, his hand placed dramatically over his heart. "I was just teasing her! Girls *love* to be teased!"

"Not this one," Carl said and motioned for Dill to move past him and into the aisle. He turned back to Robert. "And keep your damned hands to yourself. *You* may be Sales, but Dill *isn't*. She's Assessment. Keep it in mind...*asshole*."

The employees closest to the exchange whispered, and a few laughed–quiet rustles of sound that came and went quickly. Dill glanced back at Robert as she made her way up the aisle. He looked completely dejected.

Carl appeared at her side as the doors spilled them into the hallway and the crowd fanned out.

"You were kinda hard on him," she said.

"Yeah, I guess I was. A little," Carl grinned, "but he'll live, Dill, believe me. Look."

Candy and Robert were arm in arm, with Augustus trailing behind. They were laughing, and Robert reached out to goose one of the reception girls. When she turned with a look of shock, he winked, and she smiled at him, mollified.

Dill wasn't sure if the twinge she felt was anger at his mildly depraved treatment of a fellow employee or some sort of jealousy.

Two maintenance workers brushed past them, talking.

"I can't believe they brought a menzie to a meeting! A naked one, at that!"

"I know, right? Talk about a visual aid!"

They laughed together, and Dill turned to Carl, remembering.

"Why did you say 'Of course'?" she asked.

"Huh?" Carl was still watching as Candy and her boys walked away. Dill looked from Carl to Candy and back to Carl. Did he *like* like Candy? She couldn't handle the thought right now and shook it off.

"When they brought the zombie out, you said, 'Of course,' like you were kind of disgusted by something."

He pulled his eyes from Candy. "I just meant, you know…'of course', like, of course they'd use a menzie–" he shuddered, "–damn, I hate that word…but, anyway, yeah. A male zombie is going to be scarier than a lady, and a kid you'd just feel bad for. They know what they're doing. That's what I meant. Let's get up to the office. I want to check on a few things."

Dill fell in beside him, and they entered the stairwell.

"It's weird, isn't it, that someone here knew the guy in the tube?" she said.

"Why is it weird?"

"Well, because it's so safe here. Most people from the inners and outers never leave, and no new zombie outbreaks have occurred within the ZI compound for I don't even know how long…so where did that one come from?"

Carl shrugged and shot her a look over his shoulder. They were on their floor, and the wide offices of Assessment opened up in front of them. "Yeah, and?"

"It just doesn't make sense with the lack of walking dead, you know? Where is ZI getting the zombies they sell as yard zombies, for instance? Where are they getting zombies to do all that research on? That made me wonder about R&D. No one knows what they're up to. The whole division is so secretive…I mean, are they *making* new zombies or–"

Carl's reaction was immediate. He grabbed Dill's upper arm and steered her into the nearest doorway, which happened to be a small women's restroom. He tented his hand on the door to keep it from closing all the way and peered out through the crack.

"What are you doing?" Dill asked, her voice laced with shocked anger.

"Be quiet," Carl said. His tone was curt. "I'm trying to see if anyone heard you."

She opened her mouth to protest, but without turning around, Carl put his hand to her face, palm up in a 'stop' gesture. She closed her mouth and crossed her arms over her chest. After a few moments, he let the door close and turned to her. His head was down as though he were deep in thought.

"Look, Dill," he said and then fell silent again.

Dill began to feel alarmed. Whatever it was, it was serious, to him, at least.

He continued, "You can't say something like that. It would be so…so absolutely *wrong* for anyone even to *consider* doing that. Do you understand?"

"I understand it would be *wrong*…but that doesn't mean no one is going to do it. Listen, maybe making zombies is the wrong way to phrase it. Maybe they're, you know, taking advantage of convenient deaths, like, if someone dies from a fall or appendicitis or something. Instead of initiating second and final death, they just…" She shrugged and raised her hands.

Carl shook his head again. Behind Dill the sink gurgled, making her jump.

"No. There's no way," Carl said. "Aaron's high up in R&D. If something like that were going on, he'd know about it, Dill, and he would have said something to me. There's no way." He shook his head again. "No. No way."

"I get that *you* think there's 'no way' for that to be going on. I *get* it. 'No way,' you said it, like, a *hundred* times." Dill put her hands on her hips, exasperated. She was embarrassed by his response to her question and more than a little angry. He was way, way overreacting. "It's not like you know everything that goes on around here, Carl. It's not like you're such an *authority*."

"No, Dill, you're wrong. They get zombies from the outside and use them up there. Maybe that woman knew that guy from outside. It's more than plausible."

"Carl, she was like, what? Twenty? Maybe twenty-two? Did you *see* her? I can practically guarantee she's lived most of–if not her *entire*–life in the compound."

"Dill, you're twenty-seven, and you haven't lived *your* entire life in the compound. If she were twelve that might make more sense, but you can't judge something like that based on age!"

"I'm not *basing* it on her *age*!"

"On *what,* then?"

"I'm basing it on her *face*! She's *soft*, okay, Carl? I can tell that she's never–"

"You two okay in there?" The voice–slightly amused, slightly alarmed–came from just outside the door. Carl's face pinched as if he had a cramp, and he put his hand over his forehead.

"We're fine, Marcus, just a little disagreement," Carl said without opening his eyes. "I had to, uh…take my trainee to task."

"In a *bathroom*?" Marcus said, and now his voice held more amusement. Someone else tried to muffle a laugh. How many people were out there?

"It's more private than my office," Carl said. He turned, opened the door, and peered out. "Marcus…oh, hello, Dean, Angela…will you guys please leave us alone? I'm taking care of business here."

Dill couldn't see past Carl to the other Assessment personnel gathered outside, but their burst of laughter made it through loud and clear.

"Okay, ha ha…very funny," Carl said. He shook his head. "Grow up. I know you have better things to do than eavesdrop on me. Dean, is the Collier's Report done yet? Angela? Your desk cleared off for the day?"

They dispersed, and Carl turned to Dill, his back to the door. He massaged his forehead some more, his face pinched into tight lines. "Whatever your reasons may be, don't ever mention something like that to anyone else in here. It makes you sound like one of those crazy zapped idiots who–"

He stopped short, and his eyebrows drew together. "Dill," he said and then fell silent. He shook his head.

Dill's stomach rolled slowly. She didn't want to have to tell him about Z.A.P.T. and Denny…now that she was out of it, she felt more foolish than ever for having been even a nominal part of it. The thought of losing this job was one thing, but the thought of disappointing Carl was actually worse. She was surprised to realize it, but there it was. Maybe she was taking the surrogate dad feelings too far.

"Dill," he started again. "Just be careful. Be careful what you say. Be careful who you associate with. ZI is a big company, and you don't want to find yourself on the outs with anyone. Z.A.P.T. is going to have a lot of trouble now that ZI has decided to turn company attention and resources to them. You understand?"

"I don't associate with the wrong people," Dill said, "not anymore."

Carl nodded, but the concern didn't leave his eyes.

Dill wondered if he really understood what she was telling him. She wondered if he realized she'd just confessed to being involved with the group he hated most. Maybe he didn't really want to know.

That was fine with her.

"Zombies aren't…they aren't fun, Dill. They aren't some kind of made-up…creature…with no…" Carl seemed to struggle with his thoughts. He leaned forward and gripped her shoulders. He fixed her in his gaze, and her stomach rolled with a brief swell of fear. The physical contact, the eye contact–she wasn't used to it. "They were *all* people once, just like you and me. It's harder for your generation to understand it. For you, the zombies have always been around, almost like a whole separate species, but they are *not* a separate species, Dill; they *are* humans. They had lives, hopes, and ambitions. They had parents and maybe kids and…love…and…"

A faint buzz made him put a hand to his ear. "This is Carl," he said as he turned and pushed through the restroom door. Dill stopped the door from swinging closed behind him, but she stayed a moment longer in the tight room, shaken. She knew that zombies weren't fun. She knew that they weren't a separate species. She knew that.

"Yeah, sure," Carl went on. He glanced back at her and waved her forward. "Sure, Aaron, no problem. Yeah, we'll be up in fifteen. Yep. See you." He glanced at her as she fell in next to him. "Aaron has something he wants to show us. Are we good?"

She nodded but didn't speak. Couldn't. She wanted to tell him that she knew...that she was well aware of a zombie's status of former human being...but she couldn't bring herself to start.

She didn't want to think about it.

It was too hard to think about.

*

"We figured out the half-popped collar," Aaron said, "and it's a good goddamned thing we did, too. I'm glad you made it a priority, Carl. This could have been a real nightmare if you consider the number of these collars currently being used in the field. The Wranglers are going to be a busy group in the next few weeks. It'll be interesting to see how Marketing handles it!"

Carl and Dill followed Aaron down the main corridor of R&D. There were no traces of the incident with the escaped zombie and the unfortunate Randy. The enzyme was a tidy, hungry little bugger that could eat the organic matter–blood, brain, skin–from between the paint molecules. Maintenance didn't even have to patch in fresh carpet.

"There's an issue with how the charges are ordered," Aaron continued. "When the collar hits the field head on or at any angle from the right, there's no issue...the first charges to hit the field pop, thus popping the others. There is a certain angle from the left...and it's tiny, it's a tiny, tiny window of...but that doesn't matter...what I'm saying is..." He opened the door that led to his lab and office and ushered Carl and Dill through. The first cylinder contained a zombie no more than three feet tall. It was a small child, a toddler, and under its dirty tangle of long hair, it was impossible to know if it had been a boy or a girl. Carl's stomach turned, but he controlled it, breathing shallowly through his mouth. He checked to see if Dill was okay as they made their way past the cylinders. She looked dazed, almost uncomprehending. This place really got to her. She was still too sensitive, but the job would eventually steady her.

Aaron continued, "When the collar hits at that angle, the first third of the charges actually shorts out the other two thirds! That's why they never popped!" He pulled his office door closed behind them, and the smell of cold rot dissipated. "Although the charges are–essentially–simultaneous, it is that small, small hitch in the relay that did us in."

He crossed his arms and smiled triumphantly.

Carl nodded, but he was preoccupied with Dill. She still looked too white and starey. She hadn't spoken since he'd read her the riot act back at their floor. Well, but he hadn't been yelling, just trying to impress something on her. Something that was hard even for him to express. He didn't want to sound like an old loon or anything, but people…young people…took the zombie thing way too lightly. Carl could *never* take it so lightly. Not after seeing Annie. Seeing the baby as she changed in his hands. That was–

"–worse than we thought, right, Carl?" Aaron's voice.

Carl looked up, feeling slow and drugged as he tried to shove the image of the changing baby, his daughter, back down where it belonged.

"Huh?" Carl said. "Sorry, Aaron, I missed that. What did you say?"

"I was just telling Dill here that these things are often less worse than we would have thought at first. These situations, I mean." Aaron laughed. "I mean, no one got hurt yet because of this. No one was attacked." He smiled at Dill, and his smile became troubled at her blank stare. "I know some people think of us as cruel up here, but it's not true! We just want what's best for everyone. We want everyone to be able to feel safe and secure…and not to just *feel* it but to actually *be* safe and secure. We're the good guys!"

"Excuse me," Dell said and bolted from the office. They watched her through the glass as she made her way back past the cylinders and out the lab door.

"She knows that, Aaron," Carl said. "She knows we're the good guys. She's just, you know, shook up."

Aaron's eyebrows shot up in honest surprise. "By what?"

"I think the first cylinder."

"The first...? Oh! The kidzie. Yeah, well, they are disturbing. Grosser still: that one came from one of the kidzie porn raids." He shook his head, his face pinched in disgust.

"Of all the twisted shit I've seen," Carl said, "and believe me, I've seen a *lot* of twisted shit," his voice twanged like a harshly played guitar chord, "...the kidzie porn is the worst. I don't even get the regular, adult zombie porn, much less..." He jerked like a dog having a bad dream. "At least they were able to make it a crime."

"Oh, right, right," Aaron said as if remembering. "By making all zombies property of the United Five-State Republic."

"Yeah," Carl said, "it was the only way. You can't give them human rights, but at least now it's a federal crime. You can't steal from the government, buddy."

"Wouldn't want to!" Aaron said and clapped Carl on the shoulder.

*

Dill pounded from the lab and straight into the restroom across the hall. She stood with her back to the door and swallowed a sob, stopping it before tears could start. It couldn't have been what she saw. Her eyes were playing tricks because of breaking up with him last night. Because of being tired. Something. She rubbed her eyes with her fists and hitched in a breath. *Just tired*, she counseled herself. *All the emotion has...has messed with your mind.*

She hitched in another breath.

Another breath.

Okay.

Everything was okay.

There had to be an explanation. She just had to ask.

But not Aaron. She couldn't ask him.

She took another deep, calming breath and turned to the door. She looked at her hand on the doorknob and breathed again. She frowned. Something was familiar about...this was the bathroom on the security video. This was the bathroom where Denny had been hiding after that zombie attacked Randy.

She yanked open the door in a panic, and Carl stood before her, hand raised, about to knock.

"You okay?" he asked her.

"Carl, I–" she said as Aaron popped out from behind Carl.

"Is she okay?" Aaron asked. "Hey, Dill, did you get sick? You okay now?"

Dill nodded and clenched her jaw to keep her teeth from chattering.

Carl eyed her with concern. "You sure you're okay?"

She nodded again and presented them both with a tight smile.

"You want to come back to my office and sit down a second?" Aaron asked.

"No!" she said too loudly, drawing another look from Carl. "I mean, no…thanks…but I'm okay. I'm fine."

"Yeah, look," Carl said, turning to Aaron, "we have to get going anyway. That meeting bitched up my morning."

They spent another minute talking about bowling while Dill seethed silently at Carl's side. Her hand tightened and loosened on the crossbow as tension whipped through her. If they were too much longer, she'd have to walk away.

"Okay, what's going on with you?" Carl asked as soon as they hit the stairwell. "Are you upset about the kidzie in R&D?"

"No," Dill said, "no, that's not it, but…Carl, wait."

He turned to her, his hand already on the bar that would open the door to Assessment's floor. "What's up, Dill?" His features were grave with no sign of impatience.

"I did see something…or thought I saw…back in one of the cylinders."

"You're not talking about the kid? That's not what upset you? Because it can be pretty disturbing to–"

"Carl, no. I don't even…what kidzie? I don't know what you're talking about," she said. She felt close to some internal breaking point. She swallowed. "It was Denny." Her voice was faint.

"*What* was Denny? Dill, you're not making sense."

Light gray clouds seemed to coalesce at the edges of her vision. Carl became very sharp and clear even as the details of the stairwell faded around her.

"I saw Denny in R&D...in one of the cylinders. He was...he'd become a zombie." Once the words were out, she felt a strange sense of relief. It sounded so crazy, there was no way it could be true. There was no way. She laughed. The laughter was strange, too, high and shrieky and tightening her chest instead of loosening it. The light gray fog darkened by degrees. The hallway disappeared.

"Dill, are you joking or what? I don't understand what you–"

He reached for her, and his hands were huge, enormous. "Dill?" His voice echoed and bounced around her skull, which seemed suddenly light and empty. "Dill?"

She closed her eyes against the clouds.

"Dill? Shit! Dill, what's wrong? Candy! I'm glad you're...I don't know, I think she fainted...she just–"

Dill fell into the black.

# TEN

**Z.A.P.T.**
!!ZOMBIES ARE PEOPLE TOO!!
*WAKE UP* *WAKE UP* *WAKE UP*
**CALL TO ACTION!!**
• Do you think your needs and rights should be subjugated to **BIG BUSINESS**?!
• Do you think it is **FAIR** to give your life to a **CORPORATION** that uses **SCARE TACTICS** to keep sheep employees in line?!
• Would you prefer to **SUCK** the **TIT** of **ZOMBIE, INC.**, in order to live a sheep's life of **FALSE SECURITY**?!
*WAKE UP* *WAKE UP* *WAKE UP*
This is a CALL TO ACTION for all concerned citizens of the United Five-State Republic! The GOVERNMENT IS corrupt!
ZOMBIE, INC., controls the GOVERNMENT
FEAR keeps the DOWNTRODDEN in LINE!
WHAT DO YOU HAVE TO **FEAR**?!
Ask yourself this question: *WHEN WAS THE LAST TIME I SAW A ZOMBIE?!?!?!*

---

The sharp edges of the crystal bit into her fingers, but she was unaware that she still grasped the little horse in her panic-tightened hand. Her dad struggled with the zombie less than fifteen feet away.

The zombie–a dry and stringy bag of corrupted organs and crumbling blood–had tumbled him to the ground, and now he struggled to keep the monster's decayed but still dangerous mouth away from him. He snapped a horrified glance back at her. The whites of his eyes glowed in the gray afternoon.

"Run, Dillalia! Run! Run!"

She'd taken a step, two steps, her feet reluctant to disobey him. He'd raised her to do anything he said without question and without hesitation.

She couldn't leave him.

He was all she had.

He was the only person she knew.

"Run, damnit! Dillalia, run! Now!"

Her body jerked in response, and she tilted onto her toes, but she couldn't leave him. No matter what, she couldn't. She'd rather die.

"Dad!" she screamed, the churn of her frustration squeezing the word from her throat like a curse. "Dad!" Her eyes filled with tears, and her chest ached. She couldn't breathe. Her hands curled even tighter, and the crystal horse shifted and laid open a line on her palm. She hissed in response and opened her hand to see what had cut her.

Then she remembered her knife. Dad made her carry it. He'd taught her…taught her to…

"Dill, run! Run! I can't hold him! Run! Run!"

She turned his voice down, tuned out the child in her that wanted to obey. Her hand–the one not cut, her good right hand– slipped into the calf of her boot. She pulled out the knife. Twelve inches of stainless steel gleamed dully in the hazy afternoon light. Her eyes went to the zombie. It was on top of her dad, now, as he struggled to hold its head upright and away from him. His palm was pressed into the underside of its jaw, his fingers bent back and straining away from the gnashing teeth.

Her dad screamed again, but she hardly heard it. She straightened, unconsciously slipping the cut crystal horse into her pocket like a charm, like a talisman. Her dad screamed again as the zombie's head slipped from his grasp. He caught its descending chin a mere inch away from his neck and pushed back. The zombie moaned in frustration as its skeletal limbs scrabbled for purchase on the pebbled roadway.

Dill strode to her dad's side and raised the knife. She held it in both hands straight over her head, the way dad had taught her…for maximum penetration. She aimed for the dirty, corded area at the base of the zombie's skull.

"Hold him still, Dad," she whispered.

She brought the knife down in a swift, hard line and buried it in the zombie's brain, the impact making her teeth clack painfully as her shoulders and wrists cried out in shocked pain.

"Dill?"

A woman's voice, sweet, deep, and throaty.

"Dilly, baby, can you hear me?"

"She's coming around. Just give her a second."

A man's voice…Dad? Was it…?

No. Not Dad; Dad was dead. Carl. It was Carl. The next best thing.

Dill opened her eyes to the confusion of railings and the undersides of stairs going up and up. She was still in the stairwell.

"Here she is," the woman's voice said, and now Dill recognized it–Candy. Dill shifted her eyes and found Candy's powdered bosom half a foot from her face. The woman was all boob!

Candy smiled, and Carl stood just behind Candy, his gaze going from Dill to the glass window in the door.

"Can you get up, Dill? We can't stay here. Someone is going to come along," he said, and his voice was too quiet to echo up or down.

Dill nodded and pushed herself up until she was sitting. A shimmer of disorientation distorted everything for a split second, and then everything snapped back into place. Candy put a warm hand on her back, and the contact further steadied her.

"How long was I out?" Dill asked and ran a shaking hand over her forehead.

"Not even a minute," Carl said. He reached down for her hand and pulled her to her feet. Candy stood in one easy, lithe motion. "Candy came in just as you were passing out."

"You swooned right into this big guy's arms, Dillybean," Candy said and cut her eyes to Carl. "What a hero!" Her voice held a teasing note but something else, something Dill would bet Carl didn't even notice: longing.

"We have to get out of here," Carl said to Dill, ignoring Candy. "So we can talk." His eyes flashed a warning, and she understood she wasn't to say anything about Denny, not in front of Candy.

"Well, Jesus, Carl," Candy said, "you have to take this little girl to the nurse! She fainted!"

"She's all right," Carl said. "You're all right, right?" He was already starting to descend, and his footsteps clattered sharply against the cinderblock walls. "She just needs some air. We'll go out front for a minute. Come on, Dill."

Candy eyed Dill with sympathy. "You sure, honey? I'll take you to the nurse if you want. Men are just stupid about these kinds of things."

"I'm okay. Just…blood sugar or something," Dill said. She wanted to get away from Candy's commiserating and angelic blue eyes. Everything burning inside Dill–Denny and the memories of what had happened to her dad–wanted to come tumbling out, to be laid in a tangled heap at Candy's feet for her to fret and fuss over. It would feel so good to confide in someone.

"Well," Candy said and squeezed Dill's arm, "you go ahead, then. Don't keep the big guy waiting." Her eyes took on a cast of sadness even though she smiled.

Dill wanted to reach out and grasp Candy's arm in kind, but after years of no contact, it just felt wrong. She smiled, instead. "You like him," Dill said.

Candy blinked rapidly, and her smile widened, became false. "Why, I like everybody, Dillybean! I'm in Sales!"

Dill nodded and touched just her fingertips to the back of Candy's hand, then turned to follow Carl down the stairs.

She caught up to him halfway through the lobby.

"Carl, I–"

"Wait a second," he said and made a chopping motion in her direction, "let's get outside." They pushed through the lobby door into the vestibule and from there out the front doors. Carl continued across the wide sidewalk to a large cement planter that had once held plants and cigarette butts. He leaned casually against the wide concrete lip and patted a spot next to him. "Just try to look like we're getting some air. Keep your back to the building in case anyone is watching."

"It's weird to be outside, though," Dill said and pulled herself cautiously up to sit next to where Carl leaned. She glanced around. "Nobody goes outside unless they're coming in or leaving."

"*We* do. Assessment does. Also, Wranglers," Carl said and crossed his arms over his chest. He closed his eyes and tilted his head back to catch the weak, afternoon sun. "You just never noticed. Most people don't even look out windows anymore."

Dill shrugged. "Why would they?"

"Well, it used to be a thing," Carl said and cracked one eye open to look at her. He slanted a grin her way. "In the old days, it was a thing."

Dill shrugged and ran her hands over her face.

"Now tell me," Carl said, "but act casual. Try not to get upset."

"I don't know what to tell you," Dill said. She tried tilting her own face to the sun, but didn't get it. Why invite cancer, number one, and number two, who closed their eyes outside? It seemed the penultimate of stupid gestures. "They had Denny in one of the cylinders in R&D. Way in the back."

"Which one? Which row?"

"It was the second to last row, third cylinder from the wall."

Carl frowned with his eyes still closed. "There was only one that far back, and its back was turned." He shook his head and glanced at her. "You're wrong. You were panicked and freaked out and saw something that wasn't there."

A twist of anger seemed to pull her stomach closer to her throat. "I'm not wrong, Carl."

"Calm down."

"I'm calm!" she said. "And I'm not wrong."

"Dill, you're wrong," Carl said, and his voice rose. "You were thinking about what we'd just talked about, and then you saw the kidzie and you got…you were just worked up!"

"Calm *down*, Carl," Dill said, and it was a satisfaction to watch the frustration tighten his features. "I wasn't freaked out by the kidzie…who gets freaked out by that?" Dill was honestly confused that Carl insisted on her sensitivity to a kid zombie. Who cared if a zombie was a kid? In her mind, it was just a smaller monster. "I know it was Denny. He has a tattoo on his neck, just under his left ear...its real retro. A round, kind of puffed-up bird with a pissed-off look on its face? He thought it was hilarious when he got it," Dill said, remembering. "I told him not to get something on his neck, but he was...is...kind of stubborn. Was, I guess, now."

"An Angry Bird tattoo? That's what he got? Jesus, that's old as fuck."

"That's not the point."

"No," Carl said. He glanced at her. "Dill, I know you think you're sure, but it can't be. No one has changed in the compound since...since I don't know how long. Can you even remember the last time you *knew* someone who had changed?"

Dill could remember very well the last person, it had been her dad, but she pushed that aside for now. "Just because I don't know anyone and you don't know anyone doesn't mean it isn't happening. Everyone is so isolated. Look at you! Look at me! If someone disappeared from my apartment, I don't think anyone would even remark on it. People come and go, and you'd just assume they went...somewhere else. Nobody pays attention to anything anymore."

Carl crossed his arms again and dipped his chin, thinking. Regardless of what he was thinking, whether he believed her or not, Dill knew it was Denny she'd seen up in R&D.

"What are you going to do about it?" Carl asked.

Dill shrugged. "Nothing? I guess? What can I do?" The realization of her powerlessness swept across her like an empty wind. She shook her head. "I can't fight ZI. If I tried, I might end up the same way."

"Dill, ZI isn't in the business of changing their employees into zombies. There has to be an explanation. He was involved in Z.A.P.T., right? That's what you were trying to tell me the other day?" Carl said.

Dill nodded and brought her shoulders up defensively.

"That's why you broke it off with him?" Carl asked.

"Yes," Dill said and then added reluctantly, "and no. I was a member, too, Carl." She wasn't sure what to expect–maybe he would blow up at her, maybe he would denounce her on the spot, maybe he would turn her in to HR—but she would take whatever came. She'd had to tell him.

He surprised her by shrugging. "That was dumb," he said, "but understandable, I guess. Was it him on the security video?"

"Yeah, but how did you...?" She felt light-headed with relief. He didn't hate her.

"You were acting strange after Aaron showed it to us. I wasn't sure why, but it makes sense," he said. "What was he doing up there?"

"Just...as far as I know, he was putting the flyers in the bathrooms," Dill said. "I don't think he would have had anything to do with setting that zombie loose. I don't think he'd actually have gone anywhere near a zombie. For all their talk, the zapped members were kind of, you know, *all* talk."

"Most people are," Carl said, but his tone had become absent. He pulled his lower lip between his thumb and forefinger. Dill shivered and wished she had her coat, but she didn't want to do anything to jar Carl out of his reverie.

Finally, he spoke. "You don't want to be that, right?"

"Don't want to be what?" Dill asked, confused.

He grinned at her. "All talk."

*

Dill dropped her chin into her hands. Carl watched her carefully. He was glad she'd finally told him about Z.A.P.T. He'd been waiting for her to say something. This stuff about her boyfriend being a zombie up on three was just bizarre. Maybe the guilt and confusion over the break-up was making her a little crazy.

The cold of the concrete had leached into his back, and he pushed himself off the planter. He couldn't believe she'd seen her boyfriend in one of the cylinders, but at the same time, found he also didn't *not* believe it. She made a good point about isolation. He could attest to his own. If someone who was currently in his life disappeared, what would he do? If Aaron just never showed up to bowling...would he investigate? If Candy was just not at her desk one day...the thought gave him a surprising twinge of sorrow, and he pulled his mind away from it.

"Maybe we could just ask Aaron?" Dill said, her voice tentative.

At her question, Carl realized how close he was to tipping toward believing her. He said, "Are you crazy?"

"Why? Why is that crazy?"

"Because if something was going on...which it's not...then he'd be a part of it," Carl said.

"Not...not necessarily," Dill said, but her assertion was weak.

"Dill, he's in charge of the stock. Believe me, if they were changing people over...which they're not...Aaron would know."

"Do you believe me or not? You say 'if' and then 'no way'. Are they, or aren't they? Which is it?"

He sighed and crossed his arms. "I guess it's trite to say I believe *you* believe it, but as much as I believe you, I still can't imagine that ZI is involved in changing anyone over. It would be the grossest misconduct imaginable. Especially considering the final death payouts and all."

"Carl, who would they pay out to? Someone like Denny...or me, or you or most everyone...where would that money go? We none of us have families."

"It would go to your assigns," Carl said, but he shifted uneasily. Did he know anyone who had assigned heirs to their estate? How would that even be accomplished? He didn't know.

Dill shook her head. "Denny didn't have any 'assigns' lined up. He and I certainly weren't married. I don't think there are any married people at the inners. Are there a lot in the outers?"

"Married people? Christ if I'd know," Carl said. "From what I understand, it's nearly impossible to get a license, but as far as if anyone *has*...I don't know. I go to work, I go home. On the eights, we stay after work and bowl on the company lanes, but even then, I really only associate with the immediate team. Even the people who go to the gym–the one across from ZI in that community center–they aren't exactly encouraged to make conversation. There are even walls between treadmills. Shit." He scowled. "So much of our time is spent at work that you *feel* like you're socializing, you know? But really, we're not. We're not social at all compared to how it was before." He looked at Dill. "Are people in the inners very social?"

"Not in any good ways," Dill said. "Generally speaking, if you're engaging someone in conversation beyond your apartment, you're looking for something. Drugs or food or you know, whatever." She blushed and cleared her throat. "You talk to people if you do online gaming, but you don't really *talk* to them."

"Jesus Christ, is everyone as bad as us?" Carl asked. "Are we all this isolated?" He was remembering a time before the plague, when people had days off from their jobs, and they would shop and run errands, meet with friends and family over picnics or lunch dates. Even back then, around 2020 or so, most of the shopping had become an online activity; even groceries were being delivered. Schools had become unsafe, and online curriculums that allowed children to participate from the safety of their homes had become popular. Most of the schools had begun to close once the government grants for laptops and internet access had become commonplace. In some areas around big cities, the air had become slightly too toxic to breathe without a respirator, and the sun, of course, was killing anyone who ventured out without protection.

Being 'outside' was not only impractical, it had become dangerous.

Then, of course, the plague had hit, and being outside became close to impossible. Now it seemed there had been a kind of permanent adjustment in people's perspectives–no one seemed to think it odd. No one that Carl knew of had ever discussed the extreme isolation of the world. Not until now.

"I'm sure there are some married people, and I think children are still being born," Dill said. "It's just rare. That's why the ZI maternity care and leave plans are so generous. Not many takers."

"How do you know that?"

"I had looked into it," she said, and her cold-reddened cheeks became even redder. She turned her head and stared across the empty, cracked parking lot. "When Denny and I seemed serious, I talked to HR. Just to, you know, see what was what. Not that it matters now."

Carl was moved by her blush and defeated tone of voice, but he didn't know what to say. Having kids was no walk in the park at the best of times, he felt, and certainly a nightmare at the worst. Annie flashed into his mind, sweating and feverish, her face a clamped fist of pain as the baby crowned. The bite on Annie's arm was already festering, shooting out the black tendrils that signified the growing infection. If he'd been faster to cut the cord, would the baby have survived? He couldn't keep asking himself that question. He shook his head.

"You don't want a baby, Dill," he said, his voice flat and toneless.

She pulled her gaze from the empty lot and fixed it on him. "Did you...did you have kids, Carl? Before everything?"

"No," he said, "not before." He swallowed and glanced at Dill and away. "Annie, my wife, was eight months pregnant when the plague hit. We were going to have a little girl, but she didn't make it."

"Your wife didn't make it? Or the baby?" Dill asked. "Or both?"

"Both, or–" Carl shook his head, "neither. However you'd say it." A dismissive tone crept into his voice as Dill's features softened with compassion. "It was a long time ago, Dill," he said abruptly. "No need to get all mushy about it." She opened her mouth to say something, maybe offer sympathy. He didn't want it. It didn't occur to him that she might want to offer up her own story, share a common feeling. "Let's get back in. Too damn cold out here, anyway."

"What are we going to do?" Dill asked, scrambling to catch up with him.

"I'm gonna take a walk up to R&D, but I want you to stay in our office. You can enter the last few weeks of info into the file system."

"Are you going to ask Aaron about–" They were in the building now, and she glanced around cautiously. "–about what I saw?"

He shushed her with an impatient gesture. "I don't know. I'm just going to see what happens as I go along. You said he has an Angry Bird tattoo on his neck: which side? What colors?"

"It's under his right ear, and its red and black, mostly," Dill said.

Carl was glad she seemed to have lost interest in his wife and baby. He didn't know why he'd brought it up in the first place. It's not like he wanted to get into an exchange of stories with her. Everyone's story sucked. End of story.

He dropped her at two and continued up the stairs to see Aaron.

Ze Listen/Speak was as unnerving as always, but Carl held his unease in check as he waited for the system to relay a call to Aaron. It seemed to take a long time, but Aaron's voice finally clicked across the speaker.

"Hey, Carl, what's up? We're kind of busy right now." His voice was uncharacteristically sharp. Carl allowed himself to grow very still inside. Was something amiss, or was Aaron just being impatient?

"I need some info from that collar, Aaron. All right if I come in?"

ZE Listen/Speak hummed, and Carl found himself looking up at the drop ceiling as he waited. The humming began to work on his nerves, chilling him. It was so lacking in humanity.

"Uh...sure thing, Carl. I'll buzz you in. Head down to my office, and I'll meet you there in ten." Aaron's voice dissolved into the burring of the door. Carl pushed through into the bland corridor.

Quiet as ever.

He hurried down the hall to the door that led to Aaron's office and let himself into the rot-stink, dimly lit atmosphere of the holding area. At least the kidzie was gone. He hadn't been relishing the thought of seeing *that* again.

He made his way past the other cylinders–some filled, most not–barely noting the contents. The stink was not as bad as other days; the zombies were either a lot fewer in number or fresher in nature. He stopped in front of the tall zombie that Dill had indicated was Denny, her Z.A.P.T. ex-boyfriend.

He was relatively fresh, with no obvious chew wounds. His skin was gray and deeply marbled from the blood that had coagulated in his veins, and his eyes were frosted with cataracts. His hair was still intact and had not as yet started falling out in the patches that gave zombies that distinctively mangy look. His limbs still worked in a semi-smooth fashion as he stepped and stepped and stepped forward, reaching over and over to grab at Carl. He moaned, and when his mouth yawned wide, Carl could see the blackened gums and tongue, reminiscent of the mouth of a Chow.

The tattoo under his ear had begun to flake. Tattoos would lift and peel off like scabs once the blood had stopped circulating. It hadn't been unusual for a time right after the plague to find them curled in the gutters like thin and dimly colored pieces of leather.

This one was still together enough to see what it was: an Angry Bird. The game had been popular when Carl was in middle school.

"You must be Denny," Carl said and kept his voice low. "What the hell did Dill see in you?" It wasn't fair to judge Dill's taste in guys based on this walking corpse, but—

Denny's mouth opened again, but this time, only a low sigh issued forth. It was more a heavy breath than a moan, and it was thick with a vowel; a chill ran down Carl's spine. Denny stopped moving, and his limbs dropped to his sides. He whisper-breathed again, his milky eyes trained on Carl's.

Carl's stomach contracted. Was this thing trying to talk to him? Had he heard Carl say Dill's name? Carl leaned closer to the plastic.

"Denny?" he said. He splayed a hand on the plastic, palm up to the zombie. He tapped lightly. "Can you understand me?"

The zombie stood for a long moment, as if in thought. Then it sighed and began its march to nowhere.

Carl stepped back, disgusted.

"You're freaking yourself out, Carl. Get your shit together before you—"

Behind him, a door clicked open. Bad news, he'd wanted to be in Aaron's office before Aaron showed up, and he definitely didn't want to get caught staring at this particular zombie. He faded back between two cylinders on the opposite wall. Luckily, both cylinders were empty. He craned his neck until he could just make out the entrance to the stockroom. A maintenance worker in a gray overall suit dumped a small trashcan into a larger, wheeled trash cart. Then he turned and backed out, keeping his eyes lowered. People didn't like looking at zombies.

Carl let out a long, slow breath of relief.

A hand dropped onto his shoulder.

*

Dill tapped at the virtual keyboard display on the desktop's seamless surface. The process was slow...Carl's handwritten notes were hard to decipher. It had been a long time since she'd even seen handwriting–it was how her dad had taught her to read.

She glanced around nervously and wished Carl would come back. She didn't like the thought of him in R&D. *He* might doubt her assertion that it was Denny in the tube, but *she* didn't doubt it. When you didn't really know many people, the ones you knew, you knew *well*.

With Denny gone, who did she have left?

Just Carl. Just her substitute dad.

She laughed to herself, and it was an unhappy chuff. No one could replace her dad, not really, but Carl could help fill the void. Why did she even have a void? Everyone had lost people, and everyone seemed okay. Even Carl, who'd lost a wife and a baby...he seemed okay. He soldiered on.

'Soldier on' was something her dad used to say.

He'd been bit, of course.

Even though Dill killed the zombie, she'd been too late. She hadn't known right away. Her dad had rolled the finally really dead zombie off himself, and Dill had dropped to her knees to hug him. She closed her eyes and buried her face in his shoulder, and he gripped her to him, so tight she could hardly breathe, but she didn't care. It helped with the shakes that poured through her body like an electrical charge.

"Dad...Dad," she said. "I was so...I was so scared, but I did it, Dad!" She sat back on her heels to survey him. His smile was only a half smile, filled with pain, but she didn't notice that right away. She was too keyed up. "I killed that zombie, Dad! Didn't I?" She could barely get the words out from between her chattering teeth. Her hands gripped and loosened on his arms, convulsively, as if trying to convince the rest of her of his solid, upright, undead reality.

He nodded. "Dillalia...Dill, I..." He swallowed and closed his eyes.

"Dad?"

"You're so strong. You're so strong, Dill. You see that, don't you? You killed that...that monster. All on your own. You see that?"

Dill nodded and tried to smile, but an odd wisp of unease snaked into her mind. "Dad? What's wrong? Are you–"

"You're strong. You can...you *will* survive. You will." He swallowed again and opened his mouth to say something more, but then his eyes went past her, and widened. "Dill," he whispered, his eyes coming back to hers. "I love you. I will always love you. Don't forget."

The tendril of unease in her mind bloomed like black ink in water, occluding, poisoning. "What are you talking about? Why are you–"

"Move away from him."

The voice from behind her was hard and flat. She turned even as her hands clamped onto her dad's arms. A man stood near the curb–he was ordinary looking, mild even, in his rimless glasses. He nodded, and Dill had an absurd urge to nod back, but she couldn't agree to whatever this man was proposing.

"Move away from him," the man said again. He gestured with the rifle he had trained on them. "He's going to change."

"No!" Dill screamed and tilted herself in front of her dad, protecting him with her body. "You're wrong! I killed the zombie! He's not going to change. He's my dad!"

The man said nothing, but then his eyes went from Dill's to her dad's. "Tell her," the man said. "Show her." His face was neutral and patient. Immovable. Unswerving.

Dill took a breath to scream again, but her dad clutched her to him. "I'm sorry, Dill," he whispered in her ear. "I'm so sorry, baby." He lifted his arm to show her the bite on his wrist. She hadn't saved him after all.

She was frozen inside and out. Her lips felt numb. He was wrong. She had saved him, and everything would be okay. She struggled to pull away, to look into his face.

His eyes had begun to fog, the brown irises becoming gray and dead, dying by thin degrees even as she watched.

"Dad?" she said. She couldn't think straight. She couldn't process what she saw. What did she have without him? What was left for her? She was only fourteen.

She was just a kid.

As though he'd read her mind, her dad said, "You're strong. You can do it." He licked his lips and glanced at the unassuming man behind her. "Stand away from me, baby, okay? Turn your back, Dill. Don't watch."

She blinked at him, uncomprehending. "Don't watch what?" Her voice was fluttering and fractured, a bird stunned by immovable glass. "Dad?"

He pushed her then. A gentle, steady pressure that nevertheless nearly toppled her over. She was weightless, floating. Nothing was real. Nothing was…

She stood.

She turned.

The gun banged next to her, but she barely heard it. After a time, the unassuming man reached for her, but his white, white hand, floating to her over the abyss he'd just created caused her to break free from the paralysis.

She ran.

In the office, she stood abruptly, the chair rolling halfway across the floor. She pushed her fists into her eyes, massaging away tears.

She had to find Carl.

*

"You lose something, Carl?" Aaron asked, his hand clamped on Carl's shoulder.

Carl's heart galloped in his chest, but he kept his face relaxed, his features calm. He laughed, and even as he did, he assessed the sound for any cracks. He sounded okay.

"I thought I saw a rat go back here," Carl said and stepped from between the cylinders. "What's up with that?"

Aaron stared at him, his face cautious. He tilted his head. "A rat? You're sure, Carl?"

"Pretty sure, yeah. It was that or a mouse. You keep rats and mice up here?"

"For the lab, you mean? No," Aaron said. He glanced around and then back to Carl. "Who needs rodents when you have these guys?" he asked and gestured to the cylinder with Denny in it.

"Yep, I see your point," Carl said. He nodded companionably and smiled at Aaron. Then he let his eyes slide to Denny. "That one's pretty fresh. Is it tough to get fresh ones?"

Aaron shrugged. "Not tough for me. The Wranglers bring them in."

"Always?"

Aaron smiled, but it was tight. "What are you asking me, Carl? You want to know about this one, specifically?" Aaron shook his head. "Why? Do you know him?" He laughed to show that he knew–of course he knew–that Carl didn't know the zombie in the cylinder. He stopped laughing when Carl didn't join him. Aaron's features drew together.

"You *know* him?" Aaron asked and jerked his thumb at Denny. "Are you fucking *kidding* me, Carl?"

Carl looked down, thinking. If there were something going on– if ZI was involved in actively converting humans to zombies– would Aaron be a part of it? He couldn't believe it of his friend. He also couldn't understand how it was happening without Aaron's knowledge–he was in charge of the stock.

"Where did he come from, Aaron?" Carl asked, without raising his voice. He waited as Aaron sputtered.

"He...Jesus, Carl...*I* don't know...he came from wherever the Wranglers get these things!" Aaron ran a hand over his face and shook his head. His eyes shifted from Carl to the door and back to Carl. He wiped a hand across his upper lip and shrugged. "What do you want me to say?"

"Nothing," Carl said. "You can't tell me something you don't know, right?"

"That's right," Aaron said and nodded. His eyes shifted again. "I only know what they tell me." His voice dropped almost to a whisper, and he looked at Carl with grim intent. "Whatever they tell me is what I *have* to believe."

Carl glanced from the door that led to the hallway, then back to Aaron. "Let's go in your office."

Once the door closed behind them, Aaron slumped in his desk chair. He reached for the old-fashioned CD player and clicked a button. An instrumental piece filled the small office, and Aaron leaned his elbows on the desk and tented his hands. He looked far away and thoughtful.

The music dragged in spots and skipped in others, but Carl liked it anyway. He was not one to listen to music normally. It was an archaic reminder of the past.

"How did you know?" Aaron finally asked, sitting back in the chair and crossing his arms over his chest. There was something off in his posture, and Carl's wind was up.

"Know what?" Carl asked. He raised his eyebrows and half-smiled, letting his eyes fill with concern. He wanted to draw Aaron out without committing himself to anything, and part of that was making Aaron spell everything out.

"How did you know that one–" Aaron nodded toward the zombie room, "–was new up here? No one pays that much attention to the zombies anymore."

"Well, he's pretty fresh," Carl said. "That struck me as odd."

"Why?" Aaron asked. "What's odd about that?" He looked honestly concerned as though the questions had a fair amount of importance.

"Because no one inside the perimeter has been changed," Carl said.

"You can't know that, Carl," Aaron said and smiled. Was there a hint of relief in his smile? A trace of satisfaction? Carl thought there might be, and it worried him. "Besides," Aaron continued, "even if it was someone from outside, it doesn't mean he'd be a pile of rot before they brought him in. You wouldn't even have any idea of when he'd changed!" Aaron snorted and shook his head. Yes, there was definite relief there.

Carl couldn't tell Aaron that he knew for a fact that that particular zombie had been alive only yesterday. There had to be another way.

"The Wranglers gave you no indication of where they found him?" Carl asked. He was just fishing now. Feeling his way along. "That's usually written into the reports, isn't it?"

"Yes. Usually," Aaron said. His voice took on a fussed quality. "Sometimes, they don't have the info right away. You know the Wranglers are not the best bookkeepers."

Carl–who, in fact, knew that the Wranglers were sticklers for correct record-keeping and much better bookkeepers than most other departments–merely smiled. "You might be right about that, buddy," he said. "They might even just be a little late in entering it. When did they bring that one in?"

"When? Ah…that would have been…" Aaron tapped on the tablet on the corner of his desk. From where he sat, Carl couldn't see the screen directly…but he could see a miniature version of it reflected in Aaron's glasses. It was blank; he hadn't even turned it on. "Here it is. They brought him in yesterday morning. Early. Before dayshift even began." He glanced up at Carl and smiled. "That's probably why you didn't hear about it."

"Probably, yeah," Carl said. "Does it say where they found him? I'd be interested to know since I spend a good bit of time outside, you know?"

"Yes, I can imagine!" Aaron said. His voice was hearty and to Carl's ear, very, very false. He tapped on the dead tablet again. "They rounded him up in the old Willow Corners neighborhood. Seems a homeowner called in because he thought it was someone's yard zombie gone rogue."

"Huh," Carl said. He smiled at Aaron and stretched, cracking his knuckles. "Well, thanks for the info, buddy. I appreciate it."

Now it was Aaron's turn to look suspicious. "That wasn't what you wanted to see me for."

Carl, who had stood and turned toward the door, turned back. "Come again?"

Aaron stood, too, and his hand rose to his eye, not touching the scanner chip embedded there, but close. "You said you had a question about the collar you brought in. The half-popped one from the other day."

Carl hesitated, his hand dropping from the doorknob. "Yeah…yeah, I…" He glanced at Aaron and away again. Aaron tilted his head, and his hand moved a fraction of an inch closer to his eye. Carl knew he wasn't covering well, he'd forgotten the reason he'd made up to get into the stock room. He colored as his heart hammered hot blood into his face. He dropped his eyes.

"I, ah...here's the thing, Aaron," Carl said. He looked up, allowing Aaron to see his red face. Hopefully, he would read it as embarrassment. "I didn't record the number on it before I brought it up. Dill is entering the notes, and..." He shook his head and laughed, looking chagrined. "...I didn't want her to see that I had fucked up, so I thought I'd just come grab the number and enter it myself."

Aaron stared at him a moment longer, then his hand dropped. He grinned. "Can't yell at the trainee for messing up if you mess up yourself, right?" He turned to a cabinet behind his desk, shaking his head. "You're too hard on your trainees, Carl. Everyone makes mistakes, right?"

"You got that right, buddy," Carl said.

\*

Carl descended the stairs at a quick clip and nearly barreled into Dill as he turned the last corner. She yelped in surprise and stepped back into empty air. He grabbed her by the arms and righted her before she could fall.

She stared at him in wide-eyed shock, and her eyes glittered where tears had gathered to shimmer at the rims.

"Are you okay?" she asked just as he said, "You were right."

Then he said, "Are you crying?"

"No!" She shook her head and tore her arms from his grasp. She wiped under her eyes. "Yes. Just a little, though. I got...I was worried."

"About me?" His voice was a mix of amusement and astonishment. It made her cringe.

"Yes. I was...I was entering the notes, and I just got...I was thinking about...about something, and then I got worried. Scared, I guess. When you didn't come back."

"I don't understand," he said. "What were you thinking about that got you worked up?"

She dropped her eyes and swallowed. She glanced at him and away. He was a tough guy, would he understand what she was about to tell him? "I was...I was thinking about my dad and what happened to him, and just got worried, I guess." She shrugged and glanced at him again to see what he would make of what she'd said.

Carl dropped onto the second-to-last step and propped his elbows on his knees. "Tell me," he said. "Tell me what happened to your dad."

Dill ran her hand under her nose and sniffed back tears. She'd seen Carl like this with the people at the cabin: thoughtful, interested. Calm. Willing to take someone else's burden onto his own shoulders. Like a dad…just like a dad should be. It made her remember something.

"What happened to your wife, Carl? You said she and the baby didn't make it. Did she have the baby, or did she die before…?"

Carl stared at her for a long moment, but she got the impression he wasn't seeing her, he was seeing something on the internal screen of memory. Then he shifted, and his eyes refocused. He smiled a very small smile that didn't reach his eyes.

"Is that what you want to do, Dill? Exchange stories?"

She felt put off by his tone and expression. It seemed to her that he held a certain contempt for the thought of sharing his past with her. Or maybe he just thought of her as weak and needy. She *wasn't*…she was pretty sure she wasn't, anyway. Was there something wrong with wanting to know him better? With wanting to understand him? Or did she just not want to feel selfish about telling him *her* story for the comfort he might be able to give.

She dropped her eyes as her throat constricted. "I don't know," she said. It was the most honest response she could think of. She looked up at him, but this time, she didn't wipe her eyes. She didn't have to be ashamed of tears. She was astonished to see an answering glimmer in his eyes. He looked older, fatigued beyond his limits. He nodded.

"Annie–my wife–was eight months pregnant with Sarah when the plague hit. We were living down south in Delaware, and it was very rural where we were. That's what gave us a leg up in the confusion that followed those first news reports." Carl took a deep breath. He looked up at Dill and patted the spot next to him. "You might as well get comfortable," he said. His eyes were sad but kind. Resigned, almost. She sat down next to him, shoulder to shoulder but not touching. He leaned forward and clasped his hands between his knees. Then he continued.

"It was hard running with someone so pregnant. We did a lot more hiding than running, actually, but I forced us to keep going because I wanted to get her up this way. We'd heard that the military base in south Jersey was having success in holding off the walking dead."

Dill nodded and smiled.

He seemed to catch the movement from the corner of his eye, and he glanced at her and laughed unhappily. "Yeah. You know, then. Your dad must have told you. It was all a rumor. It might have been true right at the very beginning, but within a month, everything was overrun...including the base, but the rumor persisted.

"So we struggled to get up here. We were just outside of New Castle and getting ready to go over the bridge when everything went bad. Annie went into a premature labor, probably from the stress. There was a big hospital and a psychiatric center right off the Dupont Parkway that another runner had told us was still accepting patients. I don't know why I believed him." Carl shook his head and ran a hand down the side of his face. "We were so desperate, such kids. I just thought...I don't know what I thought...I just wanted to get Annie to some place safe." He swallowed and nodded as if confirming something to himself. "I was tired of feeling so responsible for her...for the baby. Christ, I was only twenty-six. I couldn't get out of my own way. I was no superhero." He shrugged and shook his head again, sighing back into his story. "The hospital looked deserted when we got there. No one in the parking lot, no one outside the building. I thought...I thought it was a good sign. I thought it meant the hospital had obtained a measure of control. Or maybe I was deliberately fooling myself.

"We pushed through the front doors, and at first, there was nothing. I sat her down at a bank of chairs, and I checked the hallways right off the lobby. No one. I thought it was deserted. I went back to Annie–she was sweating, and her face kept closing up as the pains hit–and I told her it looked empty and that we should keep going. She started crying." Carl ground his hands together. He turned his face to Dill's, and his eyes were red-rimmed and angry. "I got mad at her. Some great guy, right? Mad at my wife for being in labor, for slowing us down. Messing everything up. Man, I was…" He shook his head and swallowed again. His voice lowered. "I was such an asshole."

"You were doing the best you could," Dill said. An intense wave of empathy poured over her as she realized Carl was the age then that she is now. She felt desperate for the young him, for the pressure and fear he'd faced. How had he even got himself and his wife that far?

He continued as though she hadn't spoken.

"She asked couldn't we just stay at the hospital. Maybe someone would come along, a doctor or a nurse. Her voice got louder, more strident. My stomach knotted up. Her saying it made me somehow finally–*really*–realize that we *needed* a doctor or a nurse. Christ, it was like it was the first time I understood her pregnancy as an actual thing that was going to happen, regardless of the fact that the world was falling apart. I'd kept telling myself we still had a month to get settled somewhere. I was picturing some kind of utopia where they would welcome us in, explain that the dead weren't a problem for them and then tell us they had a bed ready and waiting with a doctor standing by to deliver the baby. So stupid. So, so stupid.

"I was just reaching for her arm when I heard it. The moaning. There was a kind of walkway way above the lobby…it was at least as high as a third floor. I looked up, and there were hundreds of them up there, doctors and nurses and patients…lining the railing, all dead. I don't know how I hadn't seen them as soon as we walked in. Distracted. Too distracted, and they hadn't started moaning until they heard Annie speak. They must not have seen us until then. I pulled her up, and she…Jesus, she screamed."

Carl shook his head. He looked white and shocked, remembering. "Her water broke all at once. She screamed again, and I was so panicked, so fucking scared. I just stood there, frozen. I didn't know what to do next.

"Then the zombies started coming over the railing. They were falling around us like…like body bombs. Annie was still screaming, but I don't know if she saw what was going on. They were hitting that marble lobby floor and…some of them were breaking apart on impact, arms flying off and heads exploding. That coffee ground shit was spattering everything. Then the second round was falling onto the pile of bodies already there. Some of them made it. They struggled toward us even if their legs had been crushed, even if they had guts trailing from them…

"I pulled her out of there. Even when we got through the doors to the outside, I could still hear that *thump, thump, thump* as they fell. They were piling up. I looked back for a second and it was this…big squirming mass of hair and bone and limbs and guts…a head rolled from the top of the pile to the bottom, and the mouth was…chomping. Chomping away at nothing, and they moaned, and it was like a chorus from hell.

"There was a small neighborhood not far away. I dragged Annie until she couldn't go any further, and then I carried her. It was almost dark. We broke into the first house, a small rancher. I thought it was clear. I checked it out, but I was distracted by Annie, by the screaming. I didn't check it out well enough.

"We stayed in the living room, and Annie had fallen asleep. I think she was just beyond exhaustion at that point. I was in and out. I kept hearing things outside. Running. Screams. The moaning. It was a nightmare. I must have slept because the next thing I knew, I was waking up and the house was on fire." Carl took a deep breath.

Above them in the stairwell, a door banged, and laughter floated down. Two voices and clattering footsteps followed the laughter. Then a door higher up opened and closed, and the voices were cut off.

Carl glanced at Dill. "I don't know how the fire got started. We didn't have a fire or anything. I think it was someone outside the house, trying to kill zombies. They didn't know there were people in there, right?" His eyes were dark and troubled as he looked at her.

Dill nodded. "I'm sure that's right."

"There was one in there with us. A young woman. Maybe she had lived there. She came up from the basement, and…she bit Annie before I even knew what was happening. I grabbed a butcher knife from the kitchen and jammed it into her eye, but it was too late. Then Annie went into labor again.

"The house was burning down around us, and I started to pull her out, but part of the ceiling caved in. She was pinned at the shoulder. Then the baby came."

Carl dropped his head into his hands and massaged his forehead. Dill didn't know if he would go on, but finally, he did.

"I delivered her...Sarah...even as Annie was changing. Annie got to see her. She got to see her daughter. I put her on Annie's stomach." He massaged his forehead harder as though that was the only way to get the words out. "Then the baby started to change." His voice dropped, and Dill had to lean close to hear. She wanted to put a hand on his shoulder, but she was afraid that would surprise him into silence.

"I didn't cut the cord, you see," he said. "I knew you were supposed to, but I didn't know...I didn't know how or where or...I picked her up, and she changed right in my arms. I don't know if Annie ever knew that part or if she was already too far gone.

"Another part of the house collapsed somewhere off the kitchen. The heat was immense, and the smoke was starting to get thick. I couldn't stop coughing. Sarah was twisting her head, trying to get to my arms. To bite me. You know what I did then? The big hero that I was?"

Dill shook her head.

"Do you *want* to know?" he asked, and the anger was back, almost a belligerence. Dill wasn't cowed; she was beyond being afraid for her job. She loved him. She loved the young, lost version of himself he was offering to her. She nodded, and his eyebrows rose slightly. Then his face tightened as if readying for a blow.

"I dropped her. I dropped the baby, and I got out. Annie grabbed at me as I went past her, but I don't know if...if she knew me by then. Did she know me? Did she know what I'd just done to Sarah and was doing to her? That I was leaving them to burn?" His bleak eyes found hers. "Do you think she knew that, Dill?"

Dill shook her head. "No, she didn't know that part." A small smile flicked across her lips. "She only knew the baby was born. She only knew the good part."

Carl stared at her bleakly, and she went on. "It was better that they...that they burned. You know that now, don't you?"

His mouth opened as if to speak, but he only sighed. Then he nodded and shrugged. "I couldn't have killed them. Not outright. I wasn't strong enough." He sat straighter, seeming to gather himself together. He rummaged his hands through his hair and blew out a long breath that dropped his shoulders. "I never told anyone about that," he said. "I don't know if it makes me feel better or not, but I'm still glad you know." He shrugged again, a man unused to expressing himself. "I don't even know *why* I'm glad that you know."

"It's just good to have someone know your story, isn't it?"

"Yeah, I guess you're right."

He sighed again and twisted his hands together. Dill felt his eyes on her, and she turned to meet his gaze. She smiled, and he half-smiled back.

"What about you, Dill?" he asked. "What's your story?"

She thought for a moment. Did she really need to tell him right now, or could she let this moment just be his? She did a quick internal scan: she felt okay. She didn't have anything to get off her chest. She was calmer now that he was here, and she knew nothing had gone wrong upstairs in R&D.

She smiled and patted his shoulder tentatively with just her fingertips. He was the first person she'd touched since starting at ZI, with the exception of Denny. Maybe the first person since her dad had died.

"Maybe another time, okay, Carl?" she said and pulled her hand back to herself like a snail retracting into its shell. "Tell me what happened upstairs. Did you see that it was Denny?"

He regarded her in silence for a long time, then stood and held out his hand to pull her up. "Let's get out of here."

# ELEVEN

**ZOMBIE, INC., SALUTES THE NEWLY ELECTED LEADERS OF**
**THE UNITED FIVE-STATE REPUBLIC**
*With a Night\* of Enchantment!*
Food,\*\* fun & dancing under the stars\*\*\* to celebrate the official incorporation of the NEW LEADERSHIP of the United Five-State Republic and to congratulate the individuals who have taken it upon themselves to steer the course of our fledgling community!
Join us at ZI Headquarters located at 100 ZI Boulevard on November 12
~ \* ~ \* ~

*\*This event will be held during normal business hours (day shift) to ensure maximum safety of all participants. ZI employees attending‡ the event will be docked for one (1) day of compensation.*

*\*\*The ZI cafeteria will have the normal menu available at a discounted rate for any employee actively participating in the event. Non-participating attendees will pay regular cafeteria charges as applied.*

*\*\*\*This event will be held indoors in the ZI cafeteria.*

*‡Attendance is mandatory although participation is not required. All day-shift employees will be docked for one (1) day of compensation regardless of participation. Night shift employees who choose to attend the event will be docked for one (1) day of*

*compensation. Since attendance (not participation) is mandatory, night-shift employees not attending and remaining on their regularly scheduled schedule will be docked for one (1) day of compensation for missing an event deemed mandatory by HR. Any employee who does not report for their shift either the day prior, the day of, or the day after the event will be docked for ALL days plus the event for a total of four (4) days deduction.*

--- --- ---

"Where are we going?" Dill asked. The tension of the morning had left her feeling wrung out and oddly calm. "It's end of shift."

"Nowhere," Carl said. "Just making rounds. I didn't want to talk in the building, and this won't ring any bells when they track the GPS of where we've been. No one cares if Assessment works late. We set our own hours."

The SUV hummed along. Dill waited for him to confirm that he'd seen Denny.

"Did you look into getting married?" Carl asked, surprising her. It seemed so off topic. "When you were thinking about having a baby with Denny?" He wheeled the SUV down a narrow street at the edge of the outers. Small houses sat facing the dead expanse of an old park. The playground equipment–large logs planted upright and roped together in the shape of a low castle bristling with swings and slides–was being reclaimed by the ground.

"No, not really," Dill said. Remembering that they'd even briefly thought about having a child together depressed her further. "I wasn't sure where to go...how to go about it. I asked a few people, but no one seemed to know."

"You have to go to the government agency under the inners," Carl said. His eyes trailed over a baseball diamond guarded by a chain-link backdrop so rusty it looked as if it would disintegrate at a touch. "People are dissuaded from doing it. That's why the knowledge of it...shit, the very idea of it...is disappearing."

"Who dissuades them?" Dill asked. "The government?"

"ZI," Carl said, "and ZI controls the government. You know that, right?"

"Yeah, I guess I knew that. It's just kind of...assumed." She shrugged. "What does that have to do with getting married?"

"ZI doesn't want people taking time off for weddings and...well, we used to have honeymoons that were basically vacations, but nobody has those anymore."

"My dad used to tell me about vacations. People used to go somewhere for a week and just lie around. Or sightsee things like old buildings or old rocks or that big hole in the west."

Carl laughed. "Yeah, sometimes. People would go to the Grand Canyon to hike and camp." He glanced at her. "That's what that 'big hole' is called...the Grand Canyon."

"Okay," Dill said but with little interest. No one would consider camping a leisure activity now. "So, people used to do that. What does that have to do with..."

"I know ZI doesn't want people taking vacations. Hell, they make it hard even to get a day off. I used to think that was the main reason they didn't want marriage, but now I think it's something else. I think they don't want people having someone legally eligible for death benefits. If you and Denny had been married, they'd owe you all that money he'd been paying in."

She shrugged, impatient. Government was a corrupt puppet of ZI...so what? Everyone knew it. No one cared as long as there were no zombies trying to kill them every day. She'd been waiting for Carl to circle back around to the topic, but she was tired of waiting. "You saw Denny...saw that it was him?" A fog of exhaustion was settling across her bones. She just wanted to lie down and sleep.

"Yes, I saw him, but Dill." He shook his head. "I don't know what it means."

She looked at him in confusion, and he continued. "I don't know if it means that ZI is somehow responsible for changing him or..."

"Carl, Denny didn't get bit or attacked or anything like that. There's no way. He's never even *around*–" She broke off, her mouth slightly open.

"He *was* around them, Dill, the day he was caught on the security tape," Carl said. "You said you thought he'd probably just been in the bathroom up there, but what if there was something else he was doing? What if he went back and something went wrong?"

"What if it's a punishment?" Dill said. "For being in Z.A.P.T.?"

"Punishment from who?" Carl asked. His tone was exasperated.

"Or what if he saw something he wasn't supposed to see? Found out what was going on and–"

"*Or*…what if he was dicking around up there–maybe trying to set a goddamned zombie free–and he got what he deserved."

Dill took a deep breath. She was glad now that she was too tired to get angry. "He didn't deserve that, Carl. Not for putting up flyers."

"Yeah, I know," he said and took a deep breath. "Look, I'm sorry, I just meant…Z.A.P.T. is going to get a lot of people hurt if they're allowed to carry on with their plans."

"Maybe, but so is ZI," Dill said. She crossed her arms over her chest. "You said so yourself at the meeting when they decided to drag one onstage."

"It's different. ZI isn't doing it under the cover of darkness…they aren't terrorists like Z.A.P.T."

"I wouldn't be so sure about that," Dill said, and then she straightened, remembering. "Hey, what did Aaron say? Did you talk to him?"

"Yeah, he was sketchy about it," Carl said. "Didn't seem to know all the details." He didn't want to tell Dill how Aaron had outright lied. That would only fuel her paranoia even as Carl was feeling more and more certain that Denny had brought whatever had happened onto his own self. Did Aaron know what had happened? Probably, yeah, and if Carl approached him the right way, he might spill this time.

"Carl, I don't understand you. You talk about ZI like they're this big, corrupt, government-owning behemoth that won't give anybody a day off and maybe they even steal money that rightfully belongs to employees or their families." She shook her head. "Then you say they won't *make* zombies? Even though the *entire* company, the entire *profit* structure, *only exists* as long as zombies exist, but that's where their *morality* kicks in?" She looked at him, eyebrows raised. "That's what you think?"

Carl let the SUV drift to a stop. What she was saying made a lot of sense, but still. "Shit," he said, head lowered. Dill stared at him until he looked at her. "I don't know, Dill; you might be right."

"No shit," she said and pushed down in her seat, setting her boots on the dash, "but what are we gonna do about it?"

"I think we should–" Carl's hand rose as a small vibration near his ear told him a call was coming through. "Hold on," he said to Dill and touched his ear. "This is Carl."

"Carl, it's Candy." Her voice was flat, all pretense of flirtation gone. "Where are you?"

"We're in the outers," Carl said. "I had a couple places I needed to check out and–"

"You have to get back here," Candy said. "Hurry."

Carl turned the wheel, directing the SUV down a street that led them back toward ZI. "I'm on my way, Candy; what's going on?"

"It's…first shift was just leaving, and…" Her voice broke, but she continued. "Augustus was out first. He was going to the gym and wanted to get there before all the machines were taken. He was…like I said, he was the first out, and that's when…that's when…"

"I'm almost there, Candy," Carl said. "We're about five minutes out. Calm down, and tell me what happened."

"There was a goddamned *zombie* out there!" Candy's tone was incredulous, insulted. "Where did a goddamned *zombie* come from, Carl? Jesus Christ, we haven't had one inside the walls since…since…"

"Candy," Carl said. "It's okay. I'm almost there."

Dill could see the top of the ZI building over the last row of houses as they made their way out of the neighborhood. She glanced at Carl and couldn't help but be amazed at his tone: soothing and confidential. No question that he had feelings for Candy.

"Is Augustus okay?" Carl asked, and then they were out of the neighborhood, the SUV humming at its top speed. The parking lot in front of ZI opened before them, the building sitting a quarter of a mile back. A scattering of people were at the front entrance along with two Wrangler trucks, but they were still too far away to see anything clearly. "How bad is it?"

"It's bad. It's really, really bad," Candy said. Tears choked her voice. "Augustus was bit, and before anyone knew what was going on, half the building had poured out the doors behind him."

"Shit," Carl said. He turned into the main entrance and sped toward the commotion. "I'm here."

"Be careful, Carl! They haven't found everyone yet. They took Augustus away, but they're still–"

"Took him away? What are you talking about?" Carl braked abruptly, still twenty yards from the front of the building. "*Who* took him *where*?"

"The Wranglers...they got one of those dog things around his neck, and...I don't know where they took him. They put him in the back of their truck, and then they were gone. I don't know. I don't know!" She sobbed steadily. "I couldn't...I couldn't see...everyone crushed back in, and I was trying to...trying to watch...but it was a panic. No one knew what to do. It's been so long. We all thought...all thought..."

"That we were safe," Carl finished for her. "Stay in your office, Candy. I'll come get you." He tapped his ear again, ending the call. He glanced at Dill. "Got your bow?"

She nodded and pulled it into her lap. She set a bolt in place. "I'm ready."

"It might not be necessary. They might have everything contained," Carl said, and the SUV began to move again. "You have to be ready. I'm going up there, but I want you to stay away from the brunt of the activity; stay near the SUV, just in case, and watch. Assess. Assess everything. Be on point. You got me, Dill?"

"Yes," she replied, her voice steady. "It's weird, though, isn't it Carl? That a zombie would pop up now?"

Carl braked again when they were close but not too close. He scanned the activity at the building and didn't say anything for a minute. "Yes," he finally said, "it's weird, and I don't like it." He spotted Aaron near one of the front doors. "Don't say anything about that to anyone." He opened his door and departed, not waiting for a response.

Carl trotted to Aaron, scanning the small crowd. Eight people stood very close to the doors, huddled together like sheep. Two Wrangler trucks were parked on the sidewalk, and a pair of Wranglers stood to either side of the people while the other two Wranglers watched from about fifteen feet away. One of the Wranglers pointed and waved an employee forward. A man dressed in Maintenance gray stepped away from the others, raising his arms away from his sides. The Wrangler scanned the man front and back, looking for bites or scrapes, or any indication of a scuffle.

"Clean. Get inside, Abby," the Wrangler said to the man who glanced from the Wrangler back to the huddle of people with confusion. Obviously he didn't know about the Wranglers' habit of referring to all non-Wranglers as 'Abby'. "You, Abby, yeah. It's you I'm talking to. Go inside. Get in the cafeteria and wait until an announcement is made." The man gazed at the Wrangler with confused distrust, then turned with caution and pushed back into the building. He moved faster and faster the further he got from the scene and was nearly running once he was past reception.

The Wrangler pointed at a woman in the whites of food service. "You're next, Abby," he said and waved her forward.

Aaron nodded to Carl as Carl approached but then turned his attention back to what the Wranglers were doing. "You missed all the excitement," he said and nodded toward the inspection. "They're almost done, now."

"What happened here, Aaron?" Carl asked. He kept his voice low with the promise of confidentiality.

Aaron shrugged. "A damn zombie came out of nowhere and attacked the first guy out. It was lucky that a few of the Wranglers just so happened to be close by." Aaron glanced at Carl and then away. "I guess everyone has learned a good lesson today. Between the meeting this morning and the attack tonight, it really brings it all home, doesn't it." His tone was flat and carried no indication that he'd just asked a question–it was all statement. "Maybe this will show everyone how dangerous the world still is."

"You think so, buddy?" Carl asked. He watched Aaron carefully, taking in his shuttered eyes and crossed arms. The last rays of the sun flashed into his glasses, turning the lenses into bright, opaque flares.

"Yes, I do think so. Don't you?" Aaron asked. His arms tightened across his chest, and his hands clamped into defensive fists. "This event, although tragic, is bound to get people thinking more seriously about their security. It's an ill wind and all, Carl, and I hate to say that so soon after this…uh, event…but it's true."

He pulled his glasses down his nose and peered at Carl with earnest intensity. "This will end up being something good for ZI. You know? Drum up awareness, drum up sales. It's good. Ultimately." He raised his eyebrows as if asking–pleading–with Carl to agree.

"How unfortunate was it?" Carl asked. "Did we lose many people?" He was scanning the ground. Three big areas of still-wet blood were surrounded by splatters and thin splashes on the sidewalk and walls.

"No…that's the good news, Carl!" Aaron said. He grinned, but the grin was taut, and two large tendons stood out from his neck. He looked reptilian. "Only three! The first guy–I think he was Sales, which is a big loss, believe me, I get that–it's kind of a surprise that the first one out was from Sales. They generally hang back to stay out of the crush…not this time, though, so that's really unfortunate…but the other two were maintenance and clerical! I mean, how lucky could you get?"

He rubbed his hands together and chortled. The four people who had yet to be checked eyed him with unease. Even the Wranglers gave him a once-over. Aaron didn't seem to notice.

"It wasn't very lucky for the clerk or the maintenance person, right, buddy?" Carl asked. He kept his voice gentle, unchallenging, but Aaron frowned.

"Everyone has become too accustomed to safety," he said and pulled his glasses off. He polished them on the pocket of his lab coat. "Something bad was bound to happen; that's what I think. Complacency will get you every time." He glanced at Carl, putting his glasses back on. "I'm just glad it wasn't worse than a few people. We could have had another pandemic on our hands. In light of everything, I think this is a good lesson for everyone."

"Yeah, you said that already, buddy," Carl said. He maintained an easy tone.

"Did I? I guess I did. Doesn't make it any less true, though."

"No. I guess it doesn't." Carl shifted his weight and glanced back at the SUV, where Dill stood watching the scene. He chose his next words carefully. "Where are they? The victims?"

"Victims!" Aaron snorted. The last person being examined glanced at Aaron and away. "The second they began to change, they were no longer victims. They were the enemy. They were monsters." Aaron eyed Carl with sharp and not very friendly interest. "You're starting to sound like one of those zapped assholes you hate so much, Carl. You weren't thinking about changing sides, were you? Because you know, ZI doesn't have much time for traitors." His voice had dropped, and he stared at Carl with flat impassivity.

"Is that right?" Carl said. "And what happens to traitors, Aaron?"

Aaron stared at him for a long time and then grinned and shrugged his shoulders. "Nothing! What could they do? Relax, Carl. Don't take everything so seriously!" He clapped Carl on the shoulder.

"We're all set over here, Abby," one of the inspecting Wranglers called across to them. "Yer sheepies 'ave all been shorn." The Wrangler's partner guffawed. The two who had more or less been on guard duty had already gotten into their truck and it jumped to gas-fueled, growling life.

"Very good," Aaron called back, but his voice was uneasy. Most people didn't like talking to Wranglers...they were too unpredictable. "Write it up and post it before you leave today."

The Wrangler, who'd been turning away, turned back and put his hands on his jeans-clad hips, his black-booted feet planted wide. He tilted his head at Aaron. "What did yer say to me, Abby, girl?"

Aaron swallowed and glanced at Carl then away. Carl suppressed a grin. He knew that the Wranglers always got their reports in...but they didn't particularly want to be told to do it. Especially by an office lag. Carl moved a few inches closer to Aaron, and his body tightened in readiness. You never knew what a Wrangler might take it into his head to do, and Carl didn't want Aaron getting hurt. Carl needed him. For now.

"Just...I meant...we need this written up. As soon as possible. HR is going to want to–"

"Fuck yer aitch ahr, Abby!" the Wrangler cried. His partner laughed again.

The Wrangler lurched a jangling step closer to Aaron, and his eyes grew darker over his mass of beard. His hick pirate accent disappeared as his voice lowered. "Anything else you wanted to say to me, Abby? Any other orders you wanted to throw my way?"

Aaron's throat worked as he swallowed. Then he straightened his shoulders. "You…you listen to me…that report has to be–"

The Wrangler huffed, and his hand dropped to the cattle prod at his belt. Then Dill stepped in between the men.

"Hey there, Floyd," she said and smiled. She was tiny against the bulk of the leather-vested man in front of her. "It's me, Abby!"

The Wrangler hesitated, and his eyes went from Dill to Aaron. He knew what she was doing. Carl held his breath. It would be easy for someone like Aaron to misjudge a Wrangler as undisciplined and maybe even stupid…everything in his office-job environment would lead him to believe it of the pirate ruffians who couldn't be tamed or shamed into civility, but it was a bad miscalculation. Hopefully, Dill's block wouldn't be.

The Wrangler considered Aaron for a long minute more and then shifted his eyes to Dill. He nodded. "Hey there, Abby," he said. His voice was quiet and still accent-free. Carl had never heard a Wrangler speak to an Abby like that. Dill had some kind of connection with him.

"Floyd!" the Wrangler half-turned and called to his partner in the truck. "It's Abby come to visit! Glad that she can since she saved us!" As his tone rose, the accent leaked back in, gathering momentum and making it seem as though he were–in some sense– coming back to himself. "Come on and see Abby, ya' lazy hoower!"

"*Our* Abby?" the second Wrangler said and burst from the truck. "There she is! The good Assessment man, herself!"

He grabbed Abby's hand and shook it until her arm looked ready to dislocate at the shoulder. Dill stood between the rough behemoths, smiling shyly. Unless Carl was mistaken, she really liked those two, and well she should, they'd saved her life. It was hard for most people, Carl included, to actively *like* the Wranglers–in theory, yes, in person…not so much.

"Where did they take the three that got bit, Aaron?" Carl asked quietly. Aaron's attention was focused on Dill and the Wranglers. His expression was that of someone watching a lion trainer who might any second get eaten up.

"Up to the stock room," Aaron said, still not paying attention to Carl, or seemingly to what he, himself was saying. "How does she *do* that?"

"What? Talk to the Wranglers?" Carl shook his head, glad that Aaron was too distracted to realize what he'd just admitted. "It's crazy, isn't it? Have you *ever* seen a Wrangler happy to talk to a non-Wrangler?"

The Wranglers were laughing as Dill spoke, the one nearly bent double, his beard near to scraping the ground. What could she be telling them?

Aaron's face soured. "No, I can't say that I have. Not that it's much of a compliment, you know." He turned to go in. Carl followed with a warning glance at Dill to stay behind.

"What do you mean, buddy?" Carl asked. Tight groups of workers filled the hall leading to the cafeteria. Conversations were quiet and tense. Many eyes followed Aaron and Carl as they crossed the lobby. At the door to the stairs, Aaron stopped and turned back to Carl.

"I mean, it's not exactly a life's goal to be liked by those animals," he said, and his eyes shot instinctively to the front of the building almost as though he were afraid they might hear him. The Wranglers were now hugging Dill, preparing to leave. Aaron sneered. "They need to learn to follow rules. It's grossly inappropriate that they get away with so much."

Carl shrugged lightly. "Well, but I guess they have a different mindset, right? Or they might not be able to do the job."

"That's what everyone says," Aaron said, but he didn't sound convinced, "but I don't see what the big deal is. I work with zombies every day, Carl. *Every* day! You don't see me yelling at…at superiors. Threatening people. It shouldn't be allowed." He shot another smoking look in the Wrangler's direction and then shook his head as if to clear it. "Anyway, I'd better get upstairs. They're going to let people go soon, and I want to make sure everything is…okay…before the night shift comes in."

Carl noted the hesitation and let it go. Aaron seemed totally unaware that he'd told Carl that the bite victims had been taken to R&D, and Carl wanted to let him remain unaware. Policy was to institute immediate second and final death to any employee who'd been changed. Not only did that (in theory) release the final death benefits, it was the decent thing to do, the safest thing to do, and the moral thing to do. Carl was more and more convinced there was very little morality on Aaron's floor.

*

"How is Candy?" Dill asked. She couldn't help a small smile, but Carl's head was down, and he didn't notice.

"She calmed down; she's tougher than she looks. Robert promised to see her home."

"You okay with that?"

"With Robert taking her home?" Carl asked and looked up with a frown. "I asked him to. He's just going to make sure she gets home safely, he's not...you know...doing anything else." He shifted, his discomfort obvious. He shook his head. "Any info from your Wrangler friends?"

"They said they were told to be there at four thirty for a vehicle inspection," Dill said. She and Carl sat in the mostly deserted cafeteria, a good distance from the handful of other employees. The day shift had finally been allowed to leave, and the night shift had taken over.

"Did that seem legitimate to them?" Carl asked. "Or did it strike them as pretty damn convenient?"

Dill shrugged. "It's hard to know with the Wranglers. They don't really *say* anything right out. Not even to me." She toyed with her empty coffee cup, spinning it one way and the other as she thought. "I asked how their vehicle inspection went, and they kind of clammed up, stared at each other...you know how I mean?"

Carl, who'd spent half his career dealing with the frustrations of recalcitrant and clannish Wranglers, knew exactly what Dill meant.

"If it was a planned attack, they could just as easily have been the ones who planted the zombie out there," Carl said. "They aren't exactly order-takers, but if they were ordered to create a small pocket of chaos, get a chance to do some zombie wrangling...what Wrangler could resist that? When you get right down to it, who knows if they'd even be on our side," he said, and

Dill looked up in surprise, the coffee cup she'd been spinning chattering to a halt.

"Our side?" she said. "You believe it, then? You believe me?"

"Yes," he said, "but I don't know what we can do about it."

Dill's frustration began to bubble the coffee sitting uneasily in her stomach. "We have to expose them," she said. "Stop them."

"Expose who? Stop who? Stop them how?" Carl shook his head. "You're talking about the biggest post-apocalyptic company in the Five-State…they control the government…shit, they *are* the government!"

"Z.A.P.T. can help," Dill said, and as Carl's face soured, she sat back and heaved a sigh. "They could help us, Carl. They could! They know the building, and they know–"

"What are they going to do? Print up a bunch of flyers?" He snorted and shook his head. "Forget it. I'm not getting mixed up with those worthless assholes."

"At least we know how to get into R&D without an escort," Dill said without realizing she had reverted to identifying with Z.A.P.T when she said 'we'. She crossed her arms over her chest and tipped back in her chair. "So…not completely worthless, huh?"

"Fine, not completely worthless," Carl said. "How?"

Dill contemplated him in silence until his face twisted in annoyance. Then she relented. "Through the parking deck off the back of the building. You can get to it from the underground parking. There's a maintenance closet at the back where we opened up one of the old, sealed doors. Once you're back there, you can access the whole building because they never sealed the other doors, they only locked them." She fished a key from her pocket and slid it across to Carl, carefully checking to make sure no one was watching. "There's a door to each floor through a maintenance stairwell. They don't even have any security. I guess they think the idea of zombies in residence is deterrent enough, but here's the thing: there aren't that many. Maybe back at the start they had more, when they were developing all the deterrents…but I think those days are gone. The ones they have now get used for everything. Used and reused."

"Like the one I saw in the corridor that day," Carl said. "It was falling apart." He drew the key the rest of the way across the table. "Well, that's good to know, and I guess the zapped assholes are good for something, after all."

"I used to be one of those assholes, Carl, remember?" Dill said.

"Not really, though," Carl said dismissively. "You were only in it because of a boy."

The absolute sureness of his tone sent a tremor of annoyance up her spine. He treated her like she was sixteen instead of twenty-six. How condescending could he be?

"You don't know anything about it," she said.

"I know enough, believe me." His tone said that he was ending the conversation. He stood. "Go home. I'm going to check out a few things, and we'll talk more tomorrow."

Dill stood, too, her chair screeching back. "No! Wait! I'm going with you!"

"Go home," he said. "I'm going to look around. If the three people from today are up there in the tubes, still zombies, then we'll have to figure something out. If not," he shrugged, "then we let it go."

"I won't let it go," Dill said. She kept her voice even and calm, not giving Carl any reason to write her off as hysterical. She turned and walked from the cafeteria, not waiting for an answer.

"See you tomorrow," Carl called after her, "Dill?"

She raised a hand but didn't turn around.

"Dammit," he said. What was she so upset about? He was only trying to protect her.

# TWELVE

**Ze Yard Stakes!®**
Zombie, Inc., introduces the newest in home security with Ze Yard Stakes!® line of undead* defense. Keep your home safe with a barrier so impenetrable that "We Guarantee!"** the undead will be unable to access your home!

*You'll sleep in comfort when you have the Zombie, Inc., Ze Yard Stakes!® giving you peace of mind!*

*The stake system is a static grid of thin wires that trip intruders onto the stakes, thus effectively pinning an intruder in place. Any zombie not staked directly through the brain will remain 'alive' and thus still pose a threat to pets, children and the elderly. Extreme caution must be used navigating the grid, as the wire will also trip humans. **ZI requires all Ze Yard Stakes!® grids be clearly marked with warning signs.***

**All warranties implied or written become void if the yard stake system is not installed by Zombie, Inc., licensed and certified contractors. For questions or to set up a free, in-home, no obligation consultation, simply stop by the ZI headquarters at One ZI Boulevard in the renovated Jackson-Levitt building or our satellite office at the Inners Mall (formerly the B. Dalton Antique Booksellers).*

*rev: 03/16/2031*

---

The parking garage was dim as usual, the handful of fluorescents doing little to push back the dark. It was cold, the air cloying and fetid. Unlike the building's offices, which had been repainted and freshly carpeted when ZI took over the building, this lowest level of the parking garage had merely been cleaned of corpses before being put back into limited use. The smell of death lingered mustily.

All but two Wrangler vehicles were in their spots. Even with their engines stilled, the vehicles gave off a sense of power and menace like big cats coiled to explode into predatory action. The electric SUVs of Assessment looked much tamer in comparison.

Carl walked to his vehicle, scanning the surrounding area for other employees–Wranglers, specifically. Few other people drove anymore, but if someone saw him now, he could just act as though he was leaving for the day.

Silence.

He skirted the SUV and trotted silently to the back of the garage. It grew even darker the further he got from the overheads, and he stood still, listening as his eyes adjusted. The back wall was gray cinderblock with old, faded markings–EXIT, NO SMOKING, REMEMBER YOUR FLOOR AND ROW NUMBER!, RESERVED SPOTS FOR MANAGEMENT ONLY!–and then– STAIRS–with an arrow.

He followed the arrow.

A single door, gray-painted metal without a window, appeared in the gloom. Attached to the front of the door was a sticker, flaked and peeling, with the following: 1$^{st}$ Floor: Visitor Registration, Information Desk, Cafeteria. 2$^{nd}$ Floor: Accounts Payable and Receivable, Customer Service. 3$^{rd}$ Floor: IT, Information Services, HR. 4$^{th}$ Floor: Executive Offices. 5$^{th}$ Floor: No Admission. The previous occupier of the building had been an insurance or financial company–Carl couldn't remember which.

He took another long look around, then fished the key from his pocket and opened the door. He slipped into the stairwell and pulled the door closed behind him, locking it. The stairwell was completely dark on this level, but there was a trickle of weak light coming from somewhere above the first set of switchback, cement stairs. Did that mean someone was up there?

He took a breath and ascended the stairs to the first floor. The door to the building was the same as the one below, solid metal with no windows, but the door opposite that led onto the first parking deck had a large glass window embedded with chicken wire mesh. A grayish light glowed through it from one small fluorescent that flickered from the ceiling just outside the door. Carl pressed himself against the building side and slid until he could see out onto the parking deck. This far back, he was enough in shadow that he wouldn't be seen by anyone unless they were right at the window. The deck looked deserted. Carl stepped cautiously to the window and peered through, craning to see as much as possible without opening the door. It was empty.

Three sides were open to the night, and Carl remembered Aaron telling him that the levels–the height–came in handy. At the time, Carl hadn't wanted to know why, but now he did. He tented his hand on the door and pushed the bar-latch, opening the door as quietly as he could. He stepped out onto the deck and hurried out from under the fluorescent. Someone standing there would be visible to anyone standing in the shadows of the deck.

Wide, square columns of cement were laid out in a grid, and Carl trotted quickly from column to column. On one side of the deck, cars from a previous life had been jammed helter-skelter. On the opposite side, a thin artificial light glowed from outside and below. The deck was deserted. Carl made his way to the back and approached the edge with caution. A low, concrete block wall, originally intended to keep cars from driving over the side, ran the perimeter. Carl stayed next to a column, hoping the shadow would conceal him, and slid to the edge.

The area behind the building must have once been very picturesque. Medium-height dogwoods and pear trees that had lost most of their leaves but would put on a bright show in the spring were dotted, park-like, around cement forms that had once held the wooden tops and benches of picnic tables. A deep, weed-clotted depression lined with slate stepping-stones and the crumbling remnants of a footbridge was probably once a pond stocked with ducks and Japanese koi. Further back, past where the grass would have been green and well tended, were the real woods–deep and dark with tangles of wild sticker bushes and guarded by the black, skeletal shapes of the pines. The woods had been burned during the purge, but what had grown back had been denser and scrubbier than before. Vines with hard, woody stems and brownish leaves hung limp and choking from trees and bushes alike.

Nothing moved in the deserted landscape.

Carl made his way to the other side, the side without the cars, and looked over the lightly glowing edge.

Spread out below was an area roughly the size of a football field, surrounded by a ten-foot stockade fence topped by barbed wire. Every twenty feet or so, a spotlight was attached to the top of the fence and turned to shine down on the yard. At least half the lights were out, and the yard, while lit, was still dim.

The area inside the fence looked like some nightmare version of an old-time sporting event. Lines and numbers had been painted onto the hard, mossy ground. Wooden structures similar to lifeguard chairs sat at the corners of the 'field', and a wide, shallow, shed-like building with doors every four feet occupied much of the back fence.

A ten-by-twenty-foot area directly below the parking deck had been dotted with wooden stakes, points up, and ends embedded deeply in the ground. At the edge of the stakes, a face-down body struggled sluggishly, a stake in its neck, shoulder and hip. There wasn't much left to it. The arms and legs were down to the bone in places, and its stomach and innards were long gone with only an oily, blackish patch below to show where they had lain until they rotted away. A steady creak, creak, creak floated up to Carl, and he squinted into the gloom. One of its forearms had a stake sticking right between the radius and ulna, where originally its meat had held it still—or at least, quiet. As it raised and lowered its arm, the bone creaked against the stake. The back of its head glowed whitely where the hair and then the flesh had melted away.

Carl backed away from the edge. So they were throwing zombies off the parking deck; so what? It was for a good reason. Defense systems had to come from somewhere, but the yard stake grids had been developed over twenty years ago. ZI had stopped selling the yard stakes once they had developed the first electrified yard grids—the stakes had too many unintended victims. The electrified yards hadn't been much safer. It wasn't until they'd started researching the collars that the shift had gone towards using the zombies *as* the defense systems as opposed to only actively keeping them out or killing them.

Back then, though, the zombies had still been plentiful.

How long had that one been stuck on that grid? It couldn't be twenty years, or it would have rotted away completely. It had certainly been back there for a long time…why hadn't it been put out of its misery?

If it wasn't twenty years, if it was recent, then why had R&D wasted a zombie on such old technology?

It didn't make sense.

He made his way back to the stairwell and continued up. This time, he merely looked out the window of the second floor door– another parking deck, this one empty, too, save for a jumble of cars pushed to one end. Carl had the impression of a space once used but since deserted. Maybe R&D didn't have as much to do as they used to.

He made his way to three.

The deck there was different. The cars still sat in a heap at one end, but the floor was crowded with ghostly shapes of machinery– old flat-screen computer monitors on long tables, treadmills, heart monitors, microscopes–barely visible under heavy plastic tarps. Everything looked gritty with dirt. Unused. Abandoned.

He turned, uneasy, and put his ear against the cold metal door that would put him on the third floor. In theory, most of R&D should have gone home with the rest of the day-shift employees, but Carl was cautious. He slid the key into the lock and opened the door a quarter inch, trying to see what lay beyond it. He should have asked Dill, but he hadn't thought of it. He had a fleeting wish that he was more like the heroes he'd seen in movies as a kid, especially the 007 movies. Those guys knew how to *do* things that Carl simply had no notion of. He was just a regular guy.

It was pitch black beyond the door. He pushed it open further. Light should be coming from somewhere. The building was never pitch black…unless. He pushed the door the rest of the way open, letting a scant amount of light in from the parking deck fluorescent. He was in a good-sized maintenance closet. Shelves lined the walls, and a cleaner's cart was pushed against the back wall. There was a thin line of light around the frame of the door that–Carl decided after some thought–sat at the end of the main corridor in R&D.

Not perfect. He'd rather the door had let him into one of the darkened offices, but at least he was oriented. He could easily make his way to Aaron's stockroom from here. He'd be on video, but did that matter? He wasn't sure. Assessment mostly had free run of the building. Mostly.

He cracked open the maintenance closet door and found himself peering down the long, main hall–he'd been right. The floor was quiet and semi-dark. Carl hesitated, unsure, wishing again that he had some James Bond knowledge. Or at least some *Die Hard* courage.

He stepped into the hall and walked quickly to the stockroom door, trying to appear purposeful instead of hurried. He let himself into the dark, abattoir-smelling room. He scanned the cylinders. Only a half dozen or so zombies, Denny still among them, moaned and walked endlessly. A low, communal moan acted almost as white noise. Augustus was not in the tubes, and none of the zombies looked very fresh.

A sense of relief relaxed Carl's shoulders. The three from today hadn't been taken up here; they had most likely been killed by the Wranglers, as was policy. He had been spooked, but none of the fears were founded. It was all coincidence, and here was the proof. He grinned, but then his eyes shifted to Denny.

Denny was still here.

Denny hadn't been decently killed.

"What the fuck does it mean?" Carl asked himself, his voice low but distressed.

"What does *what* mean?" Aaron said from behind him, his voice clipped. "And what are you doing up here, Carl? I didn't let you on the floor."

Carl turned, his heart leaping painfully like a fish on a line. Aaron's face was closed, cold. Carl swallowed and said the first thing that came to mind.

"This guy is Z.A.P.T.," he said and willed his voice not to shake. "Did you know that?" He took an accusatory step toward Aaron. "Do you know what he did?"

Aaron's eyes became slits behind his glasses, and he tilted his head. He looked at Carl a long time before he let his eyes slide to Denny.

He nodded. "Of course *I* know," he said. He grabbed Carl's bicep and pulled him toward the office at the back of the room. "How did *you* know?"

"I've been investigating," Carl said. Not wholly a lie.

"I didn't know there was an investigation," Aaron said. His voice still held traces of cautious skepticism.

"No one knows," Carl said and sat in the chair opposite Aaron's desk, and when Aaron frowned, he continued in a hurry. "EA put me onto it."

Aaron's features rounded in shock, and his mouth dropped open. "*You're* EA?"

Employee Assessment was the most feared, most mysterious group at ZI, and no one knew who they were, so unless Aaron was EA himself, Carl's bluff would hold.

"No, *I'm* not EA," Carl said. "I'm just working with them on this. They needed someone in Assessment."

"Does Dill know?"

Carl tried to think quickly. He didn't want to jeopardize Dill. If he had a secret mission, would he have told her or not?

"No," Carl said. "That's why I've been keeping her at a distance. We…EA and I…don't need any complications."

"Now *I* know," Aaron said, concern threading his voice.

Carl sighed. "Yeah. I'm sorry about that, buddy. I sure don't want to get you into any trouble. Can you keep it to yourself?"

"Geez, Carl, I guess so," Aaron said. He reached into his top desk drawer and shuffled papers back and forth. "There's only one small problem."

"What's that, buddy?" Carl asked. He was going to get away with this, he really was. Soon as he sent Aaron packing, he'd investigate those sheds across the back of the field. They had looked interesting. Just the right size to hold a zombie. "What's the problem?"

Aaron pulled a small handgun from his desk and trained it on Carl. "You're lying," Aaron said, "and I want to know why."

Carl's hand moved to the hip where his gun lay.

"Carl, don't be an idiot," Aaron said and shook his head. "This isn't a movie, and besides, you're outgunned." Aaron nodded toward his office door. Two Wranglers stood just outside, watching carefully, arms crossed over their barrel chests.

Carl said the first thing that came to mind. "They don't have guns."

"It's a figure of speech, geez, Carl," Aaron said and rolled his eyes again. "Take your gun out, and put it on my desk. Don't screw around."

Carl did as Aaron asked, but began to formulate a plan. If he could somehow make Aaron think that Carl was on his side, maybe there'd be a way out of this. A way that left him breathing.

He sighed, trying to make it not too theatrical. "You're right. I'm not working with EA on this; it's something I'm doing on my own." He glanced at Aaron, trying to seem embarrassed but also stubborn. "How did you know I'm not EA?"

Aaron laughed and shook his head. "How do you think I knew, Carl? What do you think would tip me off?"

"*You're* EA?" Carl was stunned. He'd known Aaron a long time, had bowled next to him for years. How had he missed it?

"Yes and no," Aaron said. He sat back in his chair, the gun still trained on Carl. "Technically, there is no Employee Assessment; not the way employees think of it. We're just a smallish group tasked with upholding ZI's best interests, but there's no actual name for us. We decided years ago to capitalize on a rumor that was going around the building and even started some of our own rumors…just to build the mystique, you know? But no, we're not watching employees or making reports or any of that mundane HR bullshit." Aaron dropped his head as though trying to gather his thoughts. When he spoke again, his voice had taken on an odd tone that Carl couldn't identify right away. "We're more than that, better than that," Aaron said. "We're…guardians, you could say. The guardians of ZI."

He raised his head to look at Carl, and Carl was startled by the zealous light behind his friend's mild spectacles and realized that was the tone he hadn't been able to recognize–zealotry.

"People don't know what's good for them, Carl. They don't know what they need; they don't see the big picture. We just–" He shrugged and grinned self-deprecatingly. "We just make sure the company is taken care of, and as long as ZI is healthy, we're all better off." Aaron sat forward, and the grin disappeared. "So, tell me, Carl. What is it you were doing on your own?"

Carl swallowed, trying to process the information Aaron was giving him. EA had always been the invisible boogeyman, the unseen threat keeping everyone in line. It didn't exist?

It was too much. He'd have to try to sort it out later. For now, he reverted back to task. "That zombie you have out there...the one I asked about yesterday. He *is* Z.A.P.T., high up, too."

"Yes, I *know* that...well, not about the high up part, but I know he was Z.A.P.T.," Aaron said, his voice filled with irritation. "What of it?" he asked, and Carl took heart at the hint of interest he heard behind Aaron's annoyance.

"Well...I was going to use him to flush out more of the group," Carl said. "I knew he was messing around on the different floors, putting out those flyers and shit. When I saw the video from the attack, when you showed me someone looking out the bathroom door but you didn't recognize him..." He sat back, as though reluctant to say more. Let Aaron come to him.

"You knew he was from Z.A.P.T. when you saw the video?" Aaron asked. The gun sagged in his hand as he sat forward.

"I've been following him for a while, so, yeah," Carl said, "I knew who he was."

"Why didn't you say something?"

Carl shrugged and crossed his arms over his chest. "I didn't know if I could trust you, Aaron."

"*Trust* me? Trust me to what?"

"To understand," Carl said. He lowered his voice and leaned toward Aaron. "Everyone thinks I'm crazy for hating those zapped assholes. Everyone says 'oh, they're just kids' and that they're too scattered or young or disorganized to affect any kind of real damage, but that's not true, Aaron. They are a huge threat to us, and I don't mean ZI...I mean to *all* of us. To our society." He leaned back again, pleased with Aaron's rapt expression. "No one else wants to do anything about it–" he shrugged, "–then *I'll* do something about it." He grinned. "It looks like you beat me to it, buddy."

Aaron shifted in his seat and glanced at the Wranglers outside the door. The gun sagged almost to the desk top…he seemed to have forgotten it entirely.

"Beat you to what?" Aaron asked.

Carl grinned. "I'm just saying, it's a suitable punishment," he said and shifted to the edge of his chair. "I'm a little *surprised*, I guess. I didn't think you were…well, political, let's call it. But obviously you're into it a lot deeper than I ever knew."

Aaron blinked, confused. "Punishment? Carl, I'm not sure what—"

"Turning him into a zombie," Carl said. He laughed. "It's genius! They love the walking dead so much…they should join 'em! It's perfect, Aaron. The perfect punishment for terrorists."

Aaron sat back, blinking. "I hadn't really…I hadn't thought of it in those terms, exactly," he said.

"That's why you did it, though, right? I mean…you did turn him into a zombie, didn't you?"

"No, not exactly," Aaron said. He glanced at the Wranglers again. "We found him like that but decided…instead of instituting second and final death, we just, you know…kept him."

"Because he was Z.A.P.T. though, right? As punishment?"

"No, it's more that—" Aaron sat forward. He swallowed. "Carl, I don't know if you know what dire straits we're in up here. Everything is…it's falling apart. There are so few zombies anymore," he said. "We used to have hundreds of them for research, but now, it's hard to find any. If we get one or two a week, that's a lot. With the new yard systems requiring animated product, demanding stock, the problem is exacerbated. The old systems—the ones like Ze Yard Stakes and Ze Head Blade—were killing them off so quickly that we had started to see a drastic decline in the population more than fifteen years ago. Can you imagine? What would we do…you know…without the zombies?" Aaron's eyes were filled with a baffled angst.

Carl's stomach turned over as he realized that Aaron had convinced himself of what he was saying. He kept his features sympathetic as he nodded encouragement to Aaron to go on. Aaron did.

"Our whole society is based on the undead. Our jobs, the government, the economy, our entire infrastructure…has been built up around the zombies. We all depend on them!" Aaron shook his head. "Imagine if there were no zombies. Everything we know would break down. You think Zombie, Inc., is too big to fail? Think again. We're already failing, Carl. It's already happening!" Aaron sank back in his seat, shaking his head with obvious disgust. "Everyone's gotten so cavalier about their safety. No one realizes the danger. What if there were another outbreak? What then? Is anybody prepared? No."

The petulant tone of Aaron's voice told Carl more than he wanted to know about his friend. Former friend. He really believed this ass-backwards Paulosophy he was spouting. He really believed that ZI was in the right. It scared Carl more than anything else could have. A true believer is a being beyond reason.

"Is that why there was an attack out there tonight?" Carl asked. He kept his tone sympathetic, awed, even, as though impressed with the tactic. As though he agreed with it.

Aaron nodded without looking up. "Yes. It was determined that the meeting yesterday…where we had the zombie onstage…wasn't…it didn't—" Aaron shrugged, but this time it was more a gesture of throwing off. "—it didn't seem to impress upon anyone the danger of our situation. The potential danger. Of an attack, I mean; not the danger of ZI failing. We have to…as a community…we have to be ready for another outbreak. It's all about safety."

Carl wondered if Aaron even heard his own contradictions and justifications. Probably not. Safety—that was a laugh. How could safety be a concern to someone who'd authorize an attack?

"Well," Carl said, "I think it was a damn good idea."

Aaron looked at him with frank suspicion.

"I do, Aaron," Carl said. "I think it was just what people needed to wake them up. It's been far too easy for far too long, if you want my opinion. Remember right after the outbreak? How hard it was? How scared everyone was? We were all fighting for our lives and fighting for survival. We were the first ones here, and *we* made this place safe." Carl put a tone of reminiscence in his tone. A 'buddy, we shared the war' tone, but did he really think in some twisted way that that had been a better time? Was there some deep, dark part of him that wanted to fight the war again? To fight it forever?

No.

No way.

"I'm with you, Aaron," Carl said. "Let me in on it. Let me help. It will be just like old times." He reached across the desk–carefully–and grasped Aaron's wrist. Behind him, the Wranglers began to push through the door, alerted by Carl's hand so close to his gun.

Aaron waved them off. He considered Carl for a long time without speaking. Then he put his hand over Carl's.

"Okay," Aaron said, "let me tell you what we've planned."

*

Carl stumbled out of the stairwell and leaned against the wall, breathing deeply, trying to control the shakes that wanted to start up in his knees. His midsection felt like hot Jell-O. The Wranglers had followed him most of the way down, but luckily, they hadn't followed him all the way to the basement level. Carl wasn't sure he could have held it together if they had, but they'd even waved as they turned to make their way back to three. Carl was okay; he was 'in'.

So why did he feel like he might throw up? The adrenalin. That's all.

He took a deep breath and straightened. He wanted nothing more than to get home, get a drink, and not think about this for the rest of the night. He'd think about it tomorrow. Or maybe the next day.

"Carl?"

He turned in the dark, jumping like a cat. His heart jammed into his throat, stopping his breath, and he slapped a hand over his gun.

Dill stood next to him. She must have been waiting just out of sight.

"Jesus *Christ*, Dill," he said and bent over his knees, pushing out a breath that seemed much hotter than normal. "I could have fucking *killed* you!" His voice sounded weak and whistling to his own ears; he hoped Dill didn't hear it.

"That's hardly likely," she said with a snort, "you can barely stand up. What happened up there? Are you okay? Did you find out anything?"

Carl stayed bent over, hands on his knees and breathed. A fleeting, cowardly part of him wanted to tell her that everything was fine, and that everything was normal. They'd misread everything and got it all wrong. Then he could go home, drink, *not* think...and then what? *Really* join up with Aaron and company? That wasn't about to fucking happen. *I might have a few flaws,* he thought, *but I'd never deliberately subject someone to that walking death.*

He straightened. "Come on," he said. "We'll talk once we get out of here."

"You sure you're okay, Carl?" Dill said. "You look pretty shaky."

"Yeah, well," he said, "that's what happens when someone holds a gun on you, and two big Wranglers are ready to help change you into a walking corpse."

Dill went to the passenger side of the SUV as Carl unplugged from the charging station. He glanced at her as she scanned the surrounding area, alert for danger. As a trainee, she'd come a long way in a limited time. She was a survivor, no question about it.

"Okay, get in," he said. "Let's get the hell out of here."

"Where are we going?"

"To my house," he said. "Duck down, though, in case anyone is watching."

Dill did as he asked, and they cruised silently from the dark garage to the dark outside. Carl watched the ZI building become smaller in his rearview mirror and was unexpectedly swept with a feeling almost like nostalgia. He'd spent the last fifteen years working for ZI, and it had been a good, if solitary, fifteen years. What would he do without it? What about Dee the lunch-lady, Candy and Robert...all the people who worked there...what would they do if ZI ceased to exist?

Carl didn't know, but he was sure of one thing: at the very least, they wouldn't have to worry about their employer turning them into walking dead profit.

*

"Their plan is to change just a few people at a time. They think the attack today went well–it was quickly controlled, and there was no collateral damage–so they'll probably do it again. I don't think they'll do it at ZI, though. They can't have all the 'attacks', so-called, happening there."

Carl poured whiskey into two glasses, but when he handed one to Dill, she looked at it uncertainly.

"What's this?" she asked.

"Whiskey," he said and shook the glass, swirling the amber liquid, "you've never seen whiskey?"

She shrugged. "Is it alcohol? Is that what whiskey is?"

Carl took the glass back. If she'd never had alcohol, he didn't want her to start now. She would be as worthless as a frat kid at his first big kegger.

"Forget it," he said and tipped her glass into his. "You want some water?"

She shook her head and settled onto the couch. "You should crack a window. It kind of...stinks a little in here."

"It's vomit," Carl said. His tone was matter of fact. "There are at least two Wranglers involved, eight people from R&D, one of the cleaners...they have people in almost every department, according to Aaron. What we've always thought of as 'EA' is really just a kind of ZI vigilante group."

"Like Z.A.P.T.," Dill said.

Carl turned to her, startled. "No, that's...it's different."

"Why? Because it's not company endorsed? Come on, Carl."

"Maybe you're right," Carl said and sank into a chair opposite her.

"Okay, so, what's our next move?"

Carl leaned his head back and rolled it side to side. "I don't know. We could leave, I guess. Get out of the Five-State all together."

"Leave?" Dill sat forward on the couch, her hands gripping her knees. "I don't want to leave!"

"What else can we do? I don't know who's really involved or what they're capable of." He raised his head to glare at her. "They'll do it to us. Do you understand that? They wouldn't hesitate to make us into mobile corpses. Do you want to become a sack of experimental meat? Or stand around all day and night with a shock collar on protecting some richie's house?"

"No," Dill said. She wrung her hands together and shook her head. "I don't want to leave."

"I get that, believe me," Carl said, "but Dill, ZI is dying. Even if we could flush out the bad element, the company will cease to exist and probably sooner rather than later. Aaron and the other people involved are...they're shortsighted. Aaron said he's got the big picture in mind but changing employees into zombies? That's not big-picture strategy. That's some kind of psycho justification, right there. I think–" Carl's hand flew to his ear and then hesitated. He looked at Dill with his eyebrows raised. "Phone call," he said and tapped his ear. "Yeah?"

"Carl." Candy, but her voice was so choked with tears that Carl barely recognized it at first. "Carl..."

"Candy!" He stood. "What's wrong?"

Dill stood, too, concern clouding her features.

"I've...I need...oh, God, Carl...I just...I had to! I didn't..." Her voice disintegrated into a wail.

"Candy," Carl said. He grabbed the key and motioned Dill to follow as he headed for the door. "Listen to me, Candy. Are you home? I'll come to you." He pushed out the door and glanced at Dill to make sure she carried her bow.

"Yes, I'm...oh, God, I had to...I *had* to..." She hitched and sobbed, her voice breaking across the line. "Carl, I..."

"I'm coming, Candy," Carl said. "Two minutes. Can you tell me what's happened? Can you give me an idea?"

"I...I...ki-killed Robert!" She wailed again, and Carl put his hand to his ear, wincing. "I had to, Carl...I couldn't...he...I *had* to!"

*

Dill handed Candy a cup of water. She accepted it with shaking hands and a slight, tremulous smile. Her hair was in disarray, soft tendrils curling at the sides of her face. Her makeup had been hurriedly washed off, and a combination of mascara and eyeliner still darkened the areas under her eyes. To Dill, Candy looked better without the thick coat of makeup–more human, more accessible. Less intimidating.

Candy sipped the water and glanced at the empty doorway to the kitchen. Her eyes were wide with apprehension, and her cheeks were red and feverish-looking. Dill sat next to Candy and moved to take her hand but then, restricted by the years of ZI rules, drew back, but she wanted to offer the woman something.

"He'll be back in a second, I'm sure," Dill said.

Candy swiveled her head toward Dill with an oddly mechanical movement, as though internal wires were snapping and gears were winding down. Small tremors shook her head. Shock. She was in shock.

Dill smiled, trying to be reassuring. She reached out again and then hesitated and pulled her hand back, but this time, Candy saw the small gesture, and she reached for Dill's retreating hand. She gripped it tightly, and the water in her other hand nearly spilled.

"Whoa," Dill said and took the cup from Candy's grasp. She set it on the coffee table, but it was an awkward movement as she reached over her own arm, her hand caught fast in Candy's warm, clammy grip.

"I had to...I had to..." Candy said. Her eyes swam in their pond of tears.

Dill patted Candy's hand. The contact felt odd yet satisfying. Of course, Denny had touched her, and she'd touched him, but it was mostly during the course of sex. Touching otherwise just hadn't seemed necessary.

"I know," Dill said. "You did the right thing."

"I did?" Candy tilted her head, and again the movement looked mechanical. A slow tear overflowed and rolled down her scrubbed cheek. Dill's reticence melted away, and she leaned forward to hug Candy. The woman collapsed against her shoulder with a sigh almost like contentment.

"Yes, you had to," Dill said. She tightened her arms around Candy. "You did the exact right thing. He didn't give you a choice. You had to, and it was the right thing."

Candy relaxed against her, and the small ticks and tremors faded away.

"Thank you," Candy said, "thank you, Dill, for coming here and for helping me. I can't thank you enough. I was so scared."

Finally, Candy sat back, wiping under her eyes. She sighed again–one long, shuddering outrush of breath–and then gathered herself together, patting her hair into place and smoothing her shirt. She smiled at Dill and then reached for her water again. "I'm really glad you're here."

Dill shrugged. Now that Candy was calming down, Dill felt a little shy again. She looked around the room. It was pretty and not what Dill would have expected from the Candy she'd met at ZI. It was homey and slightly shabby. The deep couch held no less than eight pillows and three soft throws. The chair opposite was plush, and the coffee table between the two was painted a buttery yellow, scarred and chipped down to the wood in places. All in all, the room gave off the impression of a comfortable nest, but not a home used to company.

Almost as though she sensed Dill's thoughts, Candy bent to pick up a pillow that had tumbled to the floor. She tucked it back with the others and straightened the edge of the throw nearest her, but she was distracted and kept glancing at the kitchen doorway.

"Do you want me to go check–" Dill started, but Candy jumped in.

"No!" she said and gripped Dill's hand again. "I mean, I'd rather you stay here."

Dill nodded and tried to think of something to say, but then a door opened at the back of the house off the kitchen. Candy flinched, and Dill squeezed her hand again; Carl appeared in the doorway.

He glanced at the women's hands and shot Dill a look she could only interpret as gratitude. Then he sat opposite them in the chair. He leaned to grasp his hands together between his knees.

"I put him in the garage," he said. His voice was so gentle that Dill thought, *Blindfolded, I might not have known it was him.* "Candy. Everything is fine. Can you tell me...us...what happened?"

When Dill and Carl had gotten to Candy's little house, she'd flown from it and into Carl's arms, hysterical. She was spattered with blood. Carl had more or less carried her back into the house, searching the surrounding homes for signs that anyone had seen them. The neighborhood was quiet and dark.

Inside, in the kitchen, they'd found Robert. Dead. With a knife handle sticking out of his chest. Candy babbled hysterically about Robert telling her that he was part of a ZI initiative that was going to save the company by generating zombies from the 'less useful' people in some of the departments. Dill and Carl had exchanged a glance at this.

While Carl had taken care of Robert's body, Dill had helped Candy clean herself up.

"Candy?" Carl said. He leaned closer to her, his voice dropping, but didn't reach for her pale hands. "Tell me what happened."

Candy swallowed and sighed. "Robert brought me home after...after Augustus was..." She swiped a hand under her eyes. "...after Augustus was attacked. I couldn't stop crying. He was so dear to me, to both of us, I thought, but Robert was acting strangely. I thought he was in shock or depressed. I asked him to come in and keep me company. I thought we could talk and that would make us both feel better. I was in the kitchen, Robert stayed out here, and I was saying how awful it was and how much I was going to miss Augustus. Then I realized that Robert wasn't saying anything." Candy grimaced and shook her head. "I won't keep crying, I promise," she said and tried to smile at Carl. He only gazed at her with calm patience, and eventually she went on. "I looked out the kitchen doorway, and he was sitting with his head in his hands and pulling at his hair; crying, but quietly, just really torn up. I went to him and put a hand on his shoulder, and when he looked up, his face was so...it was like a stranger, or worse, like a monster had taken him over. His lips were pulled back from his teeth, and his eyes were just...just crazy looking. He grabbed me. He jumped up and grabbed my arms, and he was mumbling." Candy sighed and ran a hand over her hair again as though the action would help order her thoughts. "He was saying that it had been a mistake, and that Augustus never left first, it was always clerical who streamed out the door at five. He kept asking— pleading, really—'Why did Augustus leave so fast? Why did he? Why? He wasn't supposed to,' and I started getting really scared then.

"I asked him what was going on. I said, 'Robert, please, tell me what's wrong.' I could see, you know, how distressed he was. I just didn't know that it was guilt. Really, that's what it was. He started telling me how ZI wasn't doing well; he said there weren't enough zombies anymore to keep us all employed. He said everything was falling apart because...Jesus, he actually said 'The world's too safe now. No one is afraid anymore.' I said, 'That's a *good* thing, Robert!' and he laughed. He said it wasn't good if it meant we'd all be out of a job. That's when I started to understand what he was saying, at least, a little. That's when he told me that it was planned. The attack. He said they'd meant only good to come of it." Candy laughed, and it was a dark and bitter sound. "I stayed quiet after he said that. I wanted to see how much more he'd say, and he said a lot." She shook her head. "It's funny how you can be acquainted with someone for so long but not know them at all, and then other people, you hardly ever see them, but you feel you *know* them so well." She glanced at Carl and then away. She smiled at Dill even as her eyes filled again. "I think I'm trying not to talk about this next part, but I have to. I have to tell you the rest of it."

"Take your time, Candy," Carl said, "I'm not going anywhere."

Dill noticed that he'd dropped the 'we' from his sentence. His focus was fixed on Candy entirely. A childish twist of jealousy was quickly wiped out by her admiration for him.

"He said he wanted me to be a part of it, and I refused," Candy continued. "I should have just played along, but it was too much. Poor Augustus...there was literally *no reason* for what happened to him. Worse, it was *engineered* to happen. I couldn't help myself, and I got angry. I told him what I thought of someone who'd sell out other human beings...friends, even!...because of fear. Because of money. Because of job security! Then he stopped pleading with me, and he got angry. Really angry and mean. He said...terrible things. He said I was sheltered, naïve. Ignorant. He said I was too much up my own...well, he said a lot of terrible things." Candy rubbed a hand across her forehead as if she might be getting a headache. She sighed. "He was working himself up, cycling up. Then he came at me." She sighed again. "The funny part is, he didn't know me either. Not the real me. He's only ever seen me as Sales' Candy." She sat straighter and shook her head once, sharply, throwing her hair back. "He didn't know what he was getting himself into."

Dill glanced at Carl in confusion, but a grin was surfacing on his face.

"No, he sure didn't," Carl said, and Dill opened her mouth to ask a question, but he shushed her with a gesture. "Go on, Candy."

"Instinct took over," Candy said. She gazed at Carl steadily as though he were the one thing keeping her from sinking into insanity. "I kept stepping away, deflecting him. I didn't want to hurt him; no matter what he'd said, I still didn't want to...didn't want to..."

"You're not like them," Carl said. His voice was so soft, Dill wondered if Candy registered it as her own thought.

Candy nodded, her eyes on Carl. "That's right. I'm not a killer," she said, "but he didn't give me a choice, Carl. He picked up a knife and–"

"And that was his big mistake," Carl said, and Candy nodded again, gazing at him as though hypnotized.

"I reacted. I just...*reacted*. He came at me, and I grabbed his wrist and turned it...I stabbed him," she said. She blinked rapidly. "And that was that." She tried to smile, but tears finally overflowed her lashes, and she began to crumple forward. Dill reached for her, but Carl was there first, pulling Candy up, hugging her to him.

He began to murmur words of comfort, and Dill got up, wanting to give them privacy. She turned toward the kitchen, then changed her mind and slipped quietly out the front door. *Let them have a few minutes*, she thought. She breathed deep of the cold air and smiled. Carl was pretty awesome, pretty great. He was being so good to Candy. Dill wouldn't have thought he had it in him. She hugged herself. She was, well, proud of him in some odd way. He was like that old thing, what was it? A night of shining armor? Something like that. He was all those old-fashioned things: chivalrous and manly and–

The door opened behind her, and Carl looked out.

"Dill, what the fuck are you doing out here?" He shook his head. "Get in here. We have to talk."

Okay, well, so...maybe not *that* great.

Candy was no longer in the living room when Dill followed Carl back in.

"Where's Candy?" Dill asked.

"She's getting cleaned up," Carl said and collapsed into the chair. He laced his hands together over his head. "Shit."

"What's wrong?" Dill asked, and when Carl's eyes snapped open, full of incredulity, she nearly regretted asking. Geez, he was being such a–

"Dill, what do you *think* might be wrong?" he asked, and if she wasn't immune to his sarcasm, she'd have been burned.

"Well, I mean, *besides* the obvious," she said. She rolled her eyes and put her hands on her hips. "Geez, Carl."

He blew out a long breath. "Yeah, okay. Forget it. I'm being a dick." He paused as if to give her a chance to disagree; she didn't. "I just don't know what to do."

The admission made her feel bad for him, and she took her hands off her hips and sat down on the couch. She had to push some pillows aside, and she threw one of the blankets over the back. "Cripes, how does she sit here?" she asked, not really expecting an answer.

"She sleeps out here," Carl said. "That's why there's so many pillows and stuff."

Dill rounded her eyes at Carl and raised her eyebrows. He colored.

"We have, you know, a history," he said and cleared his throat. He tipped his head back and closed his eyes. He rubbed his temples.

Dill nodded but didn't comment. She wasn't surprised by what Carl had said. She had suspected that they had feelings for each other, but she was saddened by the thought of hard-shelled, glamorous Candy sleeping on the couch.

It made her think of something Candy had just said.

"What did Candy mean when she said Robert didn't know her and you said he didn't know what he was getting into?"

Carl grinned and shook his head without opening his eyes. "Before everything, Candy was…well, it sounds crazy now, but she worked for the government." He lifted his head and cracked open one eye. "She was training to be an assassin. When she was a kid, you know, eighteen or so."

*"What?"* Dill said, making an effort to keep her voice down. She glanced down the hallway to make sure Candy wasn't listening. "No way."

"Way. I mean, not that that was her exact title," Carl said, his voice complacent. Even amused. "She told me about it after we...you know...got involved. Back in 2016, our country started having a lot of concerns about a country called North Korea. They were rumored to have nuclear weapons, and we had sanctions against them that weren't working, the UN was involved, it was a big mess."

"What's the you en?"

"Never mind; that doesn't matter. Not anymore," Carl said. "Anyway, the US–that was us–started developing a program to get to the North Korean leader without actually going to war. We were concerned about the North Korean citizens, who were rumored to be living in some really bad conditions. Poverty and starvation–there were stories as far back as '13 about people eating their children. Gruesome stuff. Anyway. The program. You see, we'd had luck with these kind of 'surgical missions' before with other terrorist leaders that we took out with just a handful of specially trained soldiers. So they decided to do something similar in North Korea."

"Candy wouldn't have even been alive in 2016, though."

"No, you're wrong–she was actually born in 2007. She's forty-six." Carl nodded at Dill's surprised expression. Then he continued. "It took the US a long time actually to do anything because the situation would get better and then worse, better and then worse, and in the meantime, we had that Second Great Depression in 2024. It's hard to explain it all. Suffice to say that Candy was part of the group that would eventually have gone in. They were being trained, but then in 2027, well–" Carl shrugged. "Candy used a lot of her training during the first wave of the plague. She was quite a fighter."

Dill felt another twist of jealousy at Carl's tone and expression. Maybe not jealousy, maybe it was just a little bit of despair. Would anyone ever talk about her with such apparent admiration?

Carl closed his eyes again, and Dill found herself wondering about Candy. It didn't seem possible that such a womanly, glamorous person could also be some kind of killer. Dill would have thought Candy would be the type to crumble at the first sign of trouble. Then Dill remembered back to when the alarms had gone off in ZI–Candy had instantly become a different person: calm, focused. Dill could start to see it.

"Now she does sales?" Dill was incredulous that you could go from one to the other.

"You'd be surprised how much my earlier training helped with that," Candy said, and Dill jumped with surprise. "Sales is a rough department. Lots of intrigue and backstabbing." Candy stood in the hallway just outside the living room. Dill would not have recognized her if she hadn't already seen Candy in half disarray.

Candy wore dark jeans tucked into boots and a tan Henley that hugged her curves. Over the Henley she wore a dark vest. Above the Henley, Candy's face was free of makeup, her hair tied back in a low, no-nonsense ponytail. Her blue eyes looked darker, guarded.

"Although," she continued as she made her way to them, "it didn't seem to help me very much tonight. It's been a long time since I've had to defend myself–in that particular way, anyway. I've discovered that I'm not at all anxious to go back to it."

"The last ten years especially," Carl said, "have been easy ones."

"And they want to change all that," Candy said and shook her head. "But the question is, what are we going to do about it?"

Carl shrugged. "We could take off. Just get out. I've heard good things about the Lower Three. Lots of sun."

"Lots of stink, too," Candy said, "and it would take months to get there."

"Sometimes, I forget how good we have it here compared to a lot of the country," Carl said. "We don't even have a car. I guess we could–"

"What about Denny and Augustus?" Dill said. She was starting to feel a little left out of their conversation. The way they talked, it was like Dill didn't have a say in the decision. She might be young enough to be their kid...but she wasn't their kid.

"What about them?" Carl asked, but Candy sat abruptly.

"You're right, Dill," Candy said. "We have to do something about them. I'd feel terrible if we left and they just went on and on until they rotted."

"Why?" Carl said. Irritation threaded his voice. "They don't know."

"It's just wrong, Carl," Candy said, and Dill nodded agreement.

"What do you want to do? Go back there? Just to kill them?" He shook his head. "Not a smart idea. We'll end up joining them instead. Would you really rather be a walking corpse than spend time in the sunny Lower Three?"

"What about everybody else?" Dill asked.

"What *about* everybody else?" Carl asked.

"Carl, they're going to start changing innocent people," Dill said, insistent, "and if they fuck it up, they're going to create another plague."

Carl raised his hands, palms up, and lifted his shoulders. "Once again…what can we do?" His eyes were tired, and Dill realized it was probably close to morning. With that thought, she, too, was overcome by a wave of exhaustion.

"We could give ZI an early death," Candy said. "Put it out of its misery. That would negate all the threat." A small smile played at the corner of her mouth. The sorrow in her eyes was partially replaced with black amusement.

Carl sat up straighter, and Dill felt a tiny zing of adrenalin at Candy's words.

"How?" Carl asked, and Candy's smile widened, dancing precariously on the edge of insanity. To Dill, it looked as though Sales Candy was trying to push through. Then Candy answered.

"We kill all the zombies."

# THIRTEEN

*Welcome!*
**To Zombie, Inc.**
*The Largest Employer\* in the Five-State since 2028*
Welcome to Zombie, Inc., the largest employer\* in the Five-State since 2028! As a new hire to the company, this **Zombie, Inc., Employee Handbook** will be your go-to resource for any questions that may arise during your 180-day probationary period.\*\*

Review this guide carefully prior to your start date and keep it handy for your first thirty days,\*\*\* minimum. Questions may arise that could be more easily answered by the book rather than involving Human Resources. HOWEVER, if you do have a question that does not seem to be answered by the guide, please refer to page 4, CONTACTING HR. Be sure that you know which division of HR handles the department you're hired into. [ALWAYS check with your direct supervisor before contacting HR. If you are unsure how to contact your direct supervisor, see page 5, CONTACTING YOUR DIRECT SUPERVISOR.]

To start your employment off on the right foot, here are:
*Some Simple Things to Remember!*
1.) Day shift start time for all\*\*\*\* departments is 8:00 AM. Please report to work no later than 7:30 AM.
2.) Night shift start time for all\*\*\*\* departments is 8:00 PM. Please report to work no later than 7:30 PM.
3.) The world has become a dangerous place, and the least dangerous place for you to be is at Zombie, Inc.,‡ so for the

benefit of our employees, we've increased the work week from six days to seven! Remember: work happens EVERY DAY! You are required to fulfill your duties EVERY DAY. We have a generous time off policy (see page 36) for cases of illness or accident. Otherwise, you are expected to report to work EVERY DAY!
*Welcome to THE TEAM at ZI!*
*We're Glad to Have YOU Aboard!*

*\*This statement is made based on assumptions and may be hyperbole.*

*\*\*Benefits do not start until after the 180-day probationary period. Time off (including mandatory in-service days) and leave (except maternity) during the 180-day probationary period will count as Unpaid Working Days [see page 56: UNPAID WORKING DAYS]. ZI is a work-at-will company, and you can be discharged at any time, for any reason, regardless of having satisfied the 180-day probationary period.*

*\*\*\*For your convenience, the Employee Handbook cost will be deducted from your first pay period. A yearly fee will be deducted for lost, missing, or used-looking Employee Handbooks (at HR discretion). When revisions occur, a new Handbook will be distributed to all ZI employees and the cost deducted from the next applicable pay period.*

*\*\*\*\*Certain departments are excepted from this rule. See the Employee Handbook with regards to the excepted departments.*

*‡ This is not implied as a guarantee of safety.*

*rev: 06/18/2031*

"I think it's a very bad idea," Carl said.

Behind him, Candy laughed. It was the deep-throated purr of Sales Candy. Dill felt an urge to look over her shoulder to see which Candy was riding in the back seat of Carl's ZI SUV.

"You're too careful," Candy said. "You have been as long as I've known you. Everything buttoned down and in line." Her tone rose and fell, implying all sorts of things that made Dill feel almost sorry for Carl. Candy seemed mostly out of his league, but when she glanced over at him, he was smiling into the rearview mirror.

"I kept *you* pretty well tethered," he said, and his voice was a low growl. Dill felt her cheeks grow hot as Candy's rumbly chuckle flowed from the backseat.

"Jesus *Christ*, you guys," Dill said. She was disgusted by the both of them. "Could you cut me a break, here? Can we get back to what the *hell* we're supposed to do now?"

Carl glanced at her and straightened his shoulders. "Yeah, Dill, you're right." He glanced at the rearview again. "Did you have some kind of actual plan? Or are we going in cold?"

Candy put a hand on Dill's shoulder and squeezed. "Sorry, Dill," she said. "Kind of like watching your parents making out, huh?" She laughed and then sat back again. "I don't have a plan. I thought we could just go up to the stockroom and start dispatching."

"I was there a couple hours ago," Carl said. "It was almost empty of zombies, and Augustus sure wasn't there."

"What about...was Denny still there?" Dill asked.

"Yeah. Denny was in the same spot, but the new ones weren't around, and there was a kidzie, too, from the other day that wasn't up there, now that I think about it," Carl said. "I think I might know where they're keeping them and all the other zombies."

Zombie, Inc., came into sight, and Carl turned off the headlights. They glided silently along the rutted street that led to the ZI parking lot. Dill shivered with unease at the sight of the half-dim building. The outline of it was blacker than the sky. Funny how less than two weeks ago she was on night shift, doing her job and dreaming of being Assessment...moving up and getting out of the inners. Even with the distraction of Z.A.P.T., she had wanted only small things: a house in the outers that was her own, the security of more money, a path. A life path. Now the path was gone. Where was her future now? With Carl and Candy in the Lower Three, living in the remains of a once-famous mouse's compound? She couldn't imagine it, but strangely enough, she also couldn't imagine a future without Carl in it. If he wanted to go south, she'd go with him, arguing comfortably the entire way.

They pulled under the building, sliding like a wraith through the tilting dark.

"Can you see?" Dill asked, her voice a quiet and shivering breath.

"Enough," Carl said. He reached across and laid one steady, weighted hand on the back of her neck. "Trust me."

She did.

*

The three of them stood at the very edge of the empty first-floor parking deck at the back of the building. The lights that lined the field below were almost entirely out, only every fifth or sixth one fighting back the gloom. The grass and dirt were nearly black, the furthest areas under the fence in deep shadow. For a second Carl was fourteen again, sitting next to MaryEllen Hess on the bleachers of the football field. It was night, and the field was dark, the bleachers ticking in the cold air as MaryEllen leaned toward him for a kiss.

"See that long shed?" Carl asked. "It's mostly in shadow now, but I could see it better earlier. It runs the whole back fence. It's shallow and has lots of doors–perfect for storing zombies. Do you see it?"

As if some helpful soul had heard his words, the rest of the lights glared to life.

Carl pulled both women back and down.

"What's going on?" Dill asked, hesitating, but Candy moved instinctively at his touch like a supple and receptive dance partner. She crouched easily, holding her breath.

Carl yanked Dill's hand again until she, too, was down below the line of light.

Voices floated up to them from the field.

"–didn't want to go this route, but with Carl knowing so much...we don't have any *choice* but to escalate!" Aaron's voice, choked with fear and excited self-righteousness. "I mean, I didn't want it to go this way, but what else can we do? We have to! We've been *forced* to!"

Carl shimmied on his stomach to the low wall and rose by degrees to peer over. Below him, less than a hundred feet away, Aaron danced and trotted around a Wrangler, gesturing wildly as he talked. The Wrangler walked easily, big arms swinging, unperturbed by Aaron's babbling. His shaggy head nodded, but Carl couldn't tell if it was with impatience or agreement.

"In the long run, of course, this is the best thing, even though no one will know it but us! Of course, there will be some collateral

198

damage...probably lots of it!...but what else can we do? Right? We *have* to do this!"

The Wrangler said something Carl couldn't catch. Then he turned and fumbled with the latch on a set of wide, double gates. He pushed, grunting, and opened the gates that led to an open area at the side of the building that eventually turned into the parking lot.

Aaron babbled on as the Wrangler proceeded to the sheds.

"Is your partner at the inners? Do you have the time synchronized? It's important that this look like a spontaneous outbreak. We don't want any fingers pointing back here once...once it's all over."

The Wrangler mumbled something else that Carl couldn't hear, but Aaron nodded.

"There will be loss of life...it's important for us to realize and remember that! We have to protect the company above all else, or there won't be *anything* for *anyone*! We have to do it! Because in the long run...in the long run..." He stopped, and his shoulders slumped like a toy winding down. "What I mean to say is–"

"You better get back," the Wrangler said, and this time, Carl heard him clearly. His voice was filled with low sarcasm. "Unless you want to increase your knowledge with a little first-hand research."

Aaron stiffened in surprise or outrage–Carl couldn't tell which– and the Wrangler laughed unkindly. Then he pushed at a lever, and all down the line of the shed, the doors opened.

Zombies poured out in a sluggish tumble.

Aaron turned and pushed past through a gate and ran up a flight of stairs to one of the small towers that lined the field. The Wrangler was right behind him, laughing. Zombies streamed by the gate less than a heartbeat later.

"No! Don't do that!" Carl yelled in horrified surprise, standing, unheedful of the light. He pulled out his gun and trained it on one of the zombies that had disentangled itself from the others and was stumbling ahead of the rest. He fired and missed as the zombie weaved awkwardly. "Dammit," Carl said and aimed again. He didn't have extra clips, they were in the SUV...he had to make the shots count.

A gunshot rang out, and the cement block pillar to Carl's right exploded into chips and chunks of cement. Carl turned away, his hand over his face. Something had hit him, cutting his cheek open in a stinging swipe. As he ducked out of sight, the Wrangler fired again from the tower.

"What's happening?" Dill asked in a harsh whisper, her hand clutching Carl's shoulder. "What are they doing?"

Carl groaned as Candy pulled his hand away from his face. Must be a pretty good-sized cut. The blood rolled hotly down his neck.

"Dill," Carl said. "Get behind that pillar; stay behind it. Shoot everything you see on the field. Go slow and *be accurate*." He gave her a small shove and turned to Candy. "You have a piece?" She nodded. "Go to the next pillar. Stay behind it! A Wrangler is shooting from about fifty feet out–the second tower."

"You want me to take out the Wrangler?" Candy asked.

"No, not yet. Just the zombies. Go!"

"Carl!" Dill said. She had attained her spot at the pillar. Her voice was horrified awe. "The field is *filled* with–"

"Zombies, yeah, fifty, at least," he said and took the spot between Candy and Dill. "Start shooting, Dill."

Candy had already squeezed off three shots. One zombie fell.

"Shoot the ones at the edges and the ones that have separated from the group," Candy said. "There's no sense in shooting at the middle." She took careful aim and fired again. Another zombie fell.

Across the field, more shots rang out. An automatic and Carl would bet that the Wrangler had plenty of ammo with him. Cement chips and dust blew back as bullets tore into the low wall and pillars.

Dill took aim on a womzie straggling away from the others. It was missing a foot and limped badly, listing to the right. Dill squeezed the trigger, and the bolt flew wide. She aimed again and took a breath. This time, the bolt buried itself in the zombie's shoulder, turning it almost completely around. She aimed again and pulled the trigger, and finally, the zombie fell, the bolt having passed almost completely through its head.

Candy fired again, and another zombie fell.

Carl's stomach lifted with hope. They had wanted to wipe out all the zombies at ZI, and now they were getting their chance. It wasn't how he had imagined doing it, but it worked out the same. He shot, and a zombie's head disintegrated.

A bolt appeared in another zombie's eye.

Candy's gun rang out again, and another zombie tumbled. She grinned at Carl in the dark, scared and triumphant.

They were doing it!

They were winning!

Carl's eyes drifted to the gate, and his stomach contracted coldly. Thirty or more zombies had piled up, funneling out. Out. They were getting out.

"Keep shooting! Keep shooting! Shoot near the gate! They're getting away!"

In his peripheral vision, Candy stepped forward and craned her neck to be able to see the gate better. The Wrangler's gun rang out. Candy spun and crumbled to the ground.

Carl half-turned toward her, but Dill yelled. "Carl, no! Keep shooting! Jesus! Keep shooting!" Her bow was shaking, and she fired into the crowd of undead, desperate and screaming. "Keep shooting!"

The Wrangler shot again, and Dill cursed, stepping further behind the pillar. It obstructed her view. Carl glanced at Candy. She was moving, sitting up. He allowed himself the barest second of relief, then turned again and shot into the crowd at the gate.

"Carl, stop!" Aaron's voice drifted over from the tower, horrified and indignant. "What are you *doing*?"

"Fuck you, Aaron!" Carl called, bellowing even as he continued to fire. "You're a fucking maniac!"

"We're going to save the company!" Aaron yelled. His voice was strident, beseeching. "Help us! Help us save ZI! I thought you were my *friend*, Carl!"

Carl stepped out from behind the pillar and fired across to the tower. "Fuck you! You fucking idiot! Fuck–"

Too late, he realized that Aaron had been trying to distract him. The Wrangler raised his gun. Even from this distance, the barrel looked big as a cannon.

"Fuuuuu–" Carl said as fire belched from the end of the Wrangler's gun. He backpedaled and flailed his arms, knowing he was about to die.

He was tackled roughly from the left and landed hard on the parking lot deck, the air pushing from his lungs in one hard huff. His head snapped back into the ground, and he saw stars. He closed his eyes and groaned. Had he been shot?

"You're okay, Carl," Dill said. She was on him, over him. She had pushed him out of the way of the Wrangler's bullet. "Take a breath."

"Keep shooting," he said, struggling to right himself. "Keep shooting, Dill!"

She rolled off him and crouched back. Her eyes in the dark were glittery. "It's too late. They're out," she said. "We didn't have enough–" She shrugged. "We didn't have enough anything."

Carl sat up. "Candy?" he said, remembering the shot, her fall.

She was leaned against the low wall, her hand over her bicep. She smiled at him in the dark. "I was lucky…it's my left arm. I can still shoot."

Carl nodded and found his gun. "We have to get up front and try to contain the rest," he said, standing shakily. He put a hand on the back of his head. His fingers came away black with blood. "Fuck. We have to…we have to alert someone…"

"Who? Who's on our side?" Dill asked. "We don't know who's involved. We don't know who would–" Her voice was harsh but watery, close to tears.

Carl gripped her shoulder and pulled her up. "We'll start with your Wranglers," he said. He reached for Candy's hand but kept his eyes on Dill. "Call them, but tell them to go to the inners."

"The inners?" Dill said. "Why? We need help here."

They were bent low, trotting to the door to the building. Behind them, the Wrangler continued to fire.

"Because they were setting some loose over there, too," Carl said. "We're probably too late, but we can try."

Carl checked the landing through the glass before entering the building. Should they go up or down? Where would they be least expected? *Who* might be expecting them?

Christ.

He wasn't up for this. His head hurt, his face...they should have just gone. They should have just packed up and left. Now it was too damn late to–

Dill slipped her hand into his, and he looked at her. Her eyes were round with fear and swimming with unshed tears. She bit her lip and blinked rapidly. How was it that he'd never seen her cry? He'd seen her close to tears, but she never broke down. A swell of pride and protectiveness made him forget his pain and his fear.

Okay. Okay, he had to figure this out. He squeezed her hand.

"We'll go down to the parking garage. It'll be dark. We can make our way out front from there," he said and squeezed Dill's hand again. He smiled, and her hand relaxed in his. Her eyes lost some of their panic. "Call your Wranglers now, Dill. Tell them to get whoever they can and get to the inners."

She nodded and turned slightly away, her fingers tapping near her ear.

Carl opened the door to the building and scanned the stairs going up and then down. Behind him, Candy seemed to be holding her breath. He cocked his head, listening, but all he heard was the soft sound of Dill's whispering voice.

"Okay. Yes. Yes," she said. "You too. Got it."

She tapped again and then turned back to Carl and Candy. She shrugged and grinned, but the tears continued to shimmer at the edges of her lashes. "They said good luck. They said–" She hitched in a breath and wiped her eyes. "They said they'd try to get back here for us." She shook her head. "I don't think that's gonna happen."

Carl gripped her shoulder. "I don't think so either, Dill." He didn't see any reason to lie to her. There was no point. She wasn't a kid.

"Let's go," he said and started down the stairs. Candy and Dill followed silently behind.

*

The parking garage was as dead and empty as it had been when they drove in twenty minutes earlier. They crossed the dark expanse in tight formation. Dill had a bolt ready, and Candy and Carl both had their guns drawn and up. Nothing could be taken for granted. Not when zombies were part of the equation.

Carl had a fleeting sense of gratitude that they hadn't turned zombies loose in the building. There weren't a lot of people working overnight, but there were enough to...fuck. He'd forgotten about the few zombies in the stock room. Would they be turned loose in the building? They had to get in there, trip the alarm.

Inside or outside? Which first?

There was nothing for it. They'd have to split up.

"Dill," he said as they neared the ZI SUV. "I don't know what happened with the zombies in the stock room up in R&D. I think there might be a chance they've been set free in the building. I'm going to drop you at the front. Get inside, and set the alarm. Get as many people notified as you can; gather them in the cafeteria. Keep them there."

"Where will you be?" she asked. Fear tweaked her voice.

"We're going to the side first. The area where the gate lets out. See how many are there; try to wipe them out. It should be easier as long as they aren't in a group."

Dill shook her head. "Not if they've started biting. Spreading it."

"Everyone is inside and if not, then they're home sleeping. We have a good head start." He gave her a light shove on her shoulder. "Get in the car. Let's go."

Candy had already gotten in, and Dill piled in next to her. Carl circled the car, scanning the garage, and climbed in behind the wheel. Still keeping the lights off, they hummed out of the building, and Carl angled the SUV toward the front of the building. They encountered no zombies. Good, that meant they hadn't gotten very far.

Carl halted at the ZI front doors. He swallowed. "Okay, Dill," he said. "Do what I said. Gather everyone in the caf. Keep them together."

"What about Sales? They have the gates. I could lower those and then–"

"No, that's no good," he said. "If someone on the verge of changing gets in, it would take too long to lift the gate for everyone to get out. It would be a slaughter." He reached across

Candy to take Dill's arm. "Keep yourself near an exit. Keep a good distance. Assess. Okay?"

She nodded. Then she opened the door and trotted to the building. Carl watched after her until she was in. She turned, waved, and disappeared behind the big reception desk.

Carl pulled away as emergency lights began to swirl in the building.

"I'm going to park right before the corner," Carl said. "We can stay in the dark and pick them off. Keep an eye out for Aaron and that Wrangler." He shook his head. "Christ. Keep an eye out for *anyone*."

Candy laughed, and he glanced at her. She had torn the sleeve off her Henley and fashioned it into a bandage on her arm. The blood was already soaking through.

"You okay?" he asked.

She nodded and laughed again. "Not that I have much choice, huh?"

Carl slowed the SUV. The area next to the building was a wide open space for about a hundred yards, and then it darkened into forest. There was enough starlight that he could make out the stumbling, awkward shapes of the undead as they slumped across the field. There were a lot.

Carl put extra clips in his pockets as Candy did the same. Then they exited the SUV.

Carl aimed at a womzie staggering nearer the building and leveled her with one shot. Her head disintegrated. He sighted another, his stomach growing hot with tension. There were so many of them. He and Candy would never be able to get them all. It was too dark, and they were too scattered. He fired again and missed. He breathed out, calming himself, and let another zombie– this one a young man, probably a teen–lurch into his field of vision. He fired, and the zombie dropped. Beside him, Candy fired steadily. Three more zombies fell. Four, five. Half a dozen.

"Jesus Christ," Candy said, and Carl glanced at her. Her face was drawn down in horror, and her gun arm had dropped almost to her side. Carl followed her gaze. Less than thirty feet away, a kidzie–the one Carl had seen in the stock room the day before– seemed to be floating toward them in the dark. He struggled, and his feet waved wildly, at least a foot above the rough grass. His head snapped left and right as if he was trying to bite his own pushed-up shoulders. His arms were out at his sides and waving awkwardly. To Carl's stunned mind, the kid looked as though he were flying.

Carl started to bring his gun back up, trying to clear the confusion from his mind. "What the fuck is–"

The kidzie dropped clumsily to the ground, and the Wrangler–who'd been carrying him as both a shield and cover–leveled his shotgun at Carl.

"Got you dead to rights, Abby," the Wrangler said. Without looking down, he stomped viciously, aiming for the kidzie's head. His teeth glinted from the midst of his deep, furry beard. "Lay down your guns. This other Abby wants you alive so's he can make you dead...but I'll kill ya for good and all, you give me the chance."

"You're killing innocent people," Carl yelled. "What are you doing this for? For the *company*?"

Candy's hand was on his arm.

"Put it down, Carl," she said and bent to lay her own gun on the ground. She looked up at him, and her lips pursed humorously. "Trust me," she said, and her eyes slid by the smallest possible fraction in the direction of the Wrangler.

Carl lowered his gun, too, crouching to do so. He kept his other hand up, palm flat in a show of surrender. He moved very slowly, drawing out each movement. Beside him, Candy held her crouched position. The Wrangler's lips skinned back, and he bared his teeth like an ape as he watched Carl and Candy with all his attention.

"Okay," Carl said, "our guns are down. Take us to Aaron." Calm assurance flowed through him. This was going to work out okay. Candy was an observant lady.

The Wrangler, finally sensing something amiss, took a step closer and growled like a wolf. "What is it you Abbys are up to? What do you think you're–"

The kidzie–whose head had not been damaged at all because the Wrangler had inadvertently stomped only on his face–jumped the Wrangler, sinking his teeth into the Wrangler's burly forearm, right above the leather wristband.

The Wrangler howled and jumped back, shaking the small zombie off and dropping his shotgun in the process. He cursed and kicked out, catching the kidzie in his chest. The kidzie went over backward, nearly flipping with the force of the kick. There was a loud crack as its spine broke.

Carl grabbed his gun and stood in one smooth motion. He shot the kidzie neatly in the back of the head and then turned his gun on the Wrangler. Candy, who'd also gained her feet, continued to shoot at the field of zombies. It was impossible to say how many, if any, had gotten out of range. If any had, they were headed directly to the ZI bedroom community of the outers.

"Shoot me! Abby! Shoot me in the head!" the Wrangler cried. "Hurry! Before it's too late." His face was a tight mask of horror, and he held his arm in his hand. Blood dripped thick and slow from under his fingers. In the moonlight, Carl couldn't see if the blood was turning black yet, crumbling. The Wrangler took one shuffling step toward Carl and then stopped. "Please, Abby. I know you don't owe me. Do it anyway. I don't want to be one of them shufflin' corpses. I don't want that fucktard doing his experiments on me."

"You're right, Floyd," Carl said. "I don't owe you anything." He pulled the trigger, and the Wrangler tensed, head flung back, eyes closed. A zombie fell behind him, and at the soft thud of its mortality, the Wrangler opened one eye. Then both. He stared from the zombie to Carl, incredulity opening his features.

Carl shot again, and this time the Wrangler didn't even flinch, only looked over his shoulder to where another zombie dropped. Then his eyes dropped to his shotgun, four feet away. He cut his eyes to Carl and feinted.

Carl shot the shotgun, spraying hard grass and dirt in a bomb. The Wrangler pulled back with another howl.

"Goddamn you, Abby!" the Wrangler said, voice breaking. "I only want to off myself! Let me do it if you won't!" His words slurred, and the blood from his arm now fell almost in clumps. It was happening; he was going over. He must have felt it within himself. He howled again, but this time it was more like a scream, terrible and wild. Insane. A soul beyond redemption. He tried again for the shotgun, a sob grunting out as he bent over.

Candy shot him. The Wrangler pitched forward and landed face-first in the dirt. The back of his head glistened wetly, opened to the night sky.

"I would have shot him," Carl said. He shot at another zombie and grunted when he missed. "Eventually, I would have."

"Sure, I know," Candy said. She smiled without taking her eyes from her target. She pulled the trigger, and another zombie fell. The field was dotted with the sad mounds of former people. "I was just getting tired of his whining."

Carl laughed. He felt better. It seemed there was a light at the end of this dirty, dead-filled tunnel. He shot another zombie, the last one.

"We're going to have to get in the car and scope out the neighborhood closest to the building," Carl said. "I think some of them might have gotten out of range."

"They did," Aaron said from behind them. Carl jumped and turned to face him. Candy stepped closer to the SUV.

Aaron waved his gun at her. "No, my dear," he said. "Drop your gun and move over next to Carl. Carl...drop your gun. *Drop* it...don't squat. You look like a damn monkey." He waved his gun again. "Let's get going. We'll go back up to three. I know I could probably let you go and let nature take its course...I'm sure the inners have fallen by now, but I can't take the chance. I held one back, just in case."

"Held one back?" Candy said. She glanced from Aaron to Carl.

"A zombie in the stock room," Carl said. "So we can be bit instead of just outright killed. No evidence of a crime that way." He walked next to Candy and didn't bother to look back at Aaron. A black depression rolled over his mind, and he thought it might drop him to his knees. He should do it, or turn and rush Aaron, force him to shoot. It would be a better ending than being turned, but he couldn't leave Candy and Dill. It seemed cowardly. He'd turned out to be not very much of a hero, but a coward? He wasn't that, either.

Carl opened the glass front door for Candy. The ZI logo seemed to mock him as he did so. He'd entered this door so many times. He thought he'd been miserable. He knew better now.

The building was half-lit and deserted looking. *Of course*, Carl thought, *everyone is in the cafeteria.* The alarm droned on and on.

They entered the stairway.

\*

Dill turned and waved to Candy and Carl through the glass front doors. She ducked behind the reception desk, dropped her bow, and mashed the red button that sat prominently at the center of the desktop. The alarm started, blaring its klaxon cry, and red lights mounted in the ceiling began to spin. From up the hall came the sound of running feet. Dill peered through the front door, but the SUV was gone.

A twinge of anger caused her to plant her hands on her hips. It wasn't fair that she'd been shooed away like a bothersome kid so Carl could be alone with Candy. In fact, it was really irritating. It seemed obvious that nothing was going on in here. She should follow the SUV. Help them take out the zombies. She took one hesitant step and then checked herself.

*Assess*, she thought. *Assess first.*

*And pick up your damn bow.*

She trotted toward the cafeteria, listening, checking each door. The alarm horn bleated every five seconds. In between each bleat, voices were filtering to her down the hall as workers from all the departments gathered.

"Cafeteria, get in the cafeteria!" Dill called.

A young man popped out of a maintenance closet and goggled at her.

She waved him forward with her bow. "Caf, now."

He looked her up and down. "You're Assessment?" His tone said that he doubted it.

"Move it, jackass," she said. It convinced him. He trotted ahead of her, glancing back uneasily.

"What's going on? Is this a drill?"

They picked up two more maintenance people as they went along.

"It's not a drill," Dill said, "there might be zombies loose in here."

"Like yesterday?" a woman asked, and Dill shook her head.

"No," Dill said. They were at the cafeteria, and she could see a sizable crowd had already gathered. "Not like yesterday. Not at all." She motioned the maintenance people in. The workers in the caf huddled in small groups, talking. They looked worried but not panicked, so they hadn't seen a zombie in the building.

"Everyone!" Dill called into the cafeteria, and they turned to her. She swallowed. "Everyone just...stay in here. Okay?"

A few people shrugged. Others rolled their eyes. A few chairs scraped along the floor as some the workers began to settle in. An older man in a maintenance jumpsuit stepped forward.

"What's going on? Is this a drill?" His voice was belligerent and demanding. "Who are you?" A lot of eyes moved from him to her, and Dill got a feeling of being weighed, tested.

"It's not a drill, so stay in there. Stay ready," she said. It hadn't come out as forceful-sounding as she'd hoped. She swallowed again. "My name's Dill. I'm...I'm from Assessment. I *am* Assessment."

The man squinted at her. "*You're* Assessment?"

Dill nodded, and to her chagrin, she swallowed again.

A voice from the back spoke up. "She's Maintenance. I've worked with her."

"I was...but I'm Assessment *now*," Dill said. She couldn't seem to help a defensive squeak on 'now'. At least she hadn't stomped her foot.

The man turned away. "Listen up," he called across the room, "we should get out of here, get back to work. We're going to get docked if we're caught goofing around in the cafeteria." He glanced back at Dill with an expression of disgust, and then addressed the crowd again. "Everyone go back to your departments. Stay calm. I'll–"

"No!" Dill said. "Stay here. It's safer!"

He rounded on her, arms thrown wide, shoulders up. "Are you kidding me? Safe from *what*? They had a problem earlier, and the *Wranglers* took care of it. There's *no more danger*." He shook his head dismissively. "Everyone do as I said. Go to your departments and get back to work. We already have a short shift because of earlier. We can't afford to waste more time with this."

A murmur started as people discussed their options. Then they began by ones and twos to move toward the cafeteria door.

"Stop!" Dill said. The crowd hesitated, and then began to move forward again. Dill ignored her instinct to back up and strode quickly forward until she was in the cafeteria with them. She pitched her voice low and caught the eyes of the people closest to the door. "Stop. Stay where you are. I don't know what's going on yet, if anything." She glanced at the older man who'd turned, hands on hips, to sneer at her. She looked at the workers again. "Are your jobs worth your lives?"

They hesitated, and then more people began to take seats.

The man snorted with derision. "Okay, stay here. Enjoy your *break*, but don't think I'm not going to write down every one of your names." He strode past Dill without looking at her and out into the hall. "Just wait until I get a hold of HR and tell them—"

A form smashed into him, knocking him out of view.

Behind Dill, the cafeteria erupted into gasps and screams as people pushed their way to the back. Chairs clattered to the floor, and a table overturned.

Dill stepped into the hall, bow up and ready, adrenaline coursing through her system like cold fire. A woman was on the maintenance man, struggling and moaning. Dill sighted the back of her head, and her finger tightened on the trigger…then paused.

Dill assessed.

The woman was not bloody, not sluggish. She wore a clean Maintenance uniform. The moans were human. The woman was human. Not a zombie. Just terrified.

"Get up," Dill said, bow still trained on the woman, just in case. "Let me see you."

The woman extricated herself from the man, struggled to her feet, and turned to Dill. She was panting. "He let them out!" she screamed. Her eyes were round with shock, and her skin was pale, almost translucent. Tears flowed unchecked down her cheeks. "I saw it! He did it on purpose!"

Behind her, the maintenance man scrambled away, hastily wiping his cheeks. Too bad he couldn't wipe away the wet spot on the front of his coverall.

"Where?" Dill asked. The only relevant question she could think of.

"On…th-th-three! I was emptying trash, and I saw…I saw…" Her teeth chattered, and she crossed her arms over her bosom. "The man in charge of the stock room…he was turning them all loose in the hall. He pr-pr-propped open the front stairwell d-d-door. It was the man in charge up there…Aaron. He was letting them out."

Dill motioned the woman into the cafeteria. She wanted the others to hear what she had to say. It was better for everyone to know everything. "Come in here. Sit down. Tell them what you just told me."

The woman dragged out a chair and began to re-tell her story. Dill turned to the Maintenance man, who sat with his back to the wall, eyes on her. She stared at him, waiting.

He swallowed. "Can I come back in there?"

A small, mean-spirited part of her wanted to shake her head no, but she couldn't; she just wasn't that cruel.

She motioned him in and closed the doors.

The workers watched the woman with caution as she related her story, and then they burst into surprised–and angry–conversation.

"Everyone," Dill called, "listen to me! We don't have time to talk this over. I need you to do what I say."

They watched her carefully. Some nodded. A few pairs of eyes shifted to the Maintenance man, who sat at a table by himself, his head in his arms.

"Who has a weapon?" Dill asked. It was not common for anyone outside of Assessment, Sales, Wranglers and Cleaners to carry weapons. There was no written policy against it, but neither was it encouraged by ZI management–they preferred to tout the 'safe' working environment. At least, until recently.

To Dill's relief, five people raised their hands: four in Maintenance coveralls and one in the blue khakis and white button down of clerical.

Dill waved them forward. "What do you have?" she asked. Two of the Maintenance people–one man, one woman–each pulled out small handguns. Another pulled a large knife out of his boot, and the fourth surprised Dill with a small hatchet that had been suspended somehow under his uniform. She blinked at him, and he grinned like a snake. The fifth person, the clerk, had yet to show his weapon.

Dill turned to him. "What do you have?"

He ran a hand through his neat black hair, mussing it. He smiled nervously and reached into his pocket. He brought forth a Swiss Army knife, no more than four inches long. Dill switched her gaze from the knife to his eyes. He was still smiling.

"Are you *sure*?" Dill asked.

His smile widened. He nodded.

"Okay, listen up," Dill said. "We're going to split into two groups, each with a gun. You and you with me," she said and indicated the clerk and one of the gun holders. "We'll take the front stairwell. You three take the back." She turned back to the caf. "I need some volunteers to bar the doors once we've gone through." A handful of people stepped forward, and Dill nodded. "Okay. Half of you with them, and half with us. Let's go."

They entered the stairwell with caution, listening. The zombies could have gotten onto other floors if they'd stumbled into the doors hard enough to release the press bars. Or they could all still be huddled at the third-floor landing.

Dill looked back through the wired glass window of the door. Two volunteers were seated, their backs pressed against it. Dill butted the door with her hip and shoulder, setting her weight against the bar. It shook but didn't open. One of the volunteers glanced up at her through the glass, and she gave him a thumbs-up.

"Okay, listen," Dill said as she turned to the men in the stairwell with her. "Stay to the right of the staircase, tight to the wall. I'll go first, and Gun, you're second. Swiss, you've got drag. Ready?"

The clerk blinked rapidly, then nodded.

Gun shrugged. "My name is Mark, but okay. I'm ready."

"Sorry. Mark," Dill said. She was anxious to begin, but controlled her impatience. She would need them to know who she was addressing if anything got out of hand. She looked to the clerk. "And you're…?"

"Ben, so, yeah. But you can call me Swiss." He swallowed. "I never had a nickname."

"You can call me Gun, then," Mark said. "That's cool."

Dill smiled. "We'll check the entire stairwell first and then sweep the floors."

She turned and pressed herself to the right-hand side of the painted cinderblock wall and began to ascend. She went silently, bow up and ready, and was gratified that her companions were just as quiet. The clerk looked younger than her, and she wondered if he had experience with zombies. The maintenance guy looked at least thirty-five. Probably why he carried a gun.

They reached the second-floor stairwell. Dill motioned for Gun to keep eyes up as she glanced through the glass of the door—Assessment's area. It was big and open, filled with row after row of large office cubicles. Like a maze. She saw no movement. Should they stick with the plan or go ahead and scan this floor before they continued up?

"Do you see any zombies?" Swiss asked in a whisper. His voice was shaky, nervous. "How many are there, anyway? Just like, two? Or, like...more than that?"

With a flash of angry regret, she wished she'd asked the hysterical maintenance lady how many zombies she had seen Aaron release. Dammit. That was stupid, stupid. This plan had seemed so simple...but what else had she missed?

"I don't know," she answered and shook her head, "I didn't ask." She expected him to become even more nervous when he realized just how inexperienced she was. To her surprise, he reached out to pat her shoulder.

"That's okay," he said, "I didn't think of it, either, and I'm really smart."

"Guys? Are we going up, or what?" Gun asked without taking his eyes from the stairwell.

"Up," Dill said, deciding. "We'll clear the stairwell first and then check the floors."

They started up again with Dill back in the lead. Cool air brushed across her face, and she remembered that the door on three had been propped open. Maybe the zombies had wandered back in there after finding the stairwell empty.

*No. They don't think about things like that. They don't reason, Dill*, she told herself. They reached the landing. No zombies. She glanced cautiously into R&D, barely peeking around the corner. The waiting area was empty, unchanged. The doors off the long hallway were all closed. A plaque was wedged at the bottom of the door, and she kicked it away. It spun and landed face up, showing a man at the apex of a mountain, the sun coming up behind him (or going down), and his hands raised over his head and clasped together. Below him was the word:

S•U•C•C•E•S•S

She hoped so.

"Okay, let's get up to four and–"

"How do we know they won't sneak up behind us?" Swiss asked.

Dill started up the stairs. "They can't open those doors from the building side. It's too complicated. Once they left the stairwell, they wouldn't be able to get back in."

The landing at four was clear, as was five. No zombies in the stairwell.

"Okay, we'll sweep this floor and then head back down to four," Dill said. The fifth floor was Medical, Archives, and Marketing. There shouldn't be anyone overnight save one emergency nurse. An emergency doctor was on call. Dill felt another rush of impatience with herself: she hadn't bothered to check if the nurse had made it to the caf at the sound of the alarm. Dammit.

"Think a second...did either of you notice if there was a night nurse in the cafeteria?" she asked.

Gun shook his head, but Swiss seemed to take her question seriously. He dropped his head, put his hand over his eyes, and stood that way without speaking.

"Swiss? Are you okay?" she asked, not sure if he was thinking or crumbling.

He ignored her, and she shifted uncomfortably. Then his head shot up.

"Yes! I did see the nurse!" He grinned and rummaged again through his hair. The knife hung at his side, loose in his hand, the little blade looking like a child's plaything. "She was all the way in the back and had a coffee in her hand. She must have already been in the caf when the alarm went."

"Okay, great," Dill said. "She should have been the only one up here. Let's go look. Ready?"

Gun nodded, and Swiss smiled, but Dill's own words echoed strangely to her. Something was telling her the zombies wouldn't be up here. Left to their own devices, they'd have stumbled *down*...the path of least resistance...and at the end of the stairs they stumbled down, going faster and faster–the door to the second floor.

She had to be methodical. Would Carl tell her to be methodical or tell her to follow her instinct? She shook her head in aggravation. She couldn't know.

She pushed back against the bar and peered cautiously through the small crack onto a waiting area and a little window where the medical receptionist would normally sit, taking names of patients as they came in with minor complaints. The receptionist was replaced at night by a small bell. Dill pushed all the way in and reached across to ding the bell, listening to the echo of it disappear down the hall. Something seemed off, and then she realized the alarm's siren had stopped. Someone downstairs must have silenced it, but the red lights still twirled, bathing everything in a nightmarish pink.

"Swiss, block the stairwell door. Just in case," Dill said, keeping her eyes on the hallway. "I know this floor; I used to do the maintenance up here. There's a main hallway that runs to the back, makes one sharp turn, bends again, and comes back around here. There are small offices off the first leg of the hallway. Archives is at the back, and that's one big room with tall shelves. Marketing is on the other side off the return hallway...it's basically a bunch of cubbies over there. I'll go first. I'm going to open each door and scan, then lock it from the inside. Ready?"

They proceeded down the hallway, Dill checking each small room and then locking the doors as they went. The end of the hallway opened into a big area lined with floor-to-ceiling shelves. Archives. They trotted quickly past the rows of files and books and outdated computer storage systems. The silence was working on her, making her anxious. They had to find the missing zombies, and she felt she was wasting too much time.

They made a left, and now they were heading back toward the stairs. On their right, big cubicles were laid out along the windows. Empty. All empty.

The thought of the second floor began to glow in Dill's mind like a banked coal. It had to be where they were. It had to.

They turned again and were back at the reception area for medical. Dill had an unreasonable urge to tap the little nurse's bell again, but restrained herself.

"Okay, now we'll do four," Dill said and opened the stairwell door. "Then run through three and then—"

"I feel like..." Swiss said and then hesitated. He looked from Dill to Gun and back to Dill. "I think we might want to go right to two."

"Why's that?" Dill asked.

Swiss shrugged and shuffled his feet. "I just think...I just *feel* like..."

"Like they're on two? Is that what you were thinking?" Dill asked, and Swiss nodded again. He opened his mouth as if to explain or justify, but Dill stopped him with a quick wave of her hand.

"I had the same feeling," she said, and Swiss smiled. Dill smiled back, feeling suddenly a little shy.

"Can we decide and then get going?" Gun asked. "I don't want to stand here all day listening to you two flirt. Badly."

Dill glanced at Gun and then back to Swiss. His face was red with embarrassed heat, but he met her eyes with his and didn't waver.

"Okay," she said, "we'll go right to two."

She turned and headed slowly down the stairs, bow up and ready. She thought she'd feel good once the decision was made— more sure of herself—but as they bypassed four and then three, another twinge of uneasiness undermined her confidence. She thought she caught a whiff of Candy's perfume, but that was impossible. She did her best to squelch her unease and concentrate on two.

It was her own floor, Assessment's area, but she didn't know it very well, not as well as she knew the other floors from years of maintenance work. Each of the associate's cubicles was big and roomy with four-foot walls...and they were generally messy. Piles of equipment and unfinished projects littered the desks and floors. In the gloom, with the red alarm lights still rotating, it was a confusion of shapes and shadowed colors. Anything could have been anything–and she couldn't turn the rest of the lights on. The systems were all controlled according to the shift times.

She waved Gun and Swiss past her into the deep hallway that ran past the cubicles. Along the hall at their backs were several doors that led to bathrooms, a kitchenette, and storage closets. Dill scanned the room, listening.

A low moan issued from the vicinity of the first cubicle. Beside her, Swiss jumped and swallowed so hard that Dill had an urge to clear her throat. She elbowed him and nodded to the knife, which he seemed to have forgotten he carried. He gripped it tighter, brought it up, and looked at it with disbelief. Gun shook his head.

"He better get behind both of us," Gun said, whispering. "That's not much protection."

Dill nodded and moved toward the moan. Her hand shook lightly, and she took a deep breath. Gun's presence at her elbow was a comfort.

She motioned them to both crouch down as they approached the cubby, and then motioned for them to stay low as she rose to look over the wall. It took her eyes two heartbeats to make out what she was seeing: a zombie–a young woman, maybe just a girl–had impaled itself on a serrated saw blade attached to a pole. An overturned chair at the zombie's feet told the story of the zombie stumbling and falling hard, straight onto the saw, piercing her thin chest and skewering her like a hunk of meat on a shish kabob fork. She struggled and moaned, then sunk over, silent. In the old days, that saw would have been used to trim high branches from a tree. In these days, an Assessment member was in the process of modifying it to work as a long-distance weapon.

Dill hoped she got the chance to tell him or her that it worked.

The zombie took two steps more, raising her arms for leverage, and more of the saw blade appeared from her back, covered in black gore. Black crumbles fell in clumps and pattered down to the ground. The zombie moaned again and took another step. Then hunched over, as if resting.

Dill waved for the other two to rise and look over the wall. Gun grunted, but Swiss gasped out a small squeak, then looked at Gun and Dill apologetically.

"I've never...never really seen one..." He swallowed again and then continued to whisper, "Never seen one so up close." The back of his hand rose to cover his nose and mouth, and he grimaced. "The smell is..."

"Breathe through your mouth," Gun said. "*Don't* throw up." He turned to Dill. "Do you want me to shoot it?"

"No," Dill said, "too loud." She glanced up the hall and then back the way they'd come in. "Keep a good lookout. At least now we know they're on this floor, and they could be anywhere."

"Well," Swiss said, "we know at least *one* is on this floor." Reasoning seemed to soothe him, and he took his hand away from his mouth. "We can't necessarily extrapolate another from just this one."

"Okay, right," Dill said, "but you sure as hell can't discount it, either. Now keep a lookout. They can...they can sneak up on you."

Swiss' eyes darkened with concern, and Dill cursed the hitch in her voice. She turned abruptly and entered the cubby. She went as silently as possible, but the zombie heard her and tried to turn. Its moans became caws of desperately hungry excitement. It twisted and turned on the saw, swinging its stick-thin arms and impaling itself further.

Dill put the bow to the zombie's temple and pulled the trigger even as her mind registered the small barrette that hung from a clump of the zombie's dirty hair. The barrette was in the shape of a butterfly.

As the bolt entered her head, the zombie slumped over, finally lifeless, and another two inches of saw blade appeared. Dill watched the zombie for three seconds, then reached down and retrieved the bolt from the side of the desk, where it had embedded itself after it went all the way through the zombie's head. Dill was careful to avoid the thing's mouth.

Gun stared back the way they'd come, head cocked and chin up. He'd seen it all before, his posture said. He didn't need to see it again, but Swiss was facing Dill.

"Gross," he said. His eyes were trained on the hanging zombie with sickly fascination. "Geez, that was...that was–"

He screamed and stumbled back, slamming into the far wall. He screamed again and kicked out, and the motion dropped him from Dill's sight as he slid down the wall.

Gun turned, his face registering surprise. He looked down, and his mouth dropped open. He raised the gun.

Dill vaulted the cubby wall and nearly landed on top of what had startled Swiss–a zombie, a menzie–was dragging itself down the hallway. Its legs were gone below the knee, and the remains of a crude prosthesis hung from the right. It huffed and moaned, then snapped at Dill's legs as she corrected her trajectory and then scrambled back.

She shook her head at Gun's gun and brought the bow up instead, slotting the bolt with shaking fingers. She'd almost jumped right on it! She'd almost done that! So stupid!

She fired, and this time, the bolt entered the zombie's eye. Its head dropped and rocked on the bolt before falling to the side.

Swiss let out a long, whistling breath. He tried to smile up at Dill and Gun, but the smile was more of a grimace. He ran a spasming hand over his head. "Geez, that was close," he said. "That was really...guys? Dill?"

Dill looked him over and beside her she could feel the tense readiness of Gun's body. He brought the gun up and trained it on Swiss a split second after Dill brought her bow up. Without taking her eyes off Swiss, she slotted another bolt.

"What are you doing? Guys?" Swiss' voice was choked with sudden tears. He pushed himself further back against the wall and then tried to gain his feet. "Guys?"

"Were you bit?" Dill asked. She kept her voice even and neutral. She also kept her finger on the bow trigger. "Swiss...listen to me: were you bit? Did it bite you?"

"No! No, it just...it grabbed at me," he said. "It just...it scared me! That's why I jumped back! Its hand was on my ankle, and...there was this pain in my ankle, and..." Swiss bent over his knees to roll up his pant leg.

Dill's heart fell at the sight of his shoes; they were casual dress loafers with no ankle protection whatsoever. He wore no socks.

He rolled his pant leg further.

His ankle was just starting to bleed.

He looked at Dill with eyes impossibly wide. His face was white and ill looking. His lips were purple.

"What happened?" he asked. His voice was faint and breathless.

"You've been bit," Dill said. She squatted next to him. "You've...the zombie bit your leg."

"It did?" Swiss asked. His eyes were wide and starey. He seemed to have trouble focusing. "Am I–"

She answered by nodding. "I'm sorry," she said, and it was a whisper. She held his gaze.

He nodded back and swallowed hard. He dug in his pocket and held his hand out, fingers curled over something. Dill put her hand under his, and he dropped the small Swiss Army knife into her open palm.

"Thanks," she said, "I'll hold onto it for you, okay?"

He nodded again and then grimaced at some deep internal pain. He gasped, and his body jerked, and a deep confusion filled his eyes. He looked from Dill to Gun and back to Dill, uncomprehending.

"Close your eyes, Swiss," Gun said, and Swiss' tortured eyes went to him.

"But, why?" Swiss asked, and Gun shook his head.

"No reason, Swiss. Just do it, okay?"

A thin, blue film swam into Swiss' eyes just before he closed them. He leaned his head back against the wall. He swallowed again.

Gun raised his eyebrows at Dill and shrugged. Should he, or would she?

Dill sighed, thinking of her dad, thinking of Carl.

She shook her head, wiped the tears from her cheeks as she stood, and shot.

*

They ran quickly through the rest of the second floor. Another zombie had wedged itself in the door to the bathroom, and another surprised them as they entered the kitchenette. Dill killed both with her bow, saving Gun's ammunition. He'd also picked up a bayonet from one of the Assessment cubicles, and he had that tucked into his belt.

Dill controlled the numbness that wanted to deaden her legs and sit her down to cry. Later she would cry. Maybe. For now, she had work to do. She hoped Carl was okay, and she hoped the Wranglers were able to put a stop to whatever was going on at the inners. She didn't have any friends there, but still...she knew people. That was enough to want to hope.

She couldn't even begin to imagine there would be a second epidemic. There was just no way. No way. After twenty-five years, they were still only barely recovered from the first.

"Do you think that's it?" Gun asked. They were back where they'd started out, near the stairwell. Dill worked hard not to look at the slumped form of Swiss sitting lonely in the darkened hall. She shook her head.

"No, I think there's more. At least *one* more, anyway." She hadn't seen Denny outside when the bulk of the zombies had been turned loose. Was it possible that she had just missed him in the dark and confusion? Yeah, but not really that likely, or at least she didn't think it likely.

If she hadn't, then he was in the building somewhere.

"We'll head back up and run through three," Dill said.

"What about...you know...Swiss?" Gun said. He shrugged. "What do we...?"

"Leave him," Dill said. She was both shocked and comforted by the calm, hard tone of her voice. "We can't do anything for him. We already did the best thing we could." She turned and entered the stairwell without glancing at Swiss again.

Time to find Denny.

# FOURTEEN

**-TERMINATION-**
Zombie, Inc., (hereafter known as ZI) values its employees and prides itself on having the best working environment in the Five-State region. Part of that successful atmosphere is in the adherence to the guidelines set down in this Employee Handbook.

READ YOUR HANDBOOK CAREFULLY AND MEMORIZE THE INFRACTIONS THAT COULD RESULT IN TERMINATION.

ZI reserves the right to terminate ANY employee, at ANY time, without warning, for ANY reason deemed acceptable to ZI HR. Please be aware that the United Five-States is a 'Work at Will' jurisdiction, and ZI will not be held liable under any circumstances for employee termination.

—   —   —

"Hurry up," Aaron said in a harsh whisper. He planted his hand in Carl's back and pushed him through the door to the third floor. Just before he pulled the door closed, two voices floated down, a man and then a woman:

*"Can we decide and then get going? I don't want to stand here all day listening to you two flirt. Badly."*

*"Okay...we'll go right to two."*

Dill, Carl realized. Why was she up there and not in the cafeteria? What was she doing?

"We'll go right to the stock room; get this over with," Aaron said and patted Carl's back. The gesture was one of sympathy and impatience. Carl's skin crawled.

"You're a shitty bowler, Aaron," Carl said and behind him, Aaron laughed. He'd dropped back to about ten feet behind them as they turned into one of the ancillary hallways. Candy pressed the back of her hand briefly to Carl's...the movement was subtle, and from Aaron's perspective, it could have looked like an accident. Carl tensed, trying to anticipate whatever she was about to do.

"I know! It really wasn't my sport at all," Aaron said and laughed again as he waved the gun for emphasis. "I'm more of a chess player, I guess. I can see ahead, see what people are going to do. It's a mark of genius, really. It's good to be able to stay one step—"

Candy lunged sideways into a doorway on her left and disappeared as the door swung shut behind her. Carl stood, gape mouthed and shocked. Aaron looked equally shocked.

"Hey, you can't...dammit!" Aaron said, his voice breaking. He turned angry, exasperated eyes on Carl and raised his hands in disgust, the gun pointed up and away. "Why did she—"

Carl saw his chance and grabbed for the doorknob. His heart hammered as he turned and spun into the room, and it seemed to take forever. He pulled the door closed a split second before Aaron shot. Carl ducked while keeping both hands on the doorknob. A hole appeared where his head had been just a breath before. His fingers fumbled over the doorknob, and he pushed the lock.

"Carl? I'm sorry, I didn't mean to shoot. I was just startled," Aaron said. "Are you okay?"

A hand stole across Carl's mouth, and he jumped and almost yelled. Then Candy whispered in his ear, "Shhh..."

He was just able to make her out as his eyes adjusted to the low emergency lighting. Her eyes glittered, and she smiled. She cupped her hand around his ear. "I'm glad you decided to join me, finally." Her breath tickled.

He shook his head at her but smiled and shrugged. He'd been slow on the uptake.

"Listen," Aaron said, "come out now, and I promise that I'll shoot you right after you get infected. I won't let you stay that way, Carl. We'll have plenty of zombies after tonight...one less won't matter. I'll just tell them I had no choice but to kill you. Besides, where are you going to go? That's an exam room...there's no exit. Carl? Are you listening?"

Aaron sighed loudly, exasperated.

"There's no way out of that room, Carl. You're stuck. I could shoot out the lock, you know." He sounded unsure of his last statement. Carl had never heard Aaron profess any kind of affinity to guns. "If you want, I'll make sure Candy gets...you know...put down pretty quickly, too. In deference to your feelings for her."

"Gee, thanks, buddy," Carl said. He tried to keep the sarcasm out of his voice, but he must not have done a very good job. Candy shook her head at him.

Aaron sighed, and the door groaned as he leaned against it. "Come on, Carl. I know you must be able to understand my position. You *must* realize that what I'm offering you is a pretty good deal." The door rattled again as Aaron shifted. "Look at it this way: we're all on borrowed time. The fact that we survived the first outbreak...we were very lucky; luckier than most. You got an extra twenty-five years, Carl! Now it's time to–"

Carl tensed at Aaron's sudden silence. What was happening? Carl stood and put his hand on the knob. He gripped it tightly, considering. He glanced at Candy, and she nodded.

"Time to what, Aaron?" Carl asked. He kept his voice low, barely above a whisper. He imagined Aaron's head mere inches away from his own, only the door between them. He twisted the doorknob slowly and caught the lock button as it popped out, silencing it. "Aaron? Buddy? Listen...I want to tell you something–"

He slammed the door open with all his might, intending to smash it into Aaron's skull, but instead, the door flung all the way back against the wall and rebounded with a hollow bang.

The hallway was empty.

*

Dill opened the door to three and found herself face to face with the barrel of a gun.

"I heard you coming and thought I'd better greet you myself. You're just in time," Aaron said and waved her through into the hallway. He waved Gun through, too. "Drop the bow. Drop the bayonet. Leave them right on the floor and move it." He motioned them to walk ahead of him. "Stop," he said at a second hallway. "Carl? Your trainee came looking for you. Why don't you come out before I shoot her?"

Silence. Dill glanced back at Aaron. His face was impassive. He didn't meet her gaze.

"Aaron?" she said. "Why are you—"

"Shut up," he said. "Carl! You and Candy come out, or I'll shoot her. I won't make it fatal, just painful."

Silence.

Aaron sighed, and it was a harsh, exasperated sound. He shot. The bullet ripped past Dill and Gun and buried itself in the floor about fifteen feet past them. The sound was immense in the tight space, and Dill's eardrums rang in reaction. She looked back at Aaron, shocked. He was half bent over, hands over his ears, grimacing. The gun rested almost against his head.

"What the *hell*?" she said and stepped toward him.

"I'm sorry! I pulled the trigger by mistake! It was just that…" The shock drained from his face as he stood and rolled his shoulders. His features hardened as he waved the gun at her. "Stay there, Dill. Next time won't be an accident."

Anger stirred in her stomach, tightening her muscles, and she stepped toward Aaron again. His eyes widened, and his hand shook. He took a half a shuffle-step back. Then Gun put a restraining hand on Dill's arm.

"You bastard," Dill said. Now Gun's hand gripped her bicep, almost painfully tight. "What are *you* getting for betraying everyone? Huh? What's your gain? Carl was your friend, Aaron. Doesn't that mean *anything*?"

Aaron shook his head. "You don't understand. You don't know what it was like before. You don't know what a horrible feeling it is to have to fight for a job, a decent wage. You never had to see your company fail."

"Your *company*?" Dill's voice was ripe with incredulity. "A company is the *people* that make it up…it's the people who *work* here who are the company, Aaron!"

His face suffused with blood, and his brows drew together. Gun's hand slipped off Dill's arm, and he stepped back, distancing himself from her. It left a cold spot on her bicep.

"You're a real smart mouth, Dill. Now I see why Carl wanted to get rid of you." The smug satisfaction tempered with anger made his words all the more peevish. He raised the gun and trained it on Dill's head. "One more dead employee won't make too much of a difference once everything calms back down."

"I never said I wanted to get rid of her," Carl said, stepping from a doorway halfway down the hall. "She's a good trainee." He glanced at Dill sourly. "Even if she has trouble following instructions."

"Where's Candy?" Aaron said. His eyes went to Carl, but the gun stayed on Dill.

Carl motioned behind him, and Candy stepped into the hallway, too. She smiled at Dill and then looked Gun up and down. "Who's your friend, Dill? He's certainly handsome."

"Save it," Aaron said. "Jesus, Candy. You're so…such a…"

She turned her eyes to Aaron and smiled again. It was a slow smile, confiding and confident, as though she and Aaron alone were privy to some deep secret. Her eyes held his, and he stared, mesmerized, his mouth hanging slightly open. The gun in his hand lowered by a few degrees.

Gun stepped into Dill, bunting her aside as he drew his own gun from its hiding place in his waistband. He fumbled it for a split second and then held it steady. Aaron let his own gun rest at his side.

Carl began to smile, and Dill let out a long sigh of relief.

"Good work!" Candy said. "I thought I saw a gun in your pants, and I knew if I distracted Aaron enough that you could…Aaron, you better drop your gun or–"

Aaron smiled. Then he laughed. Gun turned away from him and aimed at Carl and Candy, who stood shoulder to shoulder, still as statues.

"This is Mark," Aaron said and nodded once at Gun. "When you didn't come back from the cafeteria, I thought you'd gotten bit, Mark." Then Aaron sneered at Dill. "*Gun! Pssh*...what kind of stupid nickname is *that*?"

Dill's face grew hot, but she shrugged. "He had the gun," she said, "it seemed appropriate."

Carl snorted.

"Okay, enough bullshitting around," Aaron said. He waved Dill toward Carl and Candy. "Let's get to the stock room and get this over with."

Carl bumped Dill's shoulder with his own as they walked. "Did you do *anything* I told you to do?"

She glanced sideways at him, fear dissipating in her sudden annoyance. "Yeah, geez. I did exactly what you said to do, Carl. I rounded everyone up and got them into the cafeteria!"

"Shut up," Aaron said from behind them. He sounded more bored than irritated.

Carl stared ahead. Then he bumped her shoulder again. "I told *you* to stay in there, too, remember *that* part?"

She shrugged and crossed her arms tight across her chest. "What*ever*," she said. "I was trying to–"

"Jesus, will you two *please* shut up?" Aaron said. "Here we are, anyway. Turn in."

*

Carl pushed through the door and held it for Candy and Dill. He had an impulse to pull the door shut behind them, even though this door didn't have a lock. A quick glance at Mark made him reconsider...Mark was watching him with sharp concentration. He wasn't nearly as casual with his gun as Aaron.

"About halfway back, you'll see the one I saved," Aaron said. "Let's get this over with."

Carl had an odd premonition of who they were about to see in the tube. He was right; he didn't even need to hear Dill's gasp to know he was right. It was Denny.

"Sit down right there, hands behind you," Aaron said. "Mark, zip tie their hands together...but not too tight. Remember, these have to look like spontaneous attacks."

"Aaron, let me tell you something," Carl said, sitting as instructed. "There won't be anyone to investigate. You're killing the world with what you've done."

Aaron shrugged. "Then you shouldn't mind what's about to happen, since you're so defeatist." Carl thought he saw a flash of unease in Aaron's eyes.

"*Everyone* is going to change, Aaron. Change or die. There aren't that many people in the Five-State to begin with, and there's a lot of them right here in the ZI compound, and you've just doomed them all. Including yourself," Carl said. "Think about it, buddy. Think about what you're doing."

Mark zipped their hands even as Carl spoke, then moved on to their ankles. Carl wanted to kick the kid in the face, but even inept, Aaron still held the gun on them. If Carl wasn't struck, Candy or Dill might be.

"He can't think about it," Candy said. "He's more concerned about his bonus...isn't that right, Aaron? You were promised something, weren't you?"

Aaron smiled bashfully. "Well...nothing has been *officially* promised, but I do anticipate a tidy little reward. I was thinking about using it to put in a pool. That would be nice, wouldn't it?"

"Who promised it?" Carl asked. He shook his head, dazed. Who was in charge around here, anyway? Why had he never stopped to wonder?

"Management," Candy said, her voice tight and cynical. "The government. One and the same, isn't that right, Aaron? That would be my guess."

Aaron shrugged, and his mouth tightened into a moue. "What does it matter?" he said and then quickly, "Yes. They're one and the same. The government doesn't exist without ZI, and ZI doesn't exist without the government, and none of us exist without the zombies." He put his hands on his hips, again forgetting the gun. "It's as simple as that."

"Buddy," Carl said, "you're completely crazy."

"You only say that because you're on the wrong side of the gun...*buddy*," Aaron said and brought the gun back up. "Mark, do Candy first. I'm tired of her mouth. Put her shoulder up to the pass-through. This one will know what to do." He patted the tube and smiled fondly at zombie Denny, like an indulgent parent.

Mark lifted Candy by her armpits, and she struggled, whipping her body, trying to catch him with her hips, but Aaron stepped forward and grabbed her arm.

"Flip down that little panel, Mark," Aaron said. His breath began to come in thin sips of excitement. Mark reached across Candy's struggling body and opened a little four inch by four inch hinged door in the Plexiglas tube. Aaron and Mark pushed Candy forward. She screamed and threw her head back. She tried to kick out, but she was too close to the tube. Denny moaned and reached for her, his fingers crashing into the plexi. Three of his fingers bent back and broke. Candy screamed again.

Carl rolled onto his side and kicked at Mark's legs, but he was too far away. "Don't do it, Aaron!" he yelled. "I'll fucking kill you! I'll fucking–"

Beside him, Dill reached for her ankles and cut the zip tie in one quick motion. She jumped up and slammed head-first into Mark's lower back, sending him crashing into the tube. His head connected with the thick plastic. He let go of Candy as he oofed and tumbled to the ground, Dill rolling off him and away.

Candy twisted sharply and dropped all her weight, breaking Aaron's grip. Aaron yelled in surprise and brought the gun up. He shot.

The side of the tube exploded into thick shrapnel that sprayed across the room. Candy curled up, covering her head with her arms, and kicked out, catching Aaron in the shins. He yelled again and tumbled forward. The gun discharged as he fell, and half the tube disintegrated.

Denny slumped out, tripping over the low lip that was all that remained. He was peppered in the sharp shards of plastic, and he looked like a nightmare version of a human-sized porcupine as he fell onto Aaron.

Mark had gained his feet, and he wiped blood from his face, the gun in his other hand swinging wildly. "Aaron? Aaron! Where–"

Dill tackled him around the midsection, and they slammed into the ground. Mark's skull connected with the floor with a dull crack, and he lay still. He had rolled half onto Dill, and she struggled to pull herself from beneath his weight and turned her face to Carl.

"The knife! It's right behind you!" she yelled.

Carl struggled up and saw the red Swiss Army knife Dill had used to cut her bonds. He pushed himself to it and grabbed, fumbling to cut the tie without being able to see it. The small blade sunk into the meat under his thumb, and he hissed and righted the knife, cutting.

Candy pushed herself away from Aaron and the zombie, whipsawing her body like a snake with too few joints. Denny rose, mouth covered with gore. In his shadow, Aaron moved weakly, waving his arms like a drowning man.

"Candy!" Carl yelled. His arms snapped free, and he bent forward to slice the zip tie at his ankles. "Candy! Hold on!"

Denny loomed over Candy, moaning, his mouth hanging wide, a black cave. Candy kicked out and missed as Carl flung himself across the small space. The zombie bent just as Carl curled himself around Candy, squeezing tight. He closed his eyes.

*

Dill wrestled the gun from Mark's unconscious fingers and pushed his dead weight off. She rolled onto her knees and took aim on Denny's head. She fired.

Denny's head exploded in a cloud of brain, bone, and black clots of heavily coagulated blood. The force of the shot knocked him back by five feet, where he crumpled into a nearly headless heap.

Carl raised his head and glanced from Dill to Denny.

"Good shot, Dill," he said. "Some pent-up resentment there, huh?" he asked and grinned shakily, sitting up.

Dill smiled back. "Maybe, yeah." She almost laughed. It jigged in her like the beginnings of shaky hysteria.

Carl pulled Candy up and planted a quick kiss on her cheek before leaning around to cut her bonds.

Candy massaged her wrists as Carl worked on her ankles. She nodded toward Denny. "Resentment? Did you know him?"

"Yeah," Dill said. She regarded Denny for a minute before turning back to Candy. She shrugged. "He was my ex."

Candy's eyebrows rose, and she nodded. "I get it."

A moan from behind Dill caused the hair on the back of her neck to rise, wavering. Aaron. Carl looked past her, and his face froze.

"Dill–" he said, choking on her name.

Dill turned and raised the gun. With tired nonchalance, she shot Aaron between the eyes. He flipped over onto his back, the top of his head gone. She turned back to Carl and shrugged. "No biggie."

He stared at her, mouth open. "If you say so, Dill," he finally managed. A thin amusement lightened his words as he turned back to Candy. His jacket collar pulled down as he reached for her ankles. "If I'd known you were such a good shot, I would have–"

He turned back at the low moan that issued from Dill's throat. She dropped heavily as her knees gave out. A blackness like thunderclouds began to roll over her, trying to turn out the light.

"Dill? What's wrong?" Carl said. "Dill!" He reached for her as she slumped forward. Tears were hot in her eyes. His face softened with concern. "Dill? What is it?"

Her mouth worked. She felt her jaw catch like a rusty hinge. She heaved out a half sob and reached for him.

"Carl…" she said. Her voice broke and fell away. "You've been…you…"

Behind Carl, Candy screamed.

*

"You never told me," Carl said, "about your dad." He took her hand in his. Candy lay on her side nearby, passed out. The three of them were in Aaron's office. Carl hadn't wanted to look at Denny and Aaron. Not as his…not as the last thing…

Dill gripped Carl's hand. "He was–he got bit." She swallowed tears, and they burned all the way down her throat. "He saved me, and then I…I saved him, but it was too late. He got bit anyway. I didn't really save him at all."

Carl nodded and tried to smile, but his face contorted in mild pain. Then his features smoothed out. "Did you have to kill him, Dill?"

Dill dropped her eyes. Carl's grip tightened on her hand, warm and strong. *Not for long*, she thought.

"I couldn't," she said, and her voice was whispered shame. "I couldn't do it. Another man...came along and..." Her voice hitched as she held back another sob. "I fucked up. I left him."

Carl squeezed her fingers. "You were just a kid," he said and closed his eyes again. "It's not your fault." When he opened them, thin tendrils of bluish cataract had appeared.

"You're grown up, now," he said, and Dill looked at him, eyes deep with shocked pain.

"Carl, I–I can't...you–" she said, but he shushed her with one implacable shake of his head, left to right.

"You have to," he said. "I'm your dad, now. It's your job."

She nodded slowly. "Okay," she said, "you're right." The tears overflowed her lashes and streaked down her cheeks like thin trails of fire.

"I'm so glad you finally admitted it," he said and laughed, but the laugh was weak and papery. He squeezed her hand once more and closed his eyes. "Hurry, Dill. I can feel it taking me over. I don't want to–"

Dill shot.

*

She stood and dropped the gun. She regarded Carl for a long time before finally leaning over to kiss his cheek. Then she turned toward Candy.

She knelt by the woman and patted her face. "Candy? We have to get out of here. Wake up, okay?" Dill's voice was even and controlled.

She felt blessedly numb. Her limbs were light and floating. She could run forever, she felt; she could just possibly fly.

Candy moaned, and her eyes fluttered open. She scrambled up, panicked, and Dill grabbed her shoulders, steadying her.

"It's okay. You're safe," Dill said.

Candy's eyes went from Dill to Carl's lifeless body. When she looked back to Dill, Dill smiled. The smile was a trifle false, a trifle hard, but Candy didn't seem to notice.

"It's okay," Dill repeated, "are you able to walk? We have to go."

Candy nodded meekly, and Dill rose and offered Candy her hand. She pulled her up. As they walked out of Aaron's office,

Candy stared straight ahead, but Dill looked back at Carl. He looked peaceful. He looked dead and not undead, and that was right. That was the right thing. Tears tightened her throat, and so she closed her eyes for a brief second and let the numbness seep back in.

Then she turned and left the office and didn't look back again.

She led Candy down the stairs. She had given Candy the gun because she'd retrieved her bow as they left three, and now she held it up and ready. As Carl would have told her to do. As they descended, a strange sound seemed to rise up to meet them. It was almost a tidal sound, oceanic, although Dill had never heard the ocean. It was a collective sigh, mournful with longing, and at first it meshed so well with her own feelings of grief that she was able to dismiss it. Then they were at the door to the first floor.

She peered through the wire-embedded glass, and her mouth dropped along with her heart.

The first floor was overrun with zombies.

They stumbled and wandered everywhere within her sight line. Three young womzies stood at the reception desk and stared blankly out into the lobby. A menzie pushed a maintenance cart until it bumped into another menzie, and then he abandoned it and wandered in the direction of the cafeteria. Dee, the elderly lunch-lady, shuffled slowly past. She had been changed. Her apron was covered in gore, and she carried a bloodied potato peeler in one awkwardly bent hand.

Corpses littered the floor. The lucky ones who had bled out and died before they could be changed.

A zombie had gotten by them, somehow. Dill cursed weakly under her breath.

Candy tapped Dill's back.

"Is everything okay?" Candy asked. Her voice was small and shaky. She might once have been training to be an assassin, but that woman was gone. Candy was a shaking, hollow shell.

Dill shook her head and turned to her. "No," Dill said, "it's not okay at all. ZI is overrun."

Candy sank back to sit on the step. She dropped her head into her hands and whispered something.

Dill knelt beside her. "What, Candy? I didn't hear you." She took Candy's cold hands in her own. "Candy?"

Candy looked up, and she finally looked her age...older, even. Her face had fallen. Her eyes were bloodshot and filled with something Dill couldn't identify.

"I can't do this again," Candy said, whispering. "Once was too much. I can't do it again, Dill. I won't."

Dill straightened, angry, more than angry, furious. "You don't have a choice! Get yourself together, Candy. We need to find a way out of here, and I need your help, so just–" Dill had turned away to peer back out the window as she yelled at Candy. The gunshot was so loud in the small space that Dill knocked her head into the glass when she jumped.

She began to shake as she stared through the window, open mouthed with shock. Her forehead hurt where she'd bumped the glass, and she felt the growing knot tightening her skin. She didn't want to look back at Candy.

She didn't want to be here.

She just wanted it to be over.

*

The parking deck off the back of the building was quiet. No people, no zombies. Not yet, anyway. Dill trotted quickly to the open back, wondering if there were stairs or any other way to get down to ground level. The numbness was back and with it, the lightness. She would jump off if she had to. She would make it.

She had to warn everyone. Before it was too late.

She trotted quietly, scanning the edge, so intent on looking that she tripped over legs in the dark. She landed with an 'oof', and her bow skittered across the concrete. A low chuckle caused her to shriek and scramble up to reclaim her weapon.

"Calm down, Abby." The voice was rough like shifting, furry gravel. "It's just me, yer Wrangler."

"Floyd?" Dill said and peered into the deep shadow where the voice–and legs–had emanated. A big Wrangler, *her* Wrangler, sat with his back to the low wall, arms crossed over his massive chest. His leathers creaked as he shifted and put out one meaty hand to her.

"It's me all right, Abby," the Wrangler said, "and glad I am to see you've made it thus far." He grinned, and it was a flash of white behind his beard.

"I'm so glad to see you!" Dill said, and it was the truth. She was awash in joy and relief to see the big man. Relief because now she had someone who could help her fight, and help to protect her. Then she remembered where he was supposed to be: the inners. "Is everything okay? Did you get to the inners in time to warn everyone?"

To her surprise, the Wrangler laughed, hard. It was slightly wheezy around the edges. His eyes slipped closed and then opened again. "It's all done, Abby. It's all done in. Everything is gone. We might have had a chance, but there were a bunch of Abbys...they were...they..." He shook his head and closed his eyes as if the words were too much. "They were trying to...*protect*...the zombies, Abby." His voice trailed away, seeming to fade before it could get past his beard. Dill had never heard such derision and puzzlement in combination.

Of course it had been Z.A.P.T., that misguided group of which she'd once, and recently, counted herself a member. The flyers and meetings–the manifesto–child's games, children's fantasies, and she'd been part of it. She could look back on her former self with pity, but not with forgiveness. She knew so much more now.

She shook her head and crouched closer to him. His heat was great, and she put a tentative hand on his wrist. It was both hard and hairy. "It can't be gone. It can't."

"It can, and it is, Abby," the Wrangler said. He caught her eyes with his own, and they were full of sympathy but also bitter amusement. "The outers are overrun and this building, too. I came back to try and warn you, and glad I am you came out here. I was hoping you would." He smiled again and then sighed. "Time to pack it all in. That's what I think."

"Pack it in? Why?" Dill said. "You came back for me! We have to get out of here! You have to help me!" The relief she'd felt at seeing him was trickling away.

He shifted and settled himself more firmly against the wall. He smiled. "Aye, Abby, that I did. Came back for you, I did." He turned his arm over, and the bite glittered in the low moonlight.

"And I did it at a cost, Abby," he chuckled, "but don't feel bad. It was bound to happen."

She stood, shaking, willing the numbness to take her again. "I'm sorry, Floyd."

He smiled up at her and then waved her away. "Go on and try to save yourself, Abby. Someone has to make it out of this sorry mess, isn't that right?"

"Yes, that's right."

"Go on, then, and be quick about it. I've business."

"My name is Dill. Dillalia," she said and swallowed. She took another step back. "What's yours?"

She watched his face, and it was like watching the changing shape of a creek bed under fast-flowing water. His eyes filled with longing and then loss, and he opened his mouth as if to tell her. Then the grin spread across his face, and she could see what work it took for the big man to grin like that, what resolve.

"My name's Floyd," he said and winked. "I'm your Wrangler, Abby. I'll always be."

His eyes finally slid from hers. It was as though he'd set her loose, and she turned and walked away, the numbness filling her. She let it come.

She would have to jump over the edge, but she would do it where the picnic area was. The tables were down there. Maybe that would lessen the drop.

A gunshot rang out behind her, flat and somehow undramatic. *After all*, it seemed to say, *this is only how the world ends. Again and again and again.*

She crouched on the wall's lip and looked down. Dark down there. She caught a sob, swallowed it, and gripped her bow tightly to her side.

Then she dropped over the edge into the black.

# FIFTEEN

The young woman stumbled from the woods into the blackened, open field. She struggled from her knees back to her feet, careful not to drop her bow. She was thin and tired. Dirty. Her eyes were unfocused, and a bruise on her forehead was just starting to fade to green and yellow. She reached into her pocket with her free hand and let the sharp lines of the small crystal horse she found there dig into her fingers like a reminder of a different reality.

A brown and black dog, big but not as big as the others in her pack, lifted her thick snout from the rabbit trail she'd been following on the far side of the field. She caught sight of the intruder and barked once in sharp warning. She scented the air as she watched the young woman with careful regard, her legs planted wide under her barrel chest. Then she barked in sudden recognition and began to gallop across the field, tail up in excitement, ears bouncing.

The young woman knelt to greet the dog, her hands shaking.

"Hi, Maybelline," Dill said. Her voice cracked and almost broke entirely. She grinned as Maybelline licked her cheeks with her hot sponge tongue. The dog yelped and wriggled, her coat shining and soft. "Good dog," Dill said, whispering. "Good girl."

The dog doubled and then nearly disappeared as tears filled Dill's hopeless eyes. Maybelline sensed her distress and whined. She pushed herself into Dill's arms, gently, careful not to topple Dill with her weight.

Dill bent into the dog's warm shoulder and cried great, heaving sobs that seemed to want to pull her heart right out through her tightening throat. Maybelline panted and whined in sympathy and twisted her great head around to lick the salt from Dill's cheeks.

A tentative hope, buried under the unshed tears of a hard week on the road, began to rise like a bubble through Dill's mind and body.

In the middle of the burned-out field, a log cabin–nearly black itself–stood sentinel in the emptiness. A woman stepped out onto the deep, wraparound porch. She had long, gray hair pulled back in a neat horse tail and a strong face, full of steady resolve. She lifted binoculars to her eyes and found the dog and the young woman.

"Dill?" she said to herself and then turned to call back into the house. "Paul, come help me! It's Carl's girl...she needs us!"

Mary and Paul started across the field as the four other dogs ran ahead of them, a baying jumble of brown and black, and hanging pink dog tongues.

Dill watched them come, holding tight to Maybelline's comforting bulk. She wiped her face and stood but kept one hand cupped over Maybelline's head.

Together, they walked to meet the others.

-The End-

\*\*\*

If you enjoyed *Zombie, Inc.*, please consider leaving me a review on Amazon. I would greatly appreciate it. ~ Best Regards and Happy Reading, Chris

\*\*\*

Made in the USA
Middletown, DE
20 February 2018